WEDDING BELLS AT THE DOG & DUCK

Jill Steeples

www.ariafiction.com

CW00552629

About *Wedding Bells at the Dog & Duck*

Ellie Browne, landlady of The Dog & Duck, is looking forward to a relaxing Christmas Day before the arrival of her and her partner Max's baby in the New Year. But with a snowstorm brewing outside, it seems that things might not go quite to plan.

After the dramatic events of the holiday season, Ellie settles into her new life at Max's huge country mansion Braithwaite Manor, juggling work and family as best she can. When she's asked to help organise a summer wedding for one of her best friends it's only natural that her mind turns to her own, non-existent, wedding plans!

But with Max decidedly lukewarm on the subject and other family complications threatening to disrupt life further, Ellie fears there'll never be wedding bells at the Dog & Duck after all.

For Nick, Tom and Ellie

With love

One

Christmas Day

I peered outside through the leaded windows of The Dog and Duck, watching as large snowflakes fell from the sky and settled on the ground in a thick, white, crunchy carpet. Like big soft dancing petals their relentless progress was mesmerising. Inside, the fires in both bars were blazing steadily and the non-drop Blue Spruce was doing its job and standing proudly in the bay window under the weight of an assortment of brightly coloured baubles and twinkling fairy lights. Mistletoe hung in the doorways where, at every available opportunity, I loitered, puckering my lips in anticipation, waiting expectantly for Max to come along and do the honours.

'Happy Christmas,' he wished me, not for the first time that day, as he came across from the other side of the bar where he'd been entertaining some of our guests. He kissed me gently on the forehead, before dashing off again on some errand. I sighed, and looked all around me at the festive fabulousness. Freshly picked holly bursting with red berries,

1

collected from the lanes on my daily walks with Digby, adorned the many picture frames and mirrors on the walls, and gold tinsel festooned every other surface in the pub.

Honestly, if I'd gone to Harrods and asked for Christmas in a box, they couldn't have come up with anything more seasonal. *Richard Curtis eat your heart out!* Even Max who'd been totally against the idea of having Christmas at the pub had finally come round to the idea and I couldn't help but smile as I watched him, currently wafting around the bar in his Santa Claus pinny, seeing to our guests.

'I don't understand,' he'd said, a couple of months ago when we'd had the big discussion about this year's plans. 'This is our last chance to have a quiet Christmas together before the baby arrives. Just you and me, the dogs and Katy, snuggled up indoors at the manor. Instead you want to cram all the village's waifs and strays into the pub on Christmas day when you could be taking the opportunity to put your feet up and let me do all the hard work.'

'You don't really mind, do you, Max? It's just that I've already made plans for the big day and invited a few people along.'

In fairness, at the time, it *was* only a few people who I knew would be alone for Christmas, but over recent weeks the guest list had grown to such an extent that we'd had to take the decision to serve

Christmas dinner in the barn out in the beer garden just so we could fit everyone around the table. Now, with my back killing me and Junior turning somersaults in my stomach, I wondered if Max hadn't had the right idea after all. The thought of being at Braithwaite Manor curled up on one of Max's huge and squashy sofas had never seemed so appealing. It was Christmas Day, I was surrounded by all my friends from the village, who were all full of excited chatter and laughter for the day ahead, and ordinarily I'd have been feeling it too. Today though, my Christmas spirit had all but vanished and all I could think about was getting through the day, mentally counting off the hours until it was all over, when I could snuggle up into Max's embrace with Digby, my best furry friend and faithful black Labrador, at my side.

'Where is baby Jesus?' Gemma Jones's little boy, Alfie, had sidled up beside me, tugged on my skirt and was gazing up at me with wide brown eyes. I looked down at him and smiled, a warm sensation filling my stomach. Puppies, kittens, small people – just the sight of any of these at the moment was enough to bring tears to my eyes. My hormones had a lot to answer for right now.

I gulped, mulling over Alfie's question, uncertain if I was up to explaining the nativity story to him

3

right at that moment, until it dawned on me what he meant.

'He's in his crib in the barn. You'll get to see him when we go outside for our lunch.'

Alfie nodded, looking satisfied with my answer, before his little face scrunched up in contemplation. 'Are you going to have your baby in the barn?'

'Goodness me no. I'm not sure I really fancy that idea,' I said smiling. 'I'm lucky. I'll be having my baby at the hospital.'

'Are you going to call your baby Jesus too?' he asked earnestly.

'No, no we're not.' Although thinking about it, it was probably one of the few names we hadn't considered. Max and I had bandied about all sorts of possibilities for our child, some traditional, some quirky, some right out there, but anything Max liked, I didn't much fancy, and any of my suggestions were pooh-poohed by Max. I was beginning to worry that our child would be forever known as the Child with No Name. 'We don't know yet if our baby will be a little boy or a little girl so we're going to wait until they arrive before picking a name.'

Disappointment flickered over Alfie's features.

'Oh, there you are!' Gemma came rushing over and took hold of her little boy's hand. 'You're not bothering Ellie, are you?'

'No, he's fine. You were just asking me about the baby, weren't you, Alfie?'

From his vantage point at around about my kneecaps, Alfie tilted his head to look up my dress, a mischievous grin on his face, and was rewarded with a stern telling-off from his mum.

'Stop it, Alfie. That's very rude.' She turned to me, her serious expression suppressing a smile. 'Sorry! I bet you're wishing you never invited us along in the first place. You should be taking it easy while you can. You won't have much opportunity when the baby arrives.'

'Oh, but I am. I'm under strict instructions from Max not to do anything.' A sigh slipped from my mouth. My pregnancy had been relatively easy, apart from a bit of morning sickness in the early days, but now I was fed up with my body holding me hostage and people treating me like I was an invalid. Admittedly, I couldn't see my toes, barely managed a wink of sleep at nights and had developed an unbecoming waddle as I walked, but aside from that everything was hunky-dory. 'I'm just desperate to get back to some kind of normality.'

Gemma laughed ruefully. 'Are you kidding? Nothing will seem like normal for a long time to come.'

I gave a weak smile in return. I suppose with five young children of her own, Gemma would know about these things. It was all a mystery to me. Even with Junior's arrival imminent, I still couldn't quite believe I was about to become a mother. Honestly, 'out of my depth' didn't nearly cover it. It was almost as if it was happening to someone else. I put that down to the fact that none of this was planned. I'd always thought a baby was something for the future, at a time when I had my whole life in order, but life has a habit of throwing you a curveball when you least expect it. I looked down at my huge bump, cradling my arms around its fullness. Not that I'd want to change anything in the slightest.

'Still,' Gemma went on, 'you haven't got long to wait now.'

'A couple of weeks.' Although from where I was standing that seemed like a lifetime away.

'Ha, no,' said Gemma, looking from my bump to my face intently, observing me as though she was a midwife at the maternity unit, and not my barmaid. 'I reckon the next day or two.' She nodded sagely. 'You mark my words.'

Mulling over that thought, our attention was commanded by Max, who was standing at the bar, pinging a spoon against a glass.

Ah, *the Max effect*. Warm squidgy vibes engulfed me. It hadn't lessened in the slightest, in all the months that I'd known him. Just to catch a glimpse of him across the room, to see his dark wayward hair doing its own thing, his intelligent questioning eyes, the warm wide smile on his lips, still stirred feelings inside me which I wasn't sure were entirely appropriate for a heavily pregnant woman.

'Okay everyone, if you'd like to make your way out to the barn, lunch will be served shortly. Just a word of warning. You can't fail to have noticed the crazy weather out there, the snow has been coming down heavily for the last couple of hours. We have cleared and salted the path, but just be careful. We don't want any broken bones or any nasty accidents.' Max fixed his brown eyes on me, raising his brows, as though I might be prime candidate for an accident. Then as his gaze warmed and softened, I felt myself smile, a warm sensation flooding my chest.

'I can't believe this weather,' said Polly, one of my best friends and owner of Polly's Flowers, the shop next door. She was currently hanging on to the arm of her new boyfriend, George, as though her life depended on it, something to do with the number of glasses of Prosecco she'd been knocking back this morning, I imagined. Still, it was lovely to see her so happy. Seeing them, a proper couple now, so loved-up and content, only added to the festive feeling. George had moved into the village this year, taking up residence in our family home, while my parents were away working in Dubai. It took me a while to figure out what he was doing in the village, and despite my unsubtle attempts to find out, it was Katy, Max's younger sister, who put me out of my misery by informing me that George was none other than the bestselling author GG Williamson.

That had certainly caused a frisson of excitement in the village. Katy, having read all of his books, was one of his biggest fans and was now hanging onto George's other arm, leading the way out into the beer garden, chattering away excitedly.

Gemma rounded up her five kids and husband, shooing them in the direction of the back door and Dan, my right-hand man and bar manager, who'd been keeping all our guests' glasses filled over the last hour or so, took hold of his girlfriend Silke's hand and stepped backwards, waiting for everyone to go through in front of him.

I owed a huge debt of gratitude to Dan. He'd volunteered to move into the pub with Silke while I was on maternity leave to take up the role of caretaker/manager. As it happened, the narrowboat they lived on was due to go into the shipyard for urgent repairs over winter and was likely to be out of action for a couple of months, leaving them homeless, so them moving into the pub had worked out well for everyone concerned.

My move into Max's imposing Georgian house, Braithwaite Manor, wasn't half as traumatic as I suspected it might be, although I realised for most people the idea of moving into a mansion would be far from traumatic. I'd put it off to the last minute possible though, reluctant to leave The Dog and Duck, the place that had been my whole world for almost two years, telling everyone I'd be back soon. What was I thinking? For so long I'd been so emotionally invested in the pub, that I'd been reluctant to let go of the reins. It had been a whirlwind couple of years admittedly. Thinking back to when I first returned home to Little Leyton, from my busy corporate life in London, to take some time out to consider the next steps in life, I could never have imagined just how dramatically my life would change.

I'd been looking for a simpler way of life, running my own doggy day care business and working shifts at The Dog and Duck. Only I'd got so much more than I'd bargained for. When Eric, the landlord of the pub and close family friend, had expressed his intention to retire, there were concerns that the pub would be sold and turned into a carvery or, worse still, developed into a luxury private home. I was determined not to let that happen. Max had been the village's knight in shining armour, stepping in to buy the pub, in memory of his grandfather, Noel, who'd been a much-loved customer for many years, and someone we all remembered fondly. Max had no interest in managing the pub himself and had asked me if I would take over the running of it. It took me little less than a nanosecond to agree.

That was our business relationship sealed and it was only a matter of weeks before our personal relationship grew into something much stronger too. Despite my instant and overwhelming attraction to Max, I'd had my reservations. He was unlike anyone I'd ever met before. Headstrong, go-getting, undeniably drop-dead, take-my-breath-away gorgeous, oh and filthy rich too. Not that that had mattered to me in the slightest. It was just the heady combination spelled Danger with a capital D. What would the hot-shot property developer and lord of the manor have in common with me? Well, as it turned out, a mutual attraction and fascination that neither of us could ignore.

The rest, as they say, is history.

I sighed, closing my eyes for the briefest moment, the events of the last couple of years flashing through my mind in vivid technicolour. I had no reason to worry. The pub was in safe hands – Dan knew as much as I did about running a good pub and he and Silke would do a great job in my absence. While I would miss being here on a daily basis, I had other more important priorities now.

Max, our baby, Katy and Digby.

We were a little family unit and I needed to take time out of my busy working life to just enjoy this new chapter. The pub would still be here waiting for me when I was ready to return to work.

'I can't tell you how much I'm looking forward to this,' said Arthur, an old family friend and one of the pub's most long-standing customers, as he eased himself out of the cosy armchair next to the fireplace. He collected his walking stick, which had been resting against the inglenook fireplace and straightened himself, every movement made in slow motion. A smile appeared at his lips.

'My Marge would always put on a lovely spread at Christmas. The dinners we had! Mmmm. She'd do all the cooking herself, you know? She made a lovely bread sauce, and Yorkshire puddings the size of billowing clouds. We'd have everyone round, there'd be twelve or fourteen of us sometimes. A bit like today.' He nodded at the train of people heading in the direction of the barn. 'Such happy times. That was why I was so pleased when you invited me along. Brings back lovely memories,' he said wistfully.

'Aw, and I have lovely memories of you and Marge at Christmastime too. Every year you would pop round to the cottage on Christmas Eve for a glass of mulled wine and a mince pie, to drop off my present. It was the same gift every year – I would have been horrified if it wasn't – an annual and a selection box, and I can remember that feeling of excitement as I put the present beneath the tree.

Christmas Day, after all the excitement had died down, I would curl up on the sofa and read my annual and work my way through all the chocolates in the box.' I laughed, thinking how I wouldn't have minded doing the same thing right now. 'We're very happy to have you here with us today, Arthur,' I said, reaching out to take hold of his free hand, knobbly with veins, and squeezing it tight.

Josie, my best friend from way back when, and her husband, Ethan, brought up the rear, with baby Stella, my gorgeous little goddaughter, held in the arms of Eric, Josie's dad. Everyone who was important to me was here today, apart from my parents who were on standby to fly over from Dubai just as soon as my baby deigned to put in an appearance.

Just then, as we were making our way out to the barn, there was a loud and insistent banging on the door. Max had locked it earlier knowing we wouldn't be open to the general public today.

'Who on earth is that?' said Josie, almost indignantly.

'Someone wanting their Christmas Day pint, no doubt,' said Ethan.

'Tell them there's no room at the inn.' Eric chuckled to himself.

I waddled over and called through the door, 'Sorry, we're not open.'

Another bang came then, louder and more urgent this time. Maybe it was a friend or villager come to pass on their good wishes for the season. Sharing a curious look with Eric, I went to unlock the door, but he stepped in, coming over from behind me to reach up to unbolt the heavy lock. He pulled open the old oak door and a biting blast of cold air whipped through the entrance, snow flurries obscuring the view of our visitor, creating a snow globe effect.

'Crikey, that weather is insane.' Josie shivered. 'I've never seen anything like it.'

The man standing on the threshold took a step forward, coming into focus. Tall, brown hair, forty-ish, with snowflakes peppering his head and shoulders.

'Sorry to interrupt, but I saw the light on. I just wondered if you had a room available. My car is well and truly stuck in the back lane into the village.'

'But it's Christmas Day,' I said, rather unnecessarily, just in case the stranger had overlooked this vital fact. 'Where are you heading?'

'Just driving through, but in these conditions I won't be going anywhere. My car won't budge. And the way it's looking, nothing will be getting in or out of the village. Not for the next twenty-four hours at least.'

'Ellie!' Max called from the back door. 'Are you coming?'

'Oh sorry,' said the man. 'I can see you're busy. I'll leave you to it. Do you know of any bed and breakfasts in the village that might have room tonight?'

'Look, come in for a moment,' I said, eager to get the door shut before we all perished from the cold.

The man rubbed his gloveless hands together and shivered as the warmth of the pub engulfed him. His gaze met mine for a moment, dark brown eyes that looked familiar somehow. I wondered if he was from around here, or if I'd gone to school with him perhaps, but the spark of recognition was lost when a dull and insistent pain spread around my hips, taking my breath away. I winced and rubbed at the small of my back, rocking from one foot to the other to try and make myself more comfortable. Niggling pains had started early this morning and were slowly getting worse, or perhaps that was just my imagination. If I could just get through Christmas dinner, then I could make my excuses and slip away to the manor, back to a comfy sofa, some must-watch TV and a turkey sandwich. Although the man might be right, just from looking out of the window it seemed that even the short trip back to the manor might be too hazardous to consider. Snow covered the ground in a thick white blanket up to knee-level at least.

'Ellie?'

Eric's voice brought me back to the moment and made me focus on my unexpected visitor, who was leaving a puddle from his damp boots over the stone floor. Eric raised his eyebrows and shrugged his shoulders at me, and I knew what he was thinking. I could hardly turn my back on this man in his moment of need, especially in the season of goodwill.

'We don't usually let out our rooms, but there's a spare room upstairs, and I'm sure if I have a word with Dan, our manager, he'd be happy to help you out.'

'Well, that would be great, but only if you're sure. I would hate to intrude.'

'No, you're not intruding at all. You've come at the right time. We're just going to have our lunch. You're very welcome to join us, there's plenty of food.'

The man's face lit up with relief. 'Thanks.' He shrugged off his coat. 'I really appreciate your help.'

Two

'And a partridge in a pear tree!'

My gaze drifted around the long table in the barn, littered now with the colourful debris from the used Christmas crackers and party poppers, smiling at the sight of our friends and family enjoying the festivities. Max had organised a rousing rendition of the Twelve Days of Christmas, with each part of the table taking different lines of the song, with the intention of us all coming together at the end in vocal harmony. Only, with the wine flowing non-stop, the little ones growing restless – and the not so little ones getting raucous – and Digby doing his best to filch the remaining turkey from the table, the effect wasn't quite as harmonious as it might have been. We all warbled to a wobbly and out-of-key crescendo, before dissolving into fits of giggles. Even our visitor joined in, looking slightly bemused. He was sitting at the other end of the table so I hadn't had chance to get to know him any better or find out where he'd been heading, but wondered what he must be thinking having ended up here amongst this drunken rabble. He was probably planning when he might easily escape.

'Friends, can I have your attention please.' George stood up, his cheeks slightly reddened and with a big wide smile on his face. Funny to think that when he first arrived in the village, less than a year ago, he'd been a quiet and reclusive figure, who very much wanted to keep himself to himself. What I didn't know then was that he'd holed himself up in our family home because he was working on a deadline to complete the latest book in his bestselling series. He'd come to the village for work purposes only, to a place where no one knew who he was, so that he could avoid any distractions, but in a short space of time, Little Leyton had worked its charms upon him. Soon he was a regular visitor at The Dog & Duck, had become a friend to Katy, and had become romantically entangled with Polly, at a time when she was just recovering from the heartbreak of her split with Johnny Tay. When his stay in Little Leyton was coming to an end, George extended the tenancy on Ivy Lane cottage, my family home, for a further six months, which suited me as it'd meant I hadn't needed to find any new tenants. With mum and dad away in Dubai, I'd lived in the cottage for a short while when I first returned to the village, but after taking over the pub, working late nights and early mornings, it had made much more sense to move in there. Finding George, a reliable and trustworthy tenant, had been a godsend and he was now so firmly ensconced in the village that I couldn't imagine a time when he wouldn't be around. Especially as he'd made such a difference to the happiness of my friend.

'Are you going to tell us a story?' heckled Eric cheekily.

'No, don't worry, nothing like that. I'm going to keep this short. But I just wanted to say a very big thank you to our hosts Max and Ellie who, I'm sure you will agree, have put on an absolutely brilliant Christmas lunch for us all.' A spontaneous cheer of approval spread around the table and Max and I shared a glance before George continued. 'Delicious food, splendid wine and great company. I can't think of any better way of spending Christmas Day, and as a newcomer to Little Leyton, I would like to thank every single one of you sat around this table for making me so welcome in your village.'

Unexpectedly, a huge swirl of emotion caught in my throat, and my cheeks were flushed with gratitude at being amongst my friends, with the man I loved at my side, swept along by the goodwill in the room. Christmas had to be my favourite time of the year and with the birth of our baby expected in a few weeks' time, this year had an extra poignancy to it.

'Well said,' called Eric. 'Three cheers for Max and Ellie.'

When the cheers had subsided, George remained standing at his end of the table.

'Just one other thing I would like to share with you,' he said, looking hesitant for a moment. 'What I could never have imagined when I moved into this village was that I would find not only a ready group of friends who I enjoy spending time with, but also the woman I want to share the rest of my life with, Polly Samson. I am delighted to tell you all that Polly has agreed, this morning, to be my wife.'

Polly jumped to her feet and flashed the sparkliest diamond I'd ever seen.

'WHAT?!' I think my open-mouthed, wide-eyed expression must have said it all because she came running around the table to waggle her hand under my nose. 'How on earth did you hide that?'

'Oh, Ellie, I wanted to tell you just as soon as I walked through the door, but George wanted to make the grand announcement. His proposal came out of the blue. I had no idea, but when he asked me, it seemed like the most natural thing in the world. I'm so happy, Ellie. I honestly never thought this would happen to me.'

For a moment I saw tears mist in her eyes, before she shook her head, ridding herself of the emotion just bubbling beneath the surface, her blonde bob swinging defiantly. She showed off her huge rock to everyone who gathered round to have a look.

'Well, I think this calls for another toast,' said Max, standing and raising a glass to George and

Polly, the rest of the room joining in with the congratulations. Goosebumps ran along my legs and arms seeing Polly's radiance fill the room. If anyone deserved a happy ending, after the rough time she'd been through, then it was my friend Polly.

It was around this time last year that she'd had her heart broken when Johnny Tay, our old friend from school who Polly had been enjoying a whirlwind romance with, had decided on a whim that he needed to find himself and headed off to travel the world with only a rucksack on his back. To say Polly was devastated was the understatement of the century. Seeing her on a daily basis when she popped into the pub for a drink and a chat, I witnessed her heartache at first hand, saw her confusion at Johnny's behaviour, her questioning of her own behaviour – had she done something wrong to send Johnny away? – and her struggle to come to terms with what had happened. She was just getting back on her feet when George arrived in the village and he helped Polly to forget about Johnny for a short while. Their friendship slowly developed into something more serious, until Johnny arrived back in the village, just as suddenly as he'd left. Johnny being Johnny, he thought he could swan back into Little Leyton and pick up where he'd left off, but things had changed in his absence and Polly had moved on. There was a part of me that felt sorry for Johnny, I'd once had a brief romance with him myself, and I wanted to see him happy, but I'd seen how his actions had impacted on Polly and now she'd found happiness with someone else. Honestly, sometimes living in Little Leyton was like being at the centre of a soap opera.

There was a lull in the proceedings as Josie and Gemma collected the dirty crockery from our places, as the excitement of Polly and George's engagement spread around the room. I shifted in my chair, my bottom uncomfortable against the hard wooden seat, my bump keeping me a distance from the table. I held my hands to my stomach trying to soothe the aching and twinging. I'd promised myself I'd take it easy on the food front, but how could I when it was all so tempting and delicious, and we still had Christmas pudding and mince pies to go yet. I could hardly refuse when Betty Masters from the tea shop on the High Street had made them specially for me for today. Maybe just a small portion with a dollop of cream. After all, it was Christmas and I was as huge as a barrage balloon as it was, a small wodge of Christmas pudding wasn't going to make that much difference.

'You see, it's as simple as that.' Max shuffled his chair up closer to mine and rested his arm around my shoulder. The citrusy and woody notes of his aftershave, one of the presents I'd given him this morning, wafted beneath my nose.

'What's that?' I asked.

'Polly and George getting married. It's great news, isn't it?'

'Yes. And so unexpected. I'm thrilled for them both. They're so good together and Polly deserves some happiness at last.'

Max's gaze held mine, and I noticed the almost imperceptible shake of his head. Was that exasperation I saw in his eyes? I cringed, knowing what was coming next.

'Ah, so you're not against marriage as an institution then? It's just marriage to me that you don't like the idea of?'

'Please Max, don't be like that?' His red paper hat was perched on his head at a jaunty angle, there was a smile on his lips and a glint in his eye, but beneath his cheery exterior, I detected a sharp edge to his questions.

'Like what? I've asked you three times to marry me now and you've knocked me back on every occasion. I still don't understand why. We love each other. We're having a baby together. Why wouldn't we get married?'

It was a simple enough question when he put it like that, but the answer wasn't so straightforward. Well, not to me it wasn't.

'Polly and George don't seem to have had any hesitation in deciding they want to spend the rest of their lives together,' he went on, raising an eyebrow at me, making me feel like the worst girlfriend ever. 'They've been together less time than we have. Maybe you're not certain I'm the right man for you, after all.' There was that smile again, to soften the accusation in his words.

'Stop it.' I grabbed his arm and shook it playfully. 'You know how much you mean to me. And we can't compare ourselves with Polly and George. It's different and... Ow!' My thoughts and words were interrupted by a gripping pain in my lower back, my stomach tightening into a firm hard ball. I looked down at my bump accusingly.

'Are you all right?' Max's voice lowered.

'It's fine. Just a twinge, I think.'

'Hmmm, are you sure? You've had quite a few twinges today, haven't you?' His brow furrowed, a look of concern on his features. 'Mind you, you know you can't have this baby today.' He took hold of my hand. 'We'd never get you to the hospital in this weather. We wouldn't even get back to the manor. The lanes are impassable. We'll have to stay here tonight.'

'Do you think?' I said, relieved that the pain had subsided a little and even more relieved that we'd moved off the thorny topic of weddings.

'Yes, it's not worth chancing it. Certainly not in your condition. Hopefully by tomorrow the thaw will have begun. Hey, it's not that bad, is it?' he asked, seeing my face drop.

'No, it's just that I've offered the spare room to our visitor. I didn't think.' I gestured in the direction of the stranger who'd turned up on our doorstep and who was now deep in conversation with Eric and Ethan, seemingly having made himself very much at home.

'Don't worry, we'll sort something out.'

That was Max all over. For every problem there was a solution. Nothing to worry about. I liked that about him. His magnanimity, his generosity of spirt. The way he cared and looked out for people. Me especially. It was a surprise even to me that I hadn't bitten his hand off at his offer of marriage, but there was a small part of me that held back, as if guarding my heart from the damage I knew he could inflict.

'Ryan's here!' said Katy, coming up from behind us and poking her head between us. 'It's okay, isn't it?'

'Yes, of course,' I said smiling, noticing Max's twist of his mouth, stopping himself from saying something that he might later regret, I suspected.

Ever since Katy had arrived from Spain underneath a big black and brooding cloud, relations between the two siblings had been strained to say the least. In the early days there'd been lots of tears, rows and misunderstandings, but once we found out the reason for Katy's mood swings – she'd discovered that the man she thought was her father wasn't after all – and she'd confided in us, things between Katy and Max had slowly begun to improve. It hadn't been easy, Katy was only seventeen then and she and Max hadn't really grown up together as Max was considerably older than her, so this had been the first opportunity they'd had to get to know one another. Katy was devastated when she found out she and Max didn't share a father and had been worried Max wouldn't think of her in the same way, but it hadn't made the slightest difference to him. She was still his little sister, even if she was a major pain in the neck at times.

Max agreed to her staying with him at the manor and now she was doing a course at the local college in business administration and working shifts at the pub too. In a short space of time, we'd formed a very close bond as well. She was the little sister I'd always wished for, but had never had, up until now.

'Hi Ellie,' Ryan said, greeting me with a hug and nodding in deference to Max, handing us a tin of shortbread biscuits. With close cropped black hair, deep brown eyes and a rakish swagger, it wasn't hard to see why Katy had fallen so easily for Ryan's charms. The fact that he was several years older than her and rode a monster of a motorbike didn't do anything to endear him to Max, but I knew beneath his bad boy exterior, he was an absolute sweetheart. And he made Katy happy. Wasn't that the most important thing?

When Ryan came in, I noticed he wasn't alone. Behind him was the distinctive tall figure of Johnny, his eyes immediately searching out Polly. My heart squeezed knowing how her good news was likely to affect him. I was so pleased that she'd found happiness with George, but I couldn't help worrying how my old friend Johnny would react to the discovery.

'Hey Johnny, Happy Christmas!' I stood up to greet him, hugging him tight, wanting to protect him from the bad news to come. 'What's the weather like out there now?' I asked.

'Crazy! I've never seen anything like it. I fell over twice on the way, and I'd only had a couple of beers at home.' Johnny grinned, climbed out of his wellies and placed them on the doormat. 'I'm not sure how many of this lot will get home tonight.'

I smiled, trying to ignore the knot of anxiety growing ever bigger in my stomach. So much for my quiet night in at the manor with Max and Digby then.

Of course it was only a matter of time before Johnny heard the news of Polly's engagement and it was only because I knew him so well that I recognised the hurt and disappointment flicker in his eyes. In fairness to him, he went straight across to congratulate the happy couple, shaking hands with George, his face not betraying any emotions he might have been struggling with. If he'd needed any closure on his relationship with Polly, then this must surely be it. Not the best Christmas present for Johnny, I suspected.

After digestifs for those who wanted one, I was able to sit back and reflect that it had definitely been the right decision to have Christmas Day here, amongst our friends. Who knew what we might be doing next year? Our baby would have arrived and… Aargh! There it was again, another pain, much more than a twinge now though. I clutched onto the table and breathed through the pain. This baby couldn't be coming today. It wasn't time! I still had at least two weeks to go. It wasn't convenient. I had a pub full of visitors. It was Christmas Day. And outside there was a blizzard the likes of which hadn't been seen in Little Leyton before. It wasn't just inconvenient, it was bloody disastrous. Probably just a false alarm, I told myself, as the pain disappeared again. I needed to relax and not get myself into a panic, it was just my imagination running away from me.

Thankfully Johnny came over at that moment and sat down beside us, providing a welcome distraction from what was going on inside my body.

'Who is that guy over there?'

Max and I both looked across at our visitor who was now savouring a glass of red wine, deep in conversation with Katy, seemingly enraptured by every word she had to say.

'Oh, he turned up just before lunch. He was travelling through the village and his car got stuck on the road. Looks like he'll be staying for a while, at least until the weather clears,' I explained.

'Seems a bit of a dick to me,' said Johnny, who was never one to mince his words. 'What's his name?'

'I don't know,' I said, only just realising I hadn't asked. 'He seems all right though.' I was trying to appeal to Johnny's better nature, but I suspected Johnny was all out of goodwill now that the news of Polly's engagement had sunk in. 'He's probably just had a bit too much Christmas spirit. I feel sorry for him. He obviously had plans for Christmas Day and instead ended up here with a bunch of strangers. It can't be easy for him.'

Johnny rolled his eyes. 'What? You think he's the only person in the country to miss the weather forecast. All the advice was not to travel unless you had to. You're too trusting, you know that, don't you, Ellie? He's probably just a chancer after a free Christmas dinner.'

'No! Not that it matters if he is. We have enough food to feed the entire village.' I laid a hand on Johnny's leg, trying to soothe his frazzled nerves. I had my ex-boyfriend to one side of me and Max, looking on amused, from the other side. At one time, Johnny and I shared everything together. As teenagers we told each other all our secrets, our hopes and dreams, our plans for the future, and that friendship had endured for years, occasionally segueing into something more intimate, until I made the decision that we worked together much better as friends. Johnny and I were still close and would always be so, but there was a natural distancing between us now.

From the other end of the table, Ryan's voice cut through the hubbub. 'Mate, I'm not going to tell you again.' He'd stood up and his tall frame leant over our visitor with Katy looking bemused trapped between the two of them.

'What's going on?' I whispered to Max.

'I told you, the guy's a complete idiot,' said Johnny helpfully.

Max pushed his chair back and stood up, everyone's attention now focussed on the situation developing at the other end of the room.

'What's your problem? I'm just talking to Katy. You're not her keeper, are you?' said the visitor.

'Just keep your hands off her!' I swallowed hard, realising the touchpaper had been ignited in Ryan. So much for his bad boy behaviour being in the past. Wishful thinking on my part, obviously. 'What are you, some kind of perv?' He goaded now.

The guy looked at Katy, as if about to say something, then realised he had his arm around her shoulder, which he removed carefully, as though he hadn't even known it was there.

'Don't be ridiculous. Katy and I are just getting to know each other,' he said, matter-of-factly, but this whole situation was making me very uneasy.

'Yeah, well she doesn't want to know you. She's only eighteen for Christ's sake.' Ryan moved even closer to the man.

'Oi, get out of my face,' said the guy, standing up now and pushing Ryan aside.

I grimaced. Anyone who knew Ryan would know that was a big mistake. He grabbed the guy by the shirt, pulling back his arm and landing a solid punch on the man's nose, sending him staggering backwards into the Christmas tree.

'Ryan!' Max, Katy and I yelled his name in unison, a child screamed and Digby gave a terrifying warning bark. Someone knocked over a glass of red wine in the ensuing fracas, staining the lovely white starched tablecloth and Max sprinted over and pulled the men apart.

'What the hell is going on?' he shouted.

'You're a bloody psycho, do you know that,' said the man to Ryan.

'And you're a bloody creep. Leave my girlfriend alone.'

I stood up with a surge of energy I didn't know I possessed. 'Would you please just stop it. It's Christmas Day and you're spoiling everything. Think of the children, and the dog. And think of me.' I stopped, realising I was shaking, aware of everyone's eyes upon me and aware of something else too. Something unsettling. Something disturbing. Something slightly damp. Digby came up to my side and nudged me with his wet snout, but that wasn't the moistness I was worried about. What was concerning me more was the puddle forming at my feet. 'And now look what you've done,' I said, glaring at Ryan and the stranger, as though it was entirely their fault. 'My waters have broken!'

Three

Well it was a very effective way of clearing a room. On their way out, people thanked me for a lovely lunch and wished me luck, looking as though they couldn't get away fast enough, their relief palpable as they escaped into the safety of the walls of The Dog and Duck.

Max stood by the door ushering all our guests through to the main bar, clearly anxious to get everyone out of the way as quickly as possible.

'Silke, do me a favour,' he called, 'and bring some blankets and pillows through, and perhaps some towels as well.' He rushed around the barn moving tables and chairs out of the way while I staggered around, still not really believing that this was actually happening.

There was one person who loitered, however. Little Alfie came running up to my side, looking up at me with earnest brown eyes, his brow furrowed. 'I thought so. You're going to have your baby now, aren't you? It's like when baby Jesus was born in the barn.'

I gave a weak smile, unnerved by Alfie's unwavering gaze and the seriousness of his expression, suggesting an intelligence beyond his years. A little wise old man.

'Can I stay and watch?' he asked gravely.

'No you can't,' said Gemma, grabbing him by the hand and dragging him away. 'Thanks for having us. If there's anything I can do, then just let me know. You'll be fine!'

I wished everyone would stop saying that. How did they know? I closed my eyes, grimacing through another pain. My mind drifted back to earlier in the year when I was a reluctant and unwitting birth partner to Sasha, Max's ex-girlfriend. She'd moved back into the village to make a new start for herself and her baby and I'd popped round to her house to drop off a cake as a welcoming gift. It was meant to be a flying visit, but no sooner had I arrived than Sasha's waters had broken and I was thrown into a situation I couldn't have been less prepared for.

Without any family in the area, Sasha asked me to go with her to the hospital to act as her birth partner, and I cringed now to think how I had behaved. I'd run around frantically trying to look as though I knew what I was supposed to be doing, when in fact I didn't have the first idea. I'd paced up and down, grabbed towels because that was one thing I'd heard were essential for the momentous task of giving birth, and had gone in for some deep breathing, interspersed with hyperventilating. And it wasn't even me having the baby. I felt I'd been next to useless in providing a strong and supportive presence, but Sasha hadn't seemed to mind, she'd just been grateful for me being there, and I'd been impressed by the strength and stoicism she showed going through childbirth without the man she loved at her side.

Back then I could never have imagined I would soon be going through the same experience myself. But now it really was my turn and it looked as though my baby was determined to arrive today whether I liked it or not. I definitely needed to channel my inner Sasha even if my mind was entertaining a series of scary scenarios; we could take our chances and get in the jeep and see if we could make it to the hospital, but from what people were saying the roads were treacherous and it would be a dangerous and impossible trek. No, it was too risky, even to attempt the trip back to the manor and that was only five minutes down the road. Little Alfie was right: I would be having my baby here in the barn. I supposed it was preferable to going back inside the Dog and Duck, which would now be overflowing with the merry revellers.

Silke came rushing back through the door underneath a pile of linen and pillows, handing them over to Max, before quickly leaving again.

'It will be all right, won't it?' I asked Max.

He came across and took my face in his hands, nodding intently as he looked into my eyes.

'Don't worry,' said Josie, as if reading my mind. 'You'll be absolutely fine, and we'll be with you all the way.'

'What if there's a problem or if the baby gets stuck or if there's…'

She held up a hand to stop me. 'There won't be a problem. Honestly, try not to worry.' She sounded calm enough, but she wasn't looking me in the eye, and instead was bustling around, laying duvets and blankets on the ground, pouring drinks of water. 'Think of all the babies born every day across the world,' she said breezily, as she guided me over to the spot in the corner where she and Max had made a nice cosy corner for me. 'Really, it's the most natural thing ever. We can get in touch by phone with the maternity unit at the hospital if we need to and I think Dr Garrett still lives in the village, if you were really worried. Not that you should be,' she quickly added.

'Dr Garrett? He retired years ago and he's got a gammy knee and walks with a stick. It's far too slippery outside for him. He'd never get here in one piece. Oh god,' I cried, which prompted Josie to burst into laughter.

'Stop catastrophising.'

'Max?' I reached out a hand for him, fear growing inside as I realised there was no turning back.

'Josie's right.' His voice was strong and steely. 'Everything's going to be absolutely fine. Josie, would you go and check in the pub, see if anyone knows of someone in the village who might be able to help.'

Only then did I detect the note of panic in his voice as Josie dashed out of the barn.

'I don't want to do this!' I wailed.

'It's a bit late for that,' Max chuckled.

'It's not funny. I can't do it. I really can't…' I groaned, digging my nails into Max's hand as another contraction wracked my body.

'You can, you really can. Just think, soon our baby will be here and all of this will be worth it.'

'Urgh. How do you know! Oh…' I slumped down on the makeshift bed, exhaustion soaking through my limbs. 'I hate you!'

'Right. Well, I love you.' He wiped the dampness from my brow with a tissue, and I swiped his attentions away angrily. Why was he being so bloody annoying? Being there. In my face. Breathing my air. Talking to me. Although to be fair, I couldn't think of anyone better to be annoying me right at this moment. I looked up into his eyes, recognising the concern and affection there. 'I guess this wouldn't be the right time to ask you to marry me then?'

Aargh, there he went again, saying stupid annoying things. 'Noooooo! Never! After this, I'm never ever having sex again.'

*

'A beautiful baby boy!'

Jayne Sinclair, an ex-midwife who someone remembered lived locally, had been drafted in from her Christmas night festivities at the other end of the village. Johnny and Ethan had trekked along the snowy paths to collect her and escorted her back to the pub. If she'd been annoyed at being interrupted in the middle of her celebrations, she certainly didn't show it and made it just in time for our baby to make his appearance in the world.

'You did it, Ellie. And I couldn't be more proud. You've made me the happiest man in the world.' Max's words were soft and full of tenderness, his voice swelling with emotion. He kissed me on my cheek, his arm around my shoulder, tears clearly evident in his deep dark brown eyes. I looked up, overwhelmed by my love for him and the new life we'd made together, immediately regretting all the nasty thoughts and angry things I'd said earlier. Hopefully he'd appreciate that it was only the intense pain and emotion of the occasion that had made me lash out.

Our newborn baby son was laid against my naked chest and my hand rested on his tiny head, my fingers fondling his fine wispy jet black hair. My gaze drifted around the old oak beams of the barn, in awe at what had taken place in here today. Totally spent, emotional and tearful, I looked down at our baby's perfect rounded form, curled up as he had been inside me, his cries reassuring me that everything was okay.

'Oh, thank goodness,' sighed Josie, the relief apparent in her words. 'You were amazing!' she told me, peering at the baby, now wrapped in a towel. 'It's been an absolute privilege seeing your baby boy born. A little friend for Stella.' She planted a kiss on my dampened forehead. 'I'm just so relieved that everything went to plan, well sort of. Must admit I went into a bit of a panic when I realised you'd have to have the baby here.'

Max exhaled deeply, and shook his head. 'Oh god! Me too.'

'Really?' I said, pulling our baby to me tighter. 'You weren't that worried, were you?'

'Petrified. This was entirely out of my control and I hated seeing you in so much pain, when there was nothing I could do to stop it. It was such a relief when Jayne turned up,' he confessed, and I could appreciate now just how worried he'd been after all.

The ruddy-faced woman who'd come in at the eleventh hour and calmly got me through the final stages of birth smiled now. She really was a Christmas angel.

'Well, it's been a few years since I last delivered a baby, but there wasn't time to worry about that. As soon as I got here all my training kicked in. I was just pleased that it was a straightforward delivery, and that we didn't have any problems.'

'Oh, Jayne, we can't thank you enough,' I sighed, gratefully.

'It's my pleasure,' she said in awe, as though she couldn't quite believe what had happened here herself.

'You know, you were absolutely brilliant, Ellie,' said Max. 'A natural. In fact, you made it look so easy we could even start thinking about the next one now.' There was a playful glint in his eye and his mouth curled up mischievously, but if I'd had the energy I still would have sloshed him one.

'Uh-uh, no way,' I sighed wearily. 'You have no idea!' Although, funnily enough, all the pain was forgotten now, overcome as I was with bewilderment and joy that we'd managed to pull off something quite so amazing. Talk about a Christmas miracle. 'Besides, I want to enjoy this little fella first. I have everything I need now. You, my lovely friends and family, the pub, our dogs and now this precious bundle too. What more could a girl ask for?'

Max raised his eyebrows and shrugged. The smile that had formed on his lips ever since our son had arrived in the world showed no sign of departing. 'That reminds me, I should call your parents, let them know the good news.'

'Hey, what time is it?' I asked.

Josie glanced at her watch. 'Ten to midnight.'

'Oh my goodness. This little man really did want to turn up in time for the Christmas celebrations, didn't he?' His fist curled tightly around my little finger, as he nestled to my breast, and I could have stayed like that, gazing down at this tiny perfect creature, forever. 'Is everyone still in the pub? I hope I didn't spoil their Christmas.'

'There's no chance of that. The booze has been flowing freely next door with most people staying on waiting on the weather and news of the baby,' Max said, stroking my hair.

'Did that man and Ryan sort out their differences?'

'Don't worry. Johnny and Dan would have kept an eye on them. More importantly, what am I going to tell them all? They'll be dying to hear. What is this little boy's name?' asked Josie.

I looked up at Max, having no idea what we might call our little man. So many names had been suggested and yet none of them seemed to fit the small bundle currently wrapped in my arms.

'I've had an idea, Ellie,' Max said. I don't know why we didn't think of it before. How about Noel?'

'Noel?' I said the name aloud, trying it out for size on my tongue. 'After your granddad…'

'Yes, exactly! And it fits perfectly with his Christmas Day arrival.'

'Noel Golding…'

Max had adored his grandfather. It had been the reason he came to the village in the first place, to care for him in his dying days. And Noel had been a regular visitor to the pub and had been much-loved by all the staff here.

'Oh, it's perfect.' 'I looked down at our little boy who was now sleeping peacefully. 'He looks exactly like a Noel, don't you think?'

Josie and Jayne looked at each other and smiled, nodding their approval. 'It's lovely.'

'Well, I reckon as far as Christmases go, this has been a pretty successful one,' said Max, beaming. 'Friends, family, an engagement, a brilliant lunch – if I say so myself – a drunken brawl and our perfect little baby born into the middle of all the mayhem.'

'Yes,' I sighed wearily. 'A Christmas to remember, that's for sure.'

Four

The following days passed in a haze of feeds, nappy changes, impromptu meals of cold meats, cheeses and mince pies prepared by Max and Katy, snatched moments of sleep, and what seemed like a constant stream of visitors.

Exhausting, but lovely.

Jayne Sinclair popped in one morning a couple of days later, which I thought was beyond her call of duty considering she was retired now, but she'd wanted to check on us both. My actual midwife, Sunita, also managed to make her way along the snowy lanes to Braithwaite Manor and gave Noel and me a thorough checking over and declared that he was fit and well, and a very beautiful baby indeed.

Wasn't that the truth?

I'd never felt such instant and all-encompassing love in all my life before. It startled me with its raw intensity, its ability to squeeze at my heart and send goosebumps along my arms. I spent most of the time just staring at my tiny little scrap, marvelling at how wonderful and perfect he was, and how clever Max and I were to produce something quite so amazing.

'Hey, look who's here?' Max wandered in to the conservatory, where I was sat on one of the squashy sofas, followed by Polly, a big expectant smile on her face.

'Hope you don't mind me popping in again, but I just wanted to see how you were both doing.'

'Come in, come in, it's lovely to see you. It's funny, I feel like I'm in a little bubble up here. I know it's only been a few days since Noel arrived, but what with it being Christmas as well, it feels like I've been sent to an alternative universe. Having visitors reminds me that life is going on as normal out there.'

Max volunteered to make a coffee for Polly and a tea for me, before making his excuses and disappearing outside with the dogs. I suspected he was tiring of the endless conversations about Noel's sleeping and feeding routine, the state of his nappies and my engorged breasts. Though the one thing he couldn't get enough of was cuddles with his little boy.

With Noel's feed over, Polly took him out of my hands and sat down beside me, her arms wrapped around my little boy. 'So what's it like, Ellie, being a mummy?'

'Ah, well...' How could I possibly put it into words? 'It's wonderful...' I paused. 'Although I still can't believe that he actually belongs to me. Suddenly you have responsibility for this tiny defenceless person and it's huge. There's so much to think about - *Is he having enough to eat? Does he need changing? What if he's ill?* It's such a worry,' I said, laughing, but meaning every word. 'Even dressing him's hard, getting his tiny little legs and arms into one of those romper suits. I'm always afraid I'm going to break something. Babies should definitely come with an instruction manual.'

Polly laughed. 'Don't worry. All mums must feel that way at first. And if it's any consolation, you seem like you know what you're doing. You are a natural, Ellie, really! And once your parents arrive, you'll feel better. Nothing like a bit of advice from your mum to set you straight.'

I hoped that was true because, as much as I loved my beautiful baby boy, trying to do everything properly and being the best mum I could possibly be really was a struggle right now.

'Anyway, I'm blaming you both for making me feel so broody now.' Polly was looking at Noel longingly in her arms.

'Really? Does George know about this?'

'He's worse than I am. He loves children. We want to have a big family. Maybe four kids. And a couple of golden retrievers. Although we probably won't start trying until after the wedding.'

'The wedding! It's just so exciting,' I said, watching Polly swell with happiness.

Noel gave a soft gurgle as though in approval of Polly's decision, and I peered down to see his eyes fluttering, suspecting he would soon be fast asleep. I glanced at my watch wondering how long he might nap for and when he would wake for his next feed, my whole day now spent at his beck and call. Not that I minded in the least. Polly and I exchanged an indulgent look, both totally charmed and besotted by my little boy, before she placed him down carefully in his Moses basket.

'You know George got me into a bit of trouble with his proposal,' I told her.

'How come?'

'Well, Max wanted to know why you were so quick to say yes to George when you two have been going out together even less time than us.'

'Hmmm. I can imagine how that might have been awkward,' grimaced Polly.

'Yes, it was a bit, but because there was so much else going on that day we managed to gloss over it. Still I could tell he wasn't entirely happy about the whole thing.' More than that I'd seen the disappointment in his eyes. Nothing had been mentioned since because all our time and energies had been consumed by Noel but I hated knowing that I'd let him down in some way.

Polly picked up her mug from the coffee table and clasped her hands around it, thoughtful for a moment. 'What I don't understand is why you said no to Max in the first place. He clearly adores you. You love him. You're living in this beautiful house and now you have a beautiful baby together as well. Wouldn't a wedding be the icing on the cake?'

'Yes, I suppose so, but…' I floundered. My baby brain was creating a fog of conflicting ideas and thoughts inside my head, making rational thought an impossibility.

'But what, Ellie?'

'Well, I just want to make sure that it's something we really want to do, and not just rush into it because it's what's expected of us.'

Polly gave me a quizzical look and I tried to explain.

'None of this was planned. Max and I hadn't been together that long when I fell pregnant. We certainly hadn't discussed babies or marriage and I'm pretty certain Max didn't want to start a family at this point in his life. I just wonder if the only reason he asked me to marry him was because he felt that he should.'

Polly lifted her eyebrows and sniggered. 'Come on, Ellie, you must know Max isn't the sort of man to do anything he doesn't want to do. The only reason he's proposed is because he wants to spend the rest of his life with you. Simple as that. Blimey, a lot of women would jump at the chance of becoming Mrs Golding.'

She paused, her gaze drifting around the sumptuous drawing room, decorated in muted shades of cream, with bold modern artwork providing splashes of colour on the walls and with panoramic windows providing breathtaking views out over the extensive gardens.

My gaze followed hers, drinking in all the gorgeousness as though I was seeing it for the first time. I still had to pinch myself sometimes to believe that this place was actually my home now.

'I can't see what the problem is,' Polly went on. 'You do love him, don't you?'

'Yes, more so than ever now that we have little Noel. But I guess I'm just...' I paused, '...scared.' The word tripped off my tongue before I'd even realised the truth of it.

'Scared?' Polly couldn't hide her surprise. 'Of what?'

'That it's not real. That all of this is just temporary. That it might all go wrong. That he'll realise that he doesn't want to be with me after all and we'll break up. Everything will be so much more complicated and messier if we were married.'

Polly screwed up her face and shook her head despairingly. 'This isn't like you, Ellie. You're worrying unnecessarily. It's not going to go wrong. You and Max are great together. Just think what you used to tell me when I was going through a barren patch on the boyfriend front. You told me I had to stay strong and take the risk if I met someone who I thought was worth it. Max is worth that risk, isn't he?'

'Yes, definitely.' I could understand why Polly was confused. I was confused myself. And what Max must think, I just didn't know. He'd been so patient up until now. Maybe his patience would run out soon. 'I'm sure we'll get round to marrying eventually,' I said brightly, as though it were just a mere formality, trying to ignore the tears gathering in my eyes, blinking them away so that Polly wouldn't notice, only there wasn't much chance of that.

'Oh Ellie,' she jumped up and joined me at my end of the sofa, putting an arm around my shoulder. 'Everything is all right, isn't it?'

'Yeah,' I sighed, through my sobs, while chuckling at the same time and cursing my hormones too. 'It's brilliant. Just brilliant. I love my little baby. And I love Max. I'm so happy. Really I am.'

Happy and a complete soggy and messy emotional wreck too. The health visitor had reassured me that it was perfectly normal to feel this way at this stage and that it would soon pass. I really hoped she was right.

Polly looked on indulgently.

'Of course you are. When Max asks you next time to marry him, you should just say yes! Before you know it, it will be Valentine's Day and he's bound to ask you then.'

'Actually, you've reminded me,' I said, sniffing up the tears and giving myself a mental shake, glad of something else to focus on. 'I've got to put together some ideas for The Dog and Duck's Valentine's event. We always have some kind of do. I wonder what we should go for this year?'

'I remember last year's,' sighed Polly. 'I was still pining over Johnny, so I drowned my sorrows in some Martini Kisses and tried to ignore the loved-up atmosphere in the pub. If only I could go back and visit that lovelorn girl and tell her that within a year she'd be engaged to a wonderful new man. She never would have believed me.' There was a look of pure contentment on her face.

'Exactly! It just goes to show how much can change in such a short space of time. Who knows where we might all be in a year's time from now.'

'Married?' said Polly mischievously, a glint in her eye. 'You know you could always propose to Max and then we could have a double wedding in a beautiful manor house somewhere in the countryside.' She fluttered her long eyelashes exaggeratedly, looking all around her. Subtlety was never Polly's strong suit.

'Now, that would be some bash,' I said noncommittally.

'Ooh, what's that then? And am I invited?' Katy appeared in the doorway. In the skinniest of skinny jeans and a black blouse and with her dark hair, worn longer now and falling in soft waves onto her shoulder, she had that natural radiance and beauty rarely seen outside of teenage girls. A beauty she took for granted and perhaps didn't even know she possessed.

'We were just talking about Polly's wedding, not that anything's arranged yet.' I rushed to get the answer in before Polly could bring up the prospect of me marrying Max.

'Oh, I'm desperate to go to a wedding. I've only been to one and that was when I about ten years old. There are some grim photos of me wearing a floral dress, some knee-high white socks and some black patent shoes.' Katy grimaced at the memory.

'Well, you're definitely invited to mine,' said Polly laughing. 'Patent shoes not essential.'

'Thank you,' said Katy, beaming. She turned to me, her eyes bright. 'I can't wait until you and Max get married and then I can be a bridesmaid. Can't I? Wouldn't that be brilliant?'

Oh no, not Katy too!

'I can't see why not, although…'

'And my gorgeous little nephew could be a page boy. Can you imagine how sweet Noel would look in a sailor's outfit?'

Polly shrugged her shoulders at me, giving a knowing smile.

'When do you think you will get married? This coming year, right?' asked Katy, bold as you like, clearly determined not to let the subject drop.

'I really don't know.'

'Have you spoken to Max about it? Is he dragging his heels? Is that why it's taking such a time?'

'No,' I laughed. 'Besides, there's no hurry. We're happy as we are, you know.'

'I could have a word with him, if you like. Tell him to get a move on,' she continued.

'NO! Katy! Don't!' I was probably harsh in my admonition, but the last thing I needed was Katy interfering in what was already a delicate matter. 'There's no need,' I said, attempting to soften my tone. 'I don't wish to be rude, but this is something only Max and I can sort out.'

'Ooh, sorry!' Katy pulled a face, rolling her eyes at Polly. 'I was only trying to help.'

Thankfully Katy was soon distracted by the stirrings of Noel, who was making cute little babbling sounds in his Moses basket. She lifted him out and held him to her shoulder, supporting his head, while whispering into his ear.

'You be a good boy for your mummy and we'll have proper cuddles when I get home.'

Seeing Katy with little Noel warmed my heart as she revelled in her role of aunty. She was unrecognisable from the surly and tight-lipped teenager who had turned up in the village back in the spring, nursing an attitude and what turned out to be a pretty big secret. It was hardly surprising that she and Max clashed back then. They barely knew each other and with their two stubborn and fiery temperaments under one roof, it made for an explosive atmosphere, with door slamming, major sulks and Max vowing to send Katy back home again if she didn't get herself sorted. After some time, and with a bit of careful mediation from me, they came to understand each other a bit better until they were able to have a conversation without it turning into a huge argument. Nowadays, thankfully, the bust-ups were much less frequent.

'Where are you going?' I asked, surprised to see her pulling on her fur-trimmed anorak. I took Noel from her and he filled my arms, his delicious milky scent seducing my nostrils.

'Out, with Ryan. We're going to The Red Lion in Upper Leyton.'

'Not on his motorbike?' I grimaced. As much as I tried to persuade Max that Katy needed her freedom, it didn't stop me from worrying about her.

'No,' laughed Katy. 'Luke's driving. There's a group of us going.'

'Does Max know?'

'Er, not sure,' said Katy, smiling, offering a little wave as she dashed towards the door. 'Would you mind telling him?' She flashed me a wide-eyed, cute-as-pie smile that allowed her to get away with far too much. 'See you later.'

'Katy!' But it was too late. The front door slammed shut and the sound of car wheels scrunched off the gravel.

'Well, she certainly knows how to get round you,' said Polly, laughing. 'Has Max still got a downer on Ryan then?'

'Yep, even more so now after he had a pop at that guy in the pub on Christmas Day. He reckons he's a bad influence on her and doesn't trust him in the slightest. To a certain degree I can understand where he's coming from. Would you want any little sister of yours going out with a guy like Ryan?'

'Probably not, but you can see the appeal from Katy's point of view. He might be a bit down and dirty, but he's downright sexy and dangerously unpredictable too.'

We sniggered, my thoughts distracted for the moment by Ryan dressed in his black motorbike leathers.

'Polly, what are you like? You shouldn't be entertaining inappropriate thoughts about other men. Not now you're an engaged woman!'

'Well neither should you! You've just had a baby.'

'Touché.'

We heard the back door open, shortly followed by the arrival of three large, wet and overexcited dogs, who came into the living room and leapt around in a flurry of wagging tails.

'Holly, Bella, Digby – get back here!' Max's voice reverberated through the house – I don't think he'd fully taken on board yet that there might be a sleeping baby around – and the dogs obediently skittered back outside again.

A few moments later Max wandered in, and stood astride the threshold, his hands resting on the door frame. A casual enough action, but the effect sent a tidal wave of longing rushing through my bones. With his dark hair mussed up, a couple of days' dark growth on his jawline and his face shiny from the cold outside, his physical presence made a startling appearance.

What were we saying? Sexy and dangerously unpredictable? That description could easily apply to Max. Every time I saw him, whether he'd been out all day on business or if, like now, he'd just come in from the garden, my heart would respond to his presence, pitter-pattering in my chest, as though I was seeing him for the first time.

His gaze caught mine, as a smile appeared on his lips.

'You two fancy another drink?' he asked.

'No, I could sit and chat and gaze longingly at your little boy all day long,' said Polly, standing up, 'but I need to go and do some work. The shop's opening tomorrow in time for New Year and I've got some orders I need to make a start on.'

It still took me by surprise that people were going about their daily business as though nothing had changed in the world. And yet for me my whole landscape had shifted and nothing would ever be the same again. The long days between Christmas and New Year only added to the sense of being removed from reality, my whole world now existing within the confines of Braithwaite Manor.

Max saw Polly out and came back and sat down on the sofa next to me, taking Noel out of my arms. He put him over his shoulder, gently cradling him to his chest, his large hand almost totally covering Noel's white romper suit, my heart swelling at the sight. My two main men.

Max's other arm rested around my shoulder. He pulled me into his side and I laid my head on the comforting warmth of his woolly cable jumper, my eyes closing involuntarily, just for the briefest moment, until Noel started to wriggle, pulling his legs up to his chest, his tentative cries soon growing louder, reaching an insistent and ear-splitting crescendo.

Max grimaced and handed back our son, laughing as he left the room to collect his coat.

Five

'I should go,' said Max, a few minutes later, car keys in hand, above the racket Noel was making, looking as though he couldn't wait to escape. 'Hopefully the roads shouldn't be too bad.'

'You don't mind, do you?' I asked.

He chuckled and shook his head affectionately. 'Why would I mind? I love Malc and Veronica, and besides, I can't wait for them to meet their first grandchild.'

Neither could I. Just imagining Mum's face seeing Noel for the first time made me well up with emotion, and to spend some quality time with my parents was something I'd been looking forward to for weeks. I'd spoken to Mum on the phone every day since Noel's birth, but having her on hand to help with everything would be such a huge relief. Now, there was only an hour to go before their plane touched down and Max was off to the airport to collect them.

'Well, I know what you're like,' I said.

Max could be perfectly charming, but wasn't, by nature, a people person. He liked his own company, the great outdoors, doing his own thing, the peace and solitude that Braithwaite Manor set in the middle of the countryside offered him. Or might once had offered him. I glanced down at Noel who was still screaming his head off, wishing I had the magic touch that would make it all stop. Life had changed so much for me in the past twelve months, but I was also aware that Max's life had altered beyond recognition too.

'It'll be fine. It's great to have some life injected into this place.' If, by life, he meant muslins, smelly nappies and dirty crockery everywhere, then he wasn't wrong. He came over and kissed me on the cheek. 'Honestly I wouldn't have it any other way. A proper little family unit, right? Even if that does bring with it a constant stream of visitors at all times of the day. And this noisy little fella not giving me a look in. Besides, it'll be the turn of my mum and Alan in a few weeks. Now, that will be really interesting.'

Even though relations between Katy and her mum and stepdad had improved a bit in recent months, things were still on sticky ground. Max was right to feel apprehensive about having his family all under the same roof. Katy still hadn't forgiven her mum for keeping the secret of who her real father was and that had impacted badly on her relationship with Alan. She couldn't even mention his name without venom spilling from her mouth.

'Anyway, talking of happy families, is that little sister of mine not out of bed yet?'

'Yep, up and out. She left a little while ago. Meeting up with some friends.' I hoped I sounded casual enough.

'Oh,' his face dropped. 'Not Ryan?'

I nodded and Max rolled his eyes.

'For Christ's sake! What does she see in that guy?'

I shrugged, as though it was a complete mystery. Thinking back to my conversation with Polly, I could have provided a whole list of attributes, but it was probably best not to, given that Max probably wouldn't view it in the same way.

'Why can't she find someone her own age? You saw what he was like on Christmas Day. He's got a short fuse and I don't like Katy being with someone like that. You never know what a guy like that is going to do next.'

'Oh, but he would never do anything to deliberately hurt Katy. He adores her and was only looking out for her that day.' I knew Ryan from old. We'd gone to the same school and while he did have a bit of a sketchy past, I was certain that he only had Katy's interests at heart. Besides with Max breathing down his neck, he wouldn't dare step out of line.

Max didn't look convinced. 'You should talk to her. There must be some nice lads down at that college.'

'Me?'

'Well you seem to have a way with her.' Max shook his head. Truculent teenage girls were out of his comfort zone and it was true Katy and I had developed a close bond since we'd come to know each other.

'She's fine, Max. When you think how unhappy she was when she first arrived in Little Leyton and how settled she is now. That's what important, isn't it?'

'Hmm, I suppose,' he said, disapprovingly. He came across to where I'd been gently swaying in front of the crackling fire, trying to soothe Noel's sobs.

'You won't give your dad all this grief when you're older, will you?' Max ran his finger across Noel's cheek.

'I wouldn't be so sure about that. He likes to make himself heard just like his aunty. And I bet he'll be breaking a few hearts one day. What with those big blue eyes, how could he not?'

With Max off on his way and Noel still grizzly in my arms, the idea of being stuck alone in the manor for the next couple of hours didn't fill me with joy. I peered outside into the garden, seeing the snow still piled deep over the lawns, the thaw a day or two away, I suspected.

'How about we go for a little walk, Noel?' I said, lifting him above my head, nuzzling my face into his skin. It would be a change of scene for me and hopefully might send him off to sleep.

Only I could never have anticipated what a palaver it was to get one small child out of the house for something as simple as a country walk.

First of all, Noel needed another feed, his nappy changed and another outfit found, one more suited to the Arctic temperatures outside. Still, at least that wasn't a problem. This child had a wardrobe so extensive it would rival the children's department at Harrods. Then I needed to go to the loo, gather up all the baby paraphernalia, find my wellies, a winter coat, hat, scarf and gloves. Take gloves off and wrangle with the new pushchair, strap Noel in, making sure I'd done it correctly, put Holly and Bella into the utility room, and put Digby's lead on. Spend a frantic few minutes searching for gloves that I'd only minutes before taken off. Find gloves. And go.

Phew! It had only taken me thirty-five minutes.

Still, it was a starting point and I'd make it a challenge to improve on my personal best on future excursions.

Outside, as I attempted to steer the buggy across the gravel drive – no easy feat – the icy cold air greeted me, whirling around my body and stinging my cheeks with its intent. My breath gathered in wispy clouds before me and I pushed on regardless, glad to be outside, feeling energised and, dare I say, half normal again. The beauty of the landscape resonated with me deep down inside. The bare trees, their branches dusted in snow, created a stark and magical atmosphere.

Walking along the back lanes and then onto the High Street was much easier, despite a few twinges reminding me that I'd recently given birth and shouldn't overdo it. We took our time, stopping to admire the decorations adorning the fronts of the homes and shops, and the abundant wreaths hung on the doors. Lights twinkled invitingly, with the evidence of families inside enjoying the last days of their Christmas holidays. Soon we were outside the pub and I paused for a moment, looking up at the colourfully painted sign of The Dog and Duck, wondering if I should pass straight by, but it was only a fleeting thought. How could I not go in? There was a part of me that would always think of the pub as my home, more so now after the events of Christmas Day.

'Look, Noel,' I said, peering over the cover of the buggy to see a little button nose peeking out of his padded romper suit. 'This is where you were born!'

The old oak door of the pub was always heavy to open, but with a buggy it was ten times more difficult. Thankfully I was just attempting the reverse body slam manoeuvre I'd seen other mums perform when someone pulled open the door from the other side and let me in, the warmth and chatter beckoning me inside.

'Oh, look who's here,' said Jake, who was standing at the bar, 'you can't keep away Ellie, can you?' The fuss he made had everyone in the pub coming to greet us.

'Well, I thought I'd come and introduce Noel properly,' I said, feeling strangely emotional to be surrounded by so many friendly and welcoming faces.

'Why don't you come and sit in Grandpa Noel's favourite old chair,' said Eric, who was helping out behind the bar today. 'What you having, a double vodka or would a frothy cappuccino go down better this morning?'

'Thanks, Eric, that sounds lovely!' I lifted Noel out of his buggy and sat in the old rocking chair beside the inglenook fireplace which had been Noel senior's preferred spot in the pub. He'd been a lovely old man, a friend to many, including Arthur who was sat on the other side of the fireplace right now, and I'd always had a soft spot for Noel, long before I'd even met his grandson. It was poignant to imagine what he might think seeing his newborn great-grandson sitting in the very same seat where he'd spent so many happy times.

'How's it going?' I asked Dan, as I pulled Noel out from his buggy and passed him in to the waiting arms of Silke.

'Good, it's been pretty manic these last few days. Of course, everyone's been coming in wanting to hear the story of how you delivered your baby in the barn on Christmas Day. You're quite the celebrity round here now, you know.'

'I didn't plan it that way, I can assure you, but I suppose it is pretty special. Obviously, Noel wanted us to know that he intends being a regular at the pub from the very beginning.'

I looked across at my baby now, wrapped in a white crocheted blanket, and my heart expanded. Silke was gently rocking him in her arms watched by a crowd of middle-aged men who all had silly smiles on their faces.

'Everything sorted for the New Year celebrations?' I asked Dan, dead casually, not wanting him to think I didn't have anything but utter faith in his abilities. Of course I did! It was just that this time last year I'd done all the organising myself, and I was finding it very hard not to get involved now.

'Yep, all tickets have been sold. Should be a good night.'

'Well, if you need me to…'

'We won't!' Dan smiled, shaking his head, obviously knowing me only too well. 'Everything's under control.'

Of course it was. What was I expecting? That the place would fall to pieces as soon as I wasn't around? I'd been so use to doing everything myself at the pub that it was hard to let go. Ever since I'd taken over from Eric, I'd given everything I had to the business, my main priority being to ensure that the future of the Dog and Duck was secure. I'd seen so many other village pubs close down that I was determined not to let that happen in Little Leyton. Growing up in the village, it had always been at the centre of so many happy events; barbecues, summer fetes, Halloween parties and quiz nights, offering so much more than just a pint and a packet of peanuts. It was the hub of our community, a place where people of all ages could come together for friendship and support. I'd gained so much from being involved with the pub that I wanted future generations, including my children, to have the same opportunities.

'Eric, we've got a full rota of staff on for New Year so if you wanted to come to the manor instead, you'd be more than welcome. Mum and Dad will be there. Josie and Ethan too,' I said, laying a hand on his arm.

'Ah, yes, Josie mentioned something about that. I think she said she was going to call you. It's kind of you to invite me, but I prefer to work. It keeps my mind busy and stops me from dwelling on the passing of another year.' He chuckled. 'Besides, I need to keep an eye on the rabble here.'

'Old habits, eh?' I laughed.

However attached to the pub I might feel, Eric was bound to feel it even more keenly. This place had been his home and his life for almost a quarter of a century. He was happy to be back behind the bar of The Dog & Duck and it gave me a reassuring sense of security to know he was there with his whole wealth of experience to call on should it be needed.

On the way back to the manor, it occurred to me that this year would be the first in ages that I wouldn't be seeing in the New Year at the pub, but I felt only the tiniest pang of regret. Our celebrations at the manor would be more low-key, but just as special.

I'd just reached the lanes when I spotted Sasha walking towards us, looking impossibly glamorous in her long black parka, boots and fur hat, pushing Ruby in the buggy. When she was pregnant she'd decided she wanted to move back into Little Leyton to make a home for herself and her baby. At the time I'd been horrified by the thought that Max's ex would be living down the road from us, but I needn't have worried. We quickly became friends.

'Oh Ellie! How are you? I've been wanting to see you.' She came rushing over and threw her arms around me in a hug before bending down to look at Noel. 'And this little man as well. Oh my goodness, he's so adorable. And what an entrance he made into the world, eh?'

'Yes, it was a bit hairy at the time, and such a relief when he arrived safe and sound. I thought of you, and when you had Ruby. Tried to draw on the strength you'd shown. Honestly, it really helped.' Now I looked down at Noel, suddenly feeling self-conscious, my hands resting on the handle of the buggy, as though I was just trying it out for size. 'Still can't quite believe he's mine.'

'Don't worry. It takes a while,' she said with a knowing smile.

'Anyway, how are you? How was your Christmas?'

'Good. My sister, Penny, was over from Australia, it was the first time she'd been to visit since Ruby was born so it was lovely for us to spend some time together. She left for the airport this morning so I thought we'd get out for some fresh air.'

'And what about Peter?' I asked, tentatively.

'Nope.' She shook her head looking sad. 'That's all over now.'

'Really?' It wasn't the first time Sasha had told me she was ending her relationship with the father of her baby.

'Yes. It's for definite this time,' she said, as if reading my mind. 'He's been back and forwards for so long now that if one of us doesn't make a decision then we'll be carrying on like that for years and I don't want that. It's not fair on me or Ruby. I've got to accept that Peter is never going to leave his wife.'

Sasha was putting on a brave front, but I knew from the emotion in her words that she was hurting deep down inside.

'Look what are you doing for New Year's?' I asked.

She smiled ruefully, looking down at Ruby. 'Err, a quiet night in with a couple of glasses of fizz and Jools Holland.'

'Oh well in that case, why not come to us, at the manor.'

She paused, clearly considering it. 'Well I wouldn't want to intrude.'

'You wouldn't be. Mum and Dad will be there, Polly and George, Josie and Ethan too. I'm not sure yet about Katy. Maybe – if she doesn't get a better offer in the meantime. Oh, and Jools Holland will probably put in an appearance too. We're not doing anything special, just a few drinks and nibbles, but it would be lovely if you could come. We could share nappy duty. It would make sense for you to stay over as well, as it will be a late-ish night.'

'Well if you're sure, then yes I'd love to.'

There'd been a time when I'd been mistrustful of Sasha. I'd first met her when she was still with Max, and my initial impression, when I'd knocked on her door in a panic with an injured dog in my arms, had stayed with me. Tall, willowy and unquestionably gorgeous, I was taken aback by her very existence. I'd spent a long weekend with Max on a charity run, cooped up in a van with him, and he hadn't once mentioned he had a girlfriend. The discovery had rocked me, not because anything had gone on between us, but because in the space of a few days I'd developed feelings for him and allowed myself to hope that there could be something more between us in the future. Coming face to face with his stunningly attractive girlfriend had put paid to any ideas I might have had on that front. I wasn't to know that their relationship was already on dodgy ground and they were going through the process of extracting themselves from their five-year-long union. And I could never have known then that a few months later Max and I would get together. Whilst I'd been wary of Sasha in the first place she'd never shown me any animosity or jealousy whatsoever. As far as we were both concerned the past was very much in the past and we had certainly grown closer in recent months not least because of baby Ruby's arrival.

'See you tomorrow then.' Sasha turned to go down the back lane which led to Bluebell Cottages when she stopped, as though changing her mind, and that's when I noticed the hooded figure walking towards us.

'Who's that then?' I asked, realising the reason for her hesitation.

'Don't know. I saw him earlier just wandering about the lane. I've not seen him around here before and he doesn't have a dog with him. I just thought it a bit strange, that's all,' she said, surreptitiously looking over her shoulder before turning her back on him.

I gave him a glance too, not recognising him either. The thing about living in a village like Little Leyton was that you knew everyone, if only by sight. A stranger in the midst was always likely to cause comment and sometimes concern too. As he drew closer, I had the chance to get a better look.

'Oh hello there!'

I had seen him before, after all.

The man pulled his hood down and I recognised him as the visitor who had turned up at the pub on Christmas Day. What he was still doing around here when he hadn't been destined for Little Leyton in the first place I just didn't know. It took him a second but then he recognised me too.

'Ah, hello. You had your baby then?' he said, with an air of casual confidence.

'Yes, a little boy. His name's Noel,' I said, my gaze sweeping surreptitiously over the stranger. There was something about him, something I couldn't quite put my finger on, that made me feel uneasy.

'Well congratulations. Look, I don't think I had the chance of thanking you properly for taking me in on Christmas Day. Not sure what I would have done if you hadn't have helped me out.' He dropped his gaze for a moment. 'Sorry, you know, for any trouble I may have caused.'

I could see Sasha looking from me to the man curiously, but now wasn't the time to fill her in on the gossip.

'No problem.' I told him. 'But I didn't expect to see you back around here again so soon?'

'I was just driving home actually, so I thought I'd stop and take a look around. It's a lovely village, isn't it? Very picturesque. Is that Braithwaite Manor?' he asked, looking down at the Georgian house, my home, still dusted in snow.

'Er yes, that's right.'

'Yes, Katy mentioned it. It's as impressive as she made out. That's where she lives, right?'

Hearing him mention Katy's name gave me a gnawing sense of unease. 'Yes, but…'

'She was telling me about it. How amazing it was inside. The grounds etc. She seems like a sweet kid.'

'Yes, well…' I bristled against the cold and this man asking impertinent questions. I'd been only too keen to do him a favour on Christmas Day, but what was he doing here asking questions about Katy? I wasn't about to hang around to find out. 'I need to get going actually.'

The man took the hint and walked on past us. 'Yes, well Happy New Year!' he called over his shoulder. 'Perhaps I'll see you again!'

Sasha gave me a questioning look, her brow furrowed. 'What was that all about?'

'I have no idea,' I said, shaking my head. But I sincerely hoped he was wrong; I had no desire to see the man around this way again.

Six

'Is he asleep?' Max whispered hopefully.

It was New Year's Eve and I'd just tiptoed in from our cosy reading room where Noel and Ruby were sleeping in their cots, close enough for us to hear them if they woke, but far enough away so as not to be disturbed by our festivities.

'Yes. They both are. For the moment at least.' I crossed my fingers in the air and there was an audible exhalation of relief from our New Year revellers, all seven of us. Josie had rung earlier to say that they wouldn't be able to make it as they were all struggling with colds, so had opted for a quiet evening at home instead. And, as expected, Katy had received a better offer and had dashed out before Max could stop her. Our two youngest party-goers hadn't been any trouble at all. Ruby and Noel had been passed amongst all of us for cuddles and feeds and were now sleeping sweetly, totally oblivious to the excitement of their first New Year's Eve.

'With any luck Ruby should go all the way through till morning now,' said Sasha, who was looking as lovely as ever in velvet wide-legged trousers and a gold sparkly top.

'And hopefully we might get a couple of hours from Noel,' I said, taking the glass of champagne that Max proffered. I felt my body relax as I took that first delicious sip, the bubbles tickling my nostrils and giving me an immediate frisson inside. I savoured the taste on my tongue. My first alcoholic drink in months and while I hadn't missed it when I was pregnant, it tasted far far better than I remembered.

'Well, you two girls just sit back and enjoy yourselves,' said Mum who had been bustling around ever since she'd arrived and had just come in from the kitchen where she'd been removing clingfilm from plates. She'd spent the whole day preparing savoury and sweet bites for our small party and, judging by the impressive spread she had put on, she was clearly expecting the whole village to put in an appearance. 'I know what it's like when you're a young mum. It can be completely exhausting. Take the chance to relax while you can. I'm more than happy to take over the nappy and feeding duties.' It was an absolute blessing having mum around, she hadn't let me lift a finger from the moment she'd arrived.

'Now you're not to go and prod those babies to wake them up, Veronica,' said Max jokingly.

'No, I wouldn't go as far as that, but it's so lovely to have a little one in the family. And he's got a ready-made friend in Ruby, hasn't he? It's so lovely to see them together. Hasn't it made all the difference to us, Malc?'

Dad looked up and smiled his agreement before going back to supping on his beer.

I got up and followed Mum out to the kitchen.

'Is Dad okay?' I asked her.

'Why? What do you mean, love?' She glanced away, but I saw a hint in her eyes that she knew exactly what I was talking about.

'I don't know. He just doesn't seem himself, as though he's distracted by something.'

'Oh darling.' She came over, hugged me fiercely and unexpectedly, and I stepped back, surprised by her sudden show of affection.

'Mum?'

'Your dad's fine,' she said, shaking her head and returning her attentions to the food. 'He's been very busy at work. The holidays have come and he's just relaxed. You know what it's like, but he's so pleased to be here, back in Little Leyton. Don't tell him I told you, but when he heard the news that you'd had the baby, he had a little cry. We both did!'

'Really?'

I could believe it of Mum, but Dad? He had always been so strong and positive, never really showing his emotions, but always there as a source of comfort and support when we needed him. I couldn't remember seeing him cry before, not even when our much-loved golden retriever, Lady, died when I was a little girl. That lovely dog followed my dad around everywhere, the pair of them inseparable, and I knew he felt her loss just as keenly, perhaps even more so, than Mum and I had. His main concern had been for us though and he'd wrapped us both in his arms and helped us through our sadness, pushing his own feelings to one side.

My heart twisted at the thought of Dad crying at the arrival of Noel. There was a sensitivity and vulnerability I recognised in him now that I hadn't seen before. Maybe that's what happened when you had a baby, you became more sensitive to the feelings of others around you. Becoming a mother was a big emotional shift for me. Perhaps becoming a grandfather for the first time was equally as moving and life-changing. I'd not had the chance to talk to Dad alone since he'd arrived. Maybe that was what we needed. Some father and daughter one-on-one time.

'Come on then,' called Mum. 'The food's ready. Help yourself. It's all got to be eaten.'

We found our places around the big oak table in the kitchen, filling our plates from the sumptuous selection in front of us. Max ensured everyone's glass was full and it was a lovely relaxed atmosphere being with the people who mattered most to me in the world. Candles lined the windowsills that ran round the kitchen and conservatory, offering a warm, soft light. Through the full-length windows we could see out over the garden, snow still covering the ground and shrubs. The Christmas tree that Max had potted on the patio looked beautiful, covered as it was in a myriad of tiny fairy lights.

'Isn't this lovely,' said Mum, voicing my thoughts.

'Perfect,' I said, looking across at Dad, who seemed to be lost in his own world. 'I wonder how it's going down at the pub?' I mused, into the silence, wondering if he might prefer being there right now with all his pals. That was probably why he was a bit subdued. Instead he was on babysitting duties with the rest of us.

'Oh Ellie, you're always thinking about the pub,' said Polly, laughing. 'It'll be jam-packed and extremely rowdy, as we know from previous years.'

'Katy will no doubt fill us in on all the gory details when she gets home, whenever that might be,' said Max with a roll of the eyes.

'Actually,' said Polly, 'we've been thinking about the pub a bit recently, haven't we?' She turned to George who nodded and smiled indulgently.

'Oh...?' I said.

'Yes, well we've booked an appointment to see Rev. Trish Evans on Monday to firm up a date for our wedding at St Cuthbert's. We're hoping for May or June, and we've been thinking where we might have the reception. We've looked at different venues in the area, but we keep on coming back to The Dog and Duck.'

'Really? You were talking about a posh stately home do the last time we spoke,' I said, trying to hide my excitement at the possibility of my best friend having her wedding at the pub.

'I know, but we've decided we want something a bit more cosy and intimate. It's going to be a relatively quiet affair. About forty or fifty people at the most and the barn at the pub would lend itself brilliantly to that. It's so charming and quaint and perfect for an English country wedding, and that's exactly the vibe we want to go for. I mean, only if that's okay with you, Ellie, and you haven't got any other bookings for that day.'

I laughed, caught up in Polly's enthusiasm. 'Oh, don't you worry, if I have got any other bookings then I'll cancel them. You're one of my besties – of course, I'd love to host your wedding reception at The Dog and Duck if that's what you really want.'

'We do,' said Polly, her face beaming now, as she reached for George's hand. 'I keep thinking how wonderful little Stella's christening was. It was such a gorgeous, relaxed day and that's what I want for our wedding. It's near enough to the church that we can all walk to the reception. And I know if you're taking care of the arrangements, Ellie, then I won't need to worry about a thing.' Polly paused, looking around at our rapt faces. 'Listen to me though, getting carried away. You must say if you don't want to do it or can't for any reason.'

'Don't be daft. Consider it booked. Just let me know the date you decide upon and then we can start making some definite plans. Just think, a summer wedding at The Dog and Duck. How exciting it will be.' Since having Noel, I hadn't relished the idea of returning to work shifts behind the bar, not that I needed to now with such a reliable team of workers. But organising the special events, including my best friend's wedding, would be a lovely way to get me back into the swing of things at the pub.

'Lovely,' said Mum, in agreement.

'Of course, you'll all be invited,' said Polly excitedly. 'You must try and come,' she said, addressing Mum and Dad. 'This really is going to be the best year ever. George's new book comes out in March and I'm going off with him for a couple of weeks on his publicity tour around the country, and then when we get back, the wedding preparations can start in earnest.'

George coughed, clearing his throat. 'Of course, this does mean, Veronica and Malc, that I won't be renewing the tenancy on the cottage when it comes up for renewal. I'll be moving in with Polly for a while until we find a place of our own, hopefully in the village somewhere.'

'Well don't worry about that, George,' said Mum, her face lighting up, seemingly completely unruffled by the news. 'We're just pleased that you've looked after our house so well for the last year or so. We couldn't have wished for a nicer tenant. I've told all our friends in Dubai that we have a bestselling novelist living in our house and they're always so impressed.'

George laughed. 'Yes, and to think if I'd gone to a different village, I might never have met my future wife. It's funny how these things work out, isn't it?'

Max nodded his agreement to George, his lip twisting in a contemplative manner.

'Well you two are certainly in for a busy and exciting year then,' said Mum. 'And you, Ellie, and Max, and Sasha too, watching your babies grow up. They change so much in these first few months, so you must treasure the special moments, because they pass by in a flash.' She sighed, reflective for a moment. 'It can be a funny time of year though, can't it? The New Year? Not always a happy time for everyone. It's a time for reflection, to consider all that's gone on in the previous year and to make plans for the new year. Apparently, the first week in January is the busiest time for solicitors with new clients coming in wanting to start divorce proceedings.'

Dad grimaced. 'Oh dear, does that mean I'll be for the chop then?' He chuckled.

'Would you stop it, Malc,' said Mum dismissively, and I had to wonder if there was something behind Dad's jokey comment. They'd always been such a close couple, but there was definitely something going on between them. I just couldn't work out what it was at the moment.

*

The night slipped away from us as we ate good food, drank sparkling wine and gossiped.

'Oh my goodness!' Mum glanced at her watch. 'It's twenty to twelve. Not long to go now. I'll get some clean glasses out for the champagne.'

'Ellie, do me a favour and go and grab the camera,' Max asked. 'It's on the sideboard in our bedroom.'

'I can take some photos on my phone if you like,' I suggested.

Max had arranged a firework display and would be dashing off outside to set them alight just as soon as the clock had struck twelve. It looked as though I would be taking on the role of chief photographer.

'No, use the decent camera, we'll get better shots on that.'

I slipped away, checking on the babies, Noel in his Moses basket and Ruby in a travel cot, their little chests rising gently in synchronicity. I smiled, a warm squidgy feeling filling my chest. Mum was right, this really would be the best year ever.

I tiptoed upstairs, conscious of not making too much noise so that I wouldn't wake them, although they'd slept through everything else tonight, I knew Noel would be waking soon for his next feed, although hopefully not until after we'd seen in the new year. I walked along the wide galleried landing upstairs to our bedroom, and pushed open the door, the sight beyond the threshold taking my breath away. I gasped, not quite believing what I was seeing. My nose twitched at the sweet and floral scent wafting in the air.

So that's what Max had been doing when he'd disappeared earlier this evening! Rose-scented tea lights flickered in heart-shaped holders on every available surface, along the windowsills, on the dressing table and on the oak chest of drawers. Rose petals were scattered all over the cream silk eiderdown and in the centre of the bed was a makeshift heart, constructed with pastel-coloured love hearts sweets, each with a different message, and in the middle were the words 'Will you marry me?' spelled out in gold word tiles.

'Oh my goodness!' My hand flew to my mouth, as dozens of emotions flooded my head.

I didn't know if I'd been standing there a few moments or a few minutes when I heard Max's warm voice wrap around me.

'Well you didn't really think I was going to miss an opportunity like tonight?'

I span round to see him standing just outside of the door, his silhouette shadowy in the half-light. Even the outline of his tall and broad frame stirred a deep warmth and longing inside me that I couldn't ignore.

'Max? You did all this. I had no idea. It's beautiful, magical.' I couldn't help but feel thrilled but still there was a part of me that panicked.

'No less than you deserve. We have our beautiful baby boy together, a whole new year ahead of us. No, scrub that, we have the whole of the rest of our lives ahead of us. Will you marry me, Ellie? You know it makes sense.'

With a smile on his lips, he came across and took me in his arms, his face looking into mine beseechingly. My arms wrapped around his wide chest and my head rested against his shirt, the beat of his heart sounding clearly in my ear. Steady, familiar, reassuring. Funny to think that was how I thought of him now when initially I'd been attracted to his spontaneous, unpredictable and dangerous side. He was all of those things, and so much more too.

'I really don't know what to say.' I was overwhelmed by the lengths he'd gone to.

'You know you only need to say one thing,' he said, gesturing towards the message in the middle of the bed. 'That's all. It's really not that difficult.'

'Max… You know how much I love you. How happy I am to be with you, to be a family now with Noel. It's means everything to me…' I heard my voice fade away.

'But…?' He dropped his arms and shrugged. The silence between us speaking volumes. 'It's fine, Ellie. You don't owe me any explanations. I mean, I only want to marry you if you feel the same way too and clearly you don't,' he said, his expression darkening.

'No, Max, it's not that, it's…'

From downstairs I heard the distinct and insistent cries of Noel, my body reacting instinctively to his call. Max and I exchanged a look, knowing that the moment we should be sharing was lost now.

I loved Max more than anything, there wasn't anyone else I'd rather be with, but I couldn't bring myself to utter the word he longed to hear. 'Yes!' Just that one simple little word. Yet it was as if I couldn't even contemplate the idea, not when I had so many other things fighting for attention in my mind. Noel needed me, my mum and dad were staying over, my best friend was planning her wedding and I needed to lose the extra stone and a half in weight I'd gained during my pregnancy before I could even think about donning a bridal gown. Getting married was a huge, life-changing decision to make and I couldn't just agree to something like that on the spur of the moment.

'Let's talk about it in the new year,' I offered, 'once things are back to normal and when Mum and Dad have gone home.' As if everything might be clearer then.

'Whatever you think, Ellie.' He forced a smile, but I knew him well enough to know that he was stung by my rejection; yet another one, I suspected he was thinking. My gaze cast over the beautiful scene he'd created and I stood in awe for a moment, just drinking it all in, picking out the details of our names spelled out in word tiles that he'd placed around the room and the montage of photos of us in various silly poses, that I hadn't noticed before.

It was like something from a film, a feel-good romance, only in the film the heroine would have jumped up and down, and screamed and yelled, and said, 'of course, I'll marry you,' before crying tears of happiness.

I wanted to cry, tears of joy and frustration all mingled together. At that moment I may have hated myself. I turned to him reaching out my fingertips for his hand.

'I love you, Max.'

He shrugged, and took a deep breath looking all around him. Noel's cries had abated now, I suspected mum was seeing to him, but I felt torn about staying there with Max or going back downstairs. Max made the decision for me. 'Go on, you should go and see to our guests or else you'll miss the big moment. I'll just blow out these candles and then I'll be down.'

My heart twisted. The big moment had been up here in our bedroom but my lukewarm response had spoilt everything. I wondered if we shouldn't rewind five minutes and Max could ask me again if I would marry him and this time I would give him the answer he was longing to hear.

'Fancy a sweet?' he asked, laughing ruefully, scooping up the love hearts with his hand. He picked one out at random and tossed it over to me. I caught it and turned it over in my hand. 'Be mine,' it said, and as I repeated the words aloud to Max, I felt a pang of regret and loss in my chest. I gave a half-smile and cupped it in my hand, saving it for later.

'Ellie, come on,' I heard my mum calling upstairs. 'There's a glass of champagne for you both down here. There's not long to go now.'

'We can talk about this later,' I told Max, but I wasn't entirely sure he was listening, so I reluctantly left him behind, torn between staying in the bedroom and discussing it with him here and now, and returning to the festivities below.

'Ah there you are,' said Mum when I reappeared downstairs. She already had Noel in her arms and was rocking him back to sleep, his cries abating now. I hoped the heat I felt in my cheeks wasn't noticeable. I could blame it on the champagne, if necessary.

'Is Max coming?' asked Mum impatiently. We'd already started on the countdown.

'Ten, Nine, Eight, Seven...' everyone chanted.

Max slipped into the room just in time to join in. There was a warm smile on his face and no indication that we'd had any awkwardness upstairs.

'Six, Five, Four, Three, Two, One! HAPPY NEW YEAR!'

The bells chimed on midnight and party poppers rained down on us thanks to Polly and George. We all hugged and kissed, wishing each other the happiest of new years, before embarking on a ropey rendition of 'Auld Lang Syne'. Dad squeezed me tight, and Mum got all emotional, saying what a year it was and how lucky she was to have us all in our lives, Sasha poured the champagne, and Max and George disappeared off into the garden to get the firework display under way. Holly and Bella who were trained gun dogs went with them, observing from a respectable distance, while Digby sidled up against me for comfort. I reached my hand down to fondle his head. Dear Digby. He'd been with me every step of the way over the last couple of years; loyal, dependable and a constant through all the ups and downs. If he could only talk to me now and tell me what I should do.

Outside, the sky lit up in a fountain of colours, but all the deafening bangs and whistles resounding in the air couldn't silence the thoughts fighting for attention inside my head.

'Are you all right, love? You were miles away there?' Mum asked.

'I was just thinking about Noel, he'll be due his next feed soon.'

Mum seemed pretty satisfied with my answer, but it brought it home to me that I couldn't worry over it now, not while Mum and Dad were staying – she would pick up immediately on any tensions between me and Max. Not that there had been many, I thought, before tonight. Well, nothing that a good and honest conversation wouldn't sort out.

Mentally, I brought myself back to the moment, plastering a big smile on my face, looking through the French double doors at the dazzling display outside, joining in with the oohing and aahing. I should have known Max would never do things by half, the pyrotechnics flashing over the valley were so spectacular they wouldn't have looked out of place lighting up the sky over Sydney Harbour. How little Ruby could sleep through this racket, I just didn't know. She might be totally oblivious and unimpressed by the display outside, but apparently the spectacle wasn't missed by the rest of the village.

'Everyone went outside to watch them,' said Katy when she turned up later with Ryan in tow. 'They were brilliant, Max. We all said how you should make it an annual event. Fireworks over the manor bringing in the New Year.'

'I can't see why not. That's if we're still here in a year's time of course.'

We all turned to look at Max in dismay, but it was Katy who voiced our concerns.

'Max! What do you mean?' The outrage in her voice was evident

He laughed, clearly bemused by all our stricken expressions. 'Nothing in particular, I was just saying, that's all. If we're still here in a year's time, then yes, good idea!'

He shook his head, a rueful smile on his lips and returned to what he was doing, making coffee for our guests. His voice was bright enough, which allayed everyone else's concerns, but not mine. Max had always told me that he would never leave Braithwaite Manor. He intended to spend the rest of his life here. He'd spent years looking for a place where he could put down roots, somewhere that felt like home, and coming to Little Leyton to nurse his grandpa in his final months, he'd found a family connection to the village that he'd never experienced before. The fact that he would even bring up the possibility that we – I assume he was talking for both of us – may not be here this time next year was surprising to say the least. Was it a sly dig at me for not jumping at his marriage proposal?

'Max?' Katy's voice took on a sing-song quality, distracting me from my musings.

Ryan was hovering by the back door, looking as though he hadn't quite decided if he was coming or going.

'Would it be okay…' Katy trailed off, pausing for a moment before the words spilled off her tongue. 'Can Ryan stay the night? It's a bit late for him to be walking home.'

Ryan shifted on the spot, looking uncomfortable, under the intensity of Max's unwavering gaze.

'It's pitch black out there,' Katy gabbled on, 'and have you heard, Max, there's been a string of burglaries in the village over the holidays? You don't know who might be hanging about in the lanes. Four houses on the High Street were broken into apparently and their Christmas presents taken.'

'Really?' said Mum alarmed. 'Honestly, what's happening to our village? The only crime we had when you were growing up were a few thefts of

90

hanging baskets and garden gnomes. What is wrong with people now?'

'It's probably just chancers from outside the village,' said Max. 'A one-off with any luck,' he said pointedly at Ryan.

'We saw that guy in the lane the other day, didn't we, Ellie?' said Sasha. 'He seemed a bit dodgy, he was asking questions and...'

'He's been in the pub before,' I said, quickly wanting to gloss over that particular meeting. 'I'm sure he's harmless enough.' The man from Christmas Day? Could he have been a burglar scoping out the local properties? Possibly, but it seemed unlikely. Still, after all the kerfuffle before, I really didn't want to draw Max and Ryan's attention to the fact that the man was still hanging around the village.

Dad stood up, yawning. 'Well, I'll have to leave you good people to it and get to my bed. It's way past my bedtime. Thank you for a lovely evening, Max and Ellie.'

Everyone murmured their assent as Dad steadied himself on the table and then attempted to manoeuvre himself around the chairs. He swayed, a soppy grin on his face as he tried to stop his head from lolling from one side to the other. I hoped he was all right. He'd been uncharacteristically quiet, and despite Mum's assertions that everything was fine, she'd been watching him like a hawk. As he made his way deliberately through the kitchen, his movements slow and purposeful, he stepped on the debris of some party poppers strewn across the floor, his slippered foot shooting out from underneath him.

'Woah!' He tumbled over, landing in an ungainly heap on the ground. The dogs immediately rushed to his side and started licking his face and nudging him with their noses, urging him to get up.

'Malc! What have you done?' Mum rushed to his side too. 'I told you you needed to watch your drinking. I knew something like this would happen. Call an ambulance.'

'Mum!' We all turned to look at her, surprised by her reaction. This wasn't like her. She was flapping around as if Dad had done himself some serious damage when he seemed perfectly fine, without any sign of even a scratch.

'You're all right, aren't you, Dad?' I checked.

'Yes, I'm fine,' he said, sheepishly. 'You would think I'd know by now to take more water with it,' he giggled, trying and failing to get up.

'Oh Malc, let's get you up to bed.' Mum looked round helplessly, her panic evident and Max and Ryan came to her aid, helping Dad to his feet before Mum grabbed him by the arm and led him away, all the time whispering at him furiously. I couldn't help feeling sorry for him being on the end of Mum's wrath.

With Mum and Dad on their way, it seemed that everyone else was flagging too.

'Max?' Katy looked up at him hopefully, still waiting for an answer to her question.

He shrugged, and looked to me, as though I held the answers. I gave him a gentle nod trying to appeal to his better nature.

'He's not sleeping in your room,' he said gruffly.

'Oh Max, God…' Katy dropped her head in her hands. 'You're so embarrassing. No, of course not, but we've got plenty of spare rooms, haven't we? It's not a problem, is it?'

Even with Sasha and George and Polly staying over, we still had several free rooms and Katy had played a blinder, asking if Ryan could stay in front of everyone else.

'No, I suppose not. If it's all right with Ellie,' he said, waving his hand in my direction. I nodded my agreement and then he turned to Ryan. 'Fine, you're welcome to stay,' he said, not sounding wholly hospitable.

Honestly, wonders would never cease. Perhaps Max was finally thawing towards Ryan, after all. Hopefully it would be the first of many positive changes we would see in the New Year.

Seven

'Your father and I are going into town,' Mum announced after breakfast one day, just as I was squeezing Noel into his romper suit.

They'd decided to extend their stay in Little Leyton, which had come as a lovely surprise. It meant I got to spend more time with my parents, and Mum, quite willingly, took over all the domestic arrangements so I was able to focus on Noel.

Max, always an early riser, was up and out into his office in the garden every morning, a large log cabin from which he ran his property empire. Periodically during the day, he would pop back into the house for a cuppa or some lunch or more likely to snatch some time with his baby boy, before disappearing back outside to his den.

With Mum and Dad around and Noel increasingly demanding and fractious each night due to colic, there'd been little time to sit down and talk to Max about what had happened on New Year's Eve. When I'd tried, it had only ended badly.

'I'm sorry, Max,' I'd said, just as we were climbing into bed one night. 'I wasn't saying no to the concept entirely, just that it's probably best if we sit down and talk about what it is we want together.'

He'd grimaced at that comment, unable to disguise the look of disdain on his face. 'What's there to talk about?' He'd picked up his pillows and banged them with more force than was entirely necessary, I'd thought. 'It was a simple enough question. I asked you to marry me. You said no. I'd say there's nothing further to discuss.'

'Oh Max, don't be like that. I didn't mean to hurt your feelings. You know how much you mean to me. We love each other. Is it really that important if and when we get married?'

'Clearly not.' Sometimes there was just no getting through to him.

'Let's have a sensible conversation about it, Max.'

'Let's not,' he said coldly. 'For whatever reason, you don't want to get married. I've thought about it and that's fine. Don't worry. I won't ask you again.'

With that he'd harrumphed, turned his back on me and pulled the duvet over to his side of the bed, exposing my bare limbs to the cold air. It hadn't helped that when he'd been wrestling with his pillows a love heart had rolled out of the linen and onto the floor. I'd been finding those pesky sweets for days afterwards, underneath the bed and on the windowsills, a reminder of Max's grand gesture. Part of me wished I'd taken a photo of our bedroom with all of Max's special romantic touches, as I'd kept revisiting the scene in my head trying to remember the intricate details, but it wouldn't have been appropriate, not when my answer hadn't been the right one.

I hadn't told Mum because I knew she would have overreacted. Mum was Max's biggest fan and in her eyes he could do no wrong. She would never understand why I hadn't jumped at the chance to be his wife.

Dad might have seen it differently, but I didn't want to burden him with my worries, not when he was on holiday, trying to unwind. I'd noticed a change in him. Normally, he was so upbeat, full of energy and joking around, but now he was more subdued and withdrawn, older somehow. Dad had always been totally focussed on his career, but maybe it was a case of time catching up with him. He couldn't continue at breakneck speed forever, it occurred to me with a tinge of sadness. No one was invincible, not even my dad.

Today I'd planned on walking into the village and popping into the pub to discuss the Valentine's Day event with Dan, but that could wait. I wanted to make the most of the time I had with my parents.

'Good idea. We'll come with you into town. I could do with picking up some more vests for Noel.'

'No!' said Mum sharply, and I was taken aback by her response. 'You won't want to come. We've got a couple of meetings. With the bank manager. Lots of paperwork to sort out. And we're not sure how long the meetings are likely to go on for. Isn't that right, Malc? You could be hanging around for ages. I'll tell you what, why don't we fix another date for shopping and make a proper day of it. We can go for lunch as well. You know what your father's like. He gets bored after half an hour, so it would be best to leave him at home and then there'll be no need to hurry. We'll just be at the beck and call of this little man,' she said, coming over and tickling Noel under the chin.

'Okay,' I said, feeling slightly put out by mum's dismissal, but then it probably made sense for them to go alone if they had business to see to. I was just aware that they would be returning to Dubai soon and wanted to make the most of our remaining time together. I sighed inwardly. The thought of them leaving again gave me a huge pang of sadness.

I'd grown used to having my parents around, sharing the day-to-day minutiae of our lives, something that we couldn't do when they were on the opposite side of the world. I'd come to rely on Mum, asking her advice when I wasn't sure if I was caring for Noel in the right way. If his crying was normal, if he'd been sleeping too long or if he was getting enough milk from his feeds. If the terrible colic he was suffering wasn't from something I was doing. Mum was always there with a reassuring word and a kindly hug. Now, to think that she wouldn't be on hand to answer my silly questions and to make me a cup of tea when I needed one snagged at my heart. How would I cope? Not that I would ever admit as much to my parents. They had their own busy and fulfilling lives in Dubai, and I didn't want them to feel guilty about leaving me behind. When they saw Noel next, he would be several months older and would have changed so much. Still, there were always video calls. It wouldn't be the same, but it would have to do.

After seeing Mum and Dad off in the car, I made the short walk into the village, pushing Noel in his buggy, with Digby close by my side. The snow had all cleared now apart from a few stubborn traces left on the trees and rooftops. In the High Street, a snowman built by the local children was clinging on to its existence, the bright orange carrot nose and black button eyes still sticking out jauntily, but its shoulders and rotund body were slumping dejectedly to the ground. The shops had all taken down their cheery decorations and there was a back-to-business feel about today. Of course, at the pub there'd been no respite as Christmas was one of the busiest times of the year and yet this morning, before the lunchtime rush, there was a quiet peacefulness within the old walls of The Dog and Duck.

Eric was behind the bar updating the chalkboard with the latest arrivals of craft beers.

'Hello, sweetheart,' he said, his face lighting up when he saw me. 'How are you and little Noel doing?'

'Yeah, good. None of us are getting much sleep, but we're all completely besotted, it's almost as if he's always been here. Anyway, what are you doing here? You weren't down to work today, were you?' I'd drawn up the rotas so knew who should be working and when and I was certain Eric hadn't been on the list for today.

'Ah well, there lies a story. I thought Dan would have told you. I asked him to check with you first, but, well, I've moved back in here for a while. I hope that's all right with you?'

'Really? When did that happen?'

'Er, it would have been a few days after Christmas.'

I shook my head unable to hide my surprise.

This had been Eric's home for many years before he retired as landlord to go travelling the world. I'd often stayed here as a child for sleepovers with my best friend Josie, and Eric and his late wife, Miriam, were like a second family to me. Although Max had stepped in to buy the pub when the lease came up for sale and I'd been appointed as manager, I would always think of this as Eric's home. Dan had obviously forgotten to mention it, but I was still puzzling over why Eric was staying here in the first place.

'Of course, it's not a problem but I'm just wondering why, that's all.'

'Well, Josie and Ethan need some time alone together. They're a young family, they don't want her old dad looking over their shoulders all the time, getting in the way. Besides, you know what it's like,' he went on, glossing over the sadness I'd heard in his words. 'This place is in my blood. It really doesn't feel like work when I'm here. At least now I haven't got all the responsibility of managing the staff and wondering what my unpredictable landlord might do next. I have to say the new landlords are much easier to deal with,' he said, grinning.

'Well, I'm very pleased to hear that.'

Digby slinked off and collapsed in his favourite position in front of the fire. Noel had stirred and was currently in my arms, his eyes open and alert.

'Josie is okay though?' I asked, still puzzling over Eric's change of living arrangements. 'You did all have a good Christmas?'

'Well, little Stella made it of course. It's what Christmas is all about, isn't it? The little 'uns. She's such a sweetheart that one. She points at everything now, and she's becoming a right chatterbox, not that I can understand much of what she's saying. She loved all the Christmas wrapping though and the lights on the tree.' Eric paused, lost in his thoughts for a moment. 'Josie and Ethan though,' he shook his head. 'I don't know what's got into them. They need their heads banging together.'

'Really?'

Eric nodded, a rueful expression on his face. I hadn't seen Josie since Boxing Day when she'd popped round with a wicker basket of white cyclamens for me, and a beautiful gift of a crocheted blanket for Noel that she'd lovingly made. We'd exchanged a couple of texts since, but we hadn't really spoken and now I was worried. What was going on between the pair of them? I knew she and Ethan had gone through a tricky phase last year, but I thought that was all behind them. I'd believed Josie when she'd made her excuses for not attending our New Year bash, but now I had my doubts.

'I'll go round and see her,' I said decisively, as I placed Noel back into his buggy.

'She'd like that,' said Eric.

He wandered off, muttering about needing to change a barrel and disappeared down into the cellar as I fumbled beneath the buggy to find the envelope containing the posters I'd made for our Valentine's event.

'Let's have a look then,' said Dan, who came up from behind and peered over my shoulder. 'Ooh la la, we're going French, are we?' he teased. My drawing of the Eiffel Tower surrounded by hearts and balloons in various shades of red, white and blue wasn't my finest work, but it gave a flavour of what we had planned. 'Are you certain Little Leyton is ready for an evening of heady romance and music to fall in love to?' he asked, laughing.

'Well, we have to try. Who knows, we might bring two lonely souls together and it could be the start of a wonderful love affair.'

Dan raised his eyebrows, clearly thinking of our regulars at the pub and looking doubtful. He probably had a fair point.

'Well, it'll be a good night anyway. Max and I are planning on coming along. I've already lined Caroline up to babysit and if we can get a good crowd in, it should be a laugh.' This would be our first night out together since Noel's arrival and I wanted to make it special for Max.

The different events we arranged over the course of the year were one of the things I loved most about running the pub. Some of them were regular events like the monthly quiz nights, and the meetings of the various societies like the book group and the knitting and crochet circle, and others, like the beer and cider festivals, were one-off events. We also tried to fit in seasonal celebrations for Easter, Halloween and Summer and now, with our fully equipped barn outside, we were able to offer private functions as well. Engagement parties, weddings, christenings, anything our customers requested, basically.

We were just discussing the catering arrangements for the evening when the front door opened and Johnny Tay wandered in.

'Hello you,' he said, warmly. I wasn't sure if he was addressing me or Noel, until he came across and peered into the buggy, gazing down at him warmly. 'How's it going, mister?' His voice took on a low soft tone and there was genuine affection in his eyes. Sometimes it was hard to believe that we weren't still at school larking around and that we were supposed to be fully fledged grown-ups now. Looking at Johnny pulling funny faces at Noel, I suspected he had never received the memo about that one. He ordered half a lager shandy and came and sat down with us.

'I'll catch you in a while,' said Dan, who got up to see to a customer who had just walked in.

'You're starting early today?' I said to Johnny, gesturing towards his beer.

'Just been to a meeting with a new client. They've given me a rather large order for their new oak kitchen in their posh barn conversion, so I thought I'd celebrate with a quick one before going back to the workshop.'

'Well done, you!'

Johnny had always been good with his hands. He had a passion for cabinet making and would spend hours perfecting a bevelled corner or carving an intricate embellishment. I loved to visit him in his workshop to see his passion for working his wood, to breathe in the scent of the freshly sawn dust gathering on the floor. He'd walked away from it all early last year, saying he needed to get away from the village for a while, to find out what it really was he wanted from life, but it wasn't long before he was back home again and thankfully it looked as though he was here to stay now.

'You'll come to our Valentine's Day event, won't you?' I said, waving a poster underneath his nose.

He looked at my handiwork, his lip curling dismissively.

'It'll be great!' I told him. 'Music, games, bread and cheese, French beers and wine, and, who knows, love might be in the air!'

Johnny seemed wholly unimpressed. 'I'll give it a miss if you don't mind. "Romance, love and passion,"' he read the words off the poster with barely concealed contempt as though he had no idea what they could possibly mean. 'I'm not sure it's my kinda thing.'

'Come on, Johnny, don't be like that! I'm trying to drum up some business and it'll be fun.'

'What? Surrounded by loved-up couples showing me what I'm missing out on. I don't think so.' I knew he was still hankering after Polly, but it was definitely time for him to move on now, even if he might still need some convincing. He went on, grumbling. 'You and Max will be playing happy families, George and Polly will be acting out love's young dream. I think I'd rather stay at home and stick pins in myself. I know, why don't you call it the Johnny Tay Ex-girlfriends' New-Found Contentment Get-Together instead.'

He was being deliberately provocative, a disgruntled half-smile on his face, as he took a big glug of his beer.

'You'll find someone special of your own one of these days, but not if you hide yourself away at home. Who knows, it could be at our Valentine's Day Event. Go on, Johnny. Do it for me. If nothing else, we can drink a lot of French red wine and reminisce about the good old days.'

'Oh go on then,' he said, reluctantly, as though he was desperate now for me to stop going on about it. 'Put my name down. If I don't get any better offers, I'll pop in for an hour, but I can't promise to stay much longer than that.'

I threw my arm around his shoulder and gave him a kiss on the cheek. 'Thanks, Johnny. I'll make sure it's a night to remember, I promise. Anyway, I ought to get going. I want to pop in to see Josie. Perhaps she and Ethan might want to come along too… although…'

I paused, realising what I was saying, and Johnny's gaze caught mine as if he knew exactly what I was thinking. If Eric was right about them going through a tough time, then it was probably the last thing they'd want to do.

'Have you seen them?' I asked.

Johnny nodded. 'I saw Ethan the other night for a few beers. He wasn't in the best frame of mind. I don't know what's going on at home, but I don't think things are great at the moment.'

My stomach churned. The thought of Josie being unhappy and struggling in her relationship really saddened me, especially when I hadn't been around to help her through it. I'd been so wrapped up in my own life that I hadn't even thought about what Josie might be dealing with. I had a sudden urgency to see her and glanced at my watch.

'I have to go!' I picked up the pile of posters I'd brought along and left them on the bar for Dan to stick up on the oak posts around the pub. I stuffed my phone in my pocket, checked that my keys were where I'd put them in the other pocket and scooped up my handbag, throwing it over my shoulder. 'I'll see you on Valentine's Night, Johnny, if I don't see you sooner.'

I scooted towards the front door, waving goodbye to Dan and Eric on the way. I called out to Digby who came trotting obediently to my side, eager as ever to go on the next part of our journey. It wasn't until my hand clasped the brass knob of the old oak door that I heard Johnny's voice booming out at me from behind.

'ELLIE!'

I turned to look at him over my shoulder. It wasn't like him to shout.

'Aren't you forgetting something?'

I looked at him blankly, until my gaze followed his across the room to the buggy tucked in the little alcove at the back of the fireplace, my pulse picking up a pace at the realisation.

'My baby!' I said, letting out a hysterical cry, as everyone looked at me, a mix of pity and sympathy marked on their features. I rushed back to collect him, my heart soaring at the sight of his little cute form wrapped up safely beneath the covers. Poor little Noel – fancy being lumbered with a mother like me!

Eight

Obviously motherhood would take some getting used to. And forgetting about your baby, momentarily, was probably entirely normal and natural. Perhaps... I peered down at Noel hoping he wouldn't be traumatised by his ordeal, but he seemed totally oblivious to the drama and my heart swelled seeing his gorgeous little face looking up at me.

I pushed the buggy along the familiar streets of Little Leyton, vowing never to leave my beautiful baby behind ever again. Probably best not to mention my little lapse to Mum or else she'd never want to return to Dubai again. Josie, though, she'd be bound to understand.

A few minutes later when I'd arrived at her house I banged loudly on the front door.

'Ellie!' The door swung open and Josie's face lit up seeing me, but her wide smile couldn't hide her red-rimmed eyes and the weariness etched upon her features. There was a sadness in the way she moved that was almost palpable.

'Josie? Are you all right?'

'Fine,' she said. 'Well, not really, crap actually!' She laughed, slightly hysterically, I thought. 'I'll tell you all about it in a while, but it's so good to see you. Come on through. I'll go and stick the kettle on.'

Digby led the way, making himself at home by doing a crumb sweep of the carpet, before settling down in the living room.

'Where's Stella?' I asked, wrestling with Noel's little limbs as I tried to extract him from his romper suit. I still hadn't quite mastered the knack.

'Having her morning nap. I always think I'll get so much done when she's asleep, but I usually just end up collapsing on the sofa with a coffee. Still, I've got the perfect excuse today!' She sounded cheery enough as she headed into the kitchen and a few minutes later she joined me back in the living room, where I'd been giving Noel his bottle, placing the mugs of coffee down on the table. She took a deep breath. 'Look, Ellie, I'm really sorry I haven't been to see you recently, I feel really bad about that.'

'Don't be daft. You were there when I needed you most. Honestly, darling, wasn't that whole thing mad? I'd never have got through it without you.'

'Well, you did all the hard work. It was a real privilege to be there to help you through. I still find it hard to believe that I was party to Little Leyton's own little miracle. He's grown and changed so much in such a short space of time, hasn't he?'

'I know. It's scary, isn't it?' I placed Noel, fast asleep now, on the sofa next to me. 'You'll never guess what I just did down at the pub?' I said, proceeding to tell her about my major motherly oversight.

She threw her head back and laughed, a gorgeous tinkling sound that lifted the atmosphere, and reassured me that I wouldn't qualify for the Worst Mother of the Year award after all, which came as a relief. What was even better was seeing a light flicker in her eyes for the briefest moment.

'What's been going on, Josie?' I ventured. 'I've just seen your dad at the pub.'

'Ah right,' she said with a wistful smile. 'So you'll know that he's moved out?'

'Yep, he mentioned that you and Ethan needed some time alone together. What's that all about?'

She sighed, her shoulders slumping as she came and sat down on the sofa to the other side of Noel. 'Honestly? I still don't really know. Only that Ethan and I can't be in the same room together for five minutes before it erupts into a full-blown argument. It's not been right between us for a while now, but I was so looking forward to Christmas, thinking that with Dad home everything would come right. It didn't. It just seemed to make matters worse and poor Dad got caught in the crossfire. He couldn't get out of here fast enough to get back to the pub.' She paused, and gave a wry chuckle, lost in her thoughts for a moment. 'To be honest with you, I'm just glad it's over, but I do feel bad for Stella and Dad, I wanted it to be so special for them.'

'Your dad will understand. He just wants what's best for you and for you to be happy. As for Stella she wouldn't have known what was going on. I'm sure she was just excited about her presents and the tree and Father Christmas.'

'Yeah, I guess. It's just hard. You have in your mind how everything will be, you spend weeks planning for the perfect family Christmas and then when it doesn't turn out that way, it's so disappointing.' She paused, wistful for a moment. 'Anyway, enough of me boring you to tears with my marital woes, how was your Christmas, it must have been special?'

'You're not boring me, Josie, and I wish I'd known because you could have all come down to us at the manor. Mum's desperate to see you and Stella again, she was so disappointed when you couldn't make it for New Year.'

'I know.' She sighed heavily. 'I'm desperate to see them too. When is it they go back?'

'This weekend.'

'Crikey, that's gone quickly. I'll make sure I get down to see them before they go. We were all geared up to come on New Year's Eve, but then things kind of came to a head that day. Sorry for the little white lie.' She lifted her shoulders to her ears and grimaced.

'I wanted to tell you what was going on, but it didn't seem fair to unburden it all on to you. It was Christmas and you had a new baby, I didn't want to spoil that for you.'

'Oh, but you wouldn't have done. Mum and I could have provided TLC, and gin, and cake, and lots of unnecessary advice too probably. But you'd definitely have felt better after our little pep talk, even if our advice can be a bit questionable at times.'

She laughed. 'Your advice is always welcome, you know that. And I could probably have done with some that night, but instead I curled up on the sofa with a bottle of wine and a tub of Celebrations, indulging in my sorrows. Ethan moved out that day. He went back to his parents.' She saw my stricken expression. 'It's probably for the best until we decide what it is we want to do.'

I fell silent for a moment, the enormity of Josie's words hitting me hard. 'I'm so sorry, darling.' I reached out for her hand over a sleeping and totally oblivious Noel, his mouth moving in his dreams, those to-die-for long eyelashes fluttering as he slept. 'I really had no idea.'

'Why would you?'

'It's only a temporary thing though?'

'Who knows? Some time apart will give us the chance to work out what it is we both want. We couldn't continue the way we'd been going on.

Something had to change and with the new year upon us, well, I think we both realised it was crunch time. All of this, it's been building for a while.'

'How did things get so bad?' I asked, still struggling to accept the news.

'To be honest, things haven't been the same since Stella arrived. Don't get me wrong. She's the best thing that's ever happened to us and we both love her dearly, but somewhere along the way, Ethan and I, we've lost sight of each other.'

I nodded sympathetically, a cold fear gripping in my chest. Was this really where marriage, domesticity and familiarity led?

'He says I'm moody and bad-tempered, but that's only because I'm dead on my feet most of the time. According to him, he comes in from work and all I do is nag, but what does he expect? He doesn't offer to do anything around the house or help with Stella, so if I don't tell him what to do then nothing would ever get done. He either goes straight out to football practice or collapses on the sofa in front of the TV and doesn't move for the rest of the night. Then he's surprised when I don't want to have sex with him. Really?'

I grimaced, crossed my legs and shuddered. I really wished she hadn't mentioned the 'S' word. I was still at the stage where I couldn't imagine having, or even wanting, sex, ever again.

Josie laughed at my reaction and waved a hand around dismissively. 'Don't worry, it's a bit like riding a horse. As soon as you get back in the saddle you'll know exactly what to do.' Which went no way to making me feel any better about the entire subject. 'But me and Ethan, if he can't even be bothered to talk to me, why should I want to be intimate with him?'

It seemed like a fair point to me, but I really hoped they could somehow find their way back to each other.

'I'm sure it's just a bad patch. You're probably both just worn out and finding it hard to make time for each other. Look, I know this is a really tough time for you, Josie, but if you need to take some time off work or even take a break for a few weeks, then you just need to say.'

'Aw thanks, Ellie, but it's work that's been keeping me sane these last few weeks. It's given me something else to focus on. I don't know what will happen between me and Ethan, but for the time being I think it's probably better if we live apart.'

'I hate the thought of you being on your own,' I said, sadly. 'Why hasn't your Dad moved back in?'

'Well I think he's hoping the separation is only a temporary thing and Ethan will be back soon. Mind you, I think it's probably good for me to have some space and time alone at the moment. I get to see Dad most days so it's fine.'

'Come here.' I stood up and beckoned her into my arms, hugging her tight. I'd known Josie long enough to know when she was putting on a brave front. That underneath her strong outer appearance she was trying desperately to hold it all together. 'Please, Josie, promise you'll call me whenever you need to. For a chat or a cuppa or a major rant, whatever it is, whatever the time of day, you know I'm only down the road. You've always been there for me and I want you to know that I'm here for you too.'

Now it was her turn to hug me tight and I could feel the emotion swelling in her body.

'Thanks for coming, Ellie. Tell your mum I'll come and see her very soon.' She pulled back and shooed me away. 'Don't forget your baby on the way out,' she said, laughing now.

Nine

'I'm going out.' It was midway through the afternoon later on in the week when Max appeared in the kitchen changed out from his old work clothes and now wearing blue chinos, a red and blue checked shirt and with the scent of his unmistakable and distinctly sexy cologne wafting in the air. My nostrils couldn't resist taking a surreptitious sniff.

'Oh!' I couldn't hide my disappointment. 'I was going to cook us a special meal tonight. Mum and Dad are out with Caroline and Paul, Katy's staying over with a college friend and we have the house to ourselves. Thought it might be nice to do something, just the two of us.'

'Sorry, Ellie, I'm meeting with a new client at a potential development site.' He glanced at his watch. 'It shouldn't take too long though. I could always pick up a takeaway on the way home.'

'No. Let me make dinner.'

Max's face furrowed and he seemed decidedly underwhelmed by the idea, but then he didn't know what I had planned. It would make a lovely surprise. A romantic dinner date for two. Just like the first time I'd visited the manor when I'd been abuzz with excitement at being alone with Max in his wonderful house, full of anticipation for what was to come. Imagining how he might kiss me under the blue fairy lights hanging in the conservatory. I shivered, remembering how he'd done exactly that and the effect it had upon me. Maybe some more of that magic could be conjured up tonight.

In truth, the idea had popped into my head when I was in the village earlier today. I'd bumped into Arthur just as I was leaving the pub and he'd embraced me in an enthusiastic hug.

'Ah, here's my favourite girl with her little lad. I do miss seeing you at the pub every day, Ellie, but I know you have other more important things in your life now. And there's nothing more important than family. Do you know, you always remind me of my Marge? She was a pretty thing just like you.' He grew wistful, obviously conjuring up images of his lovely wife. 'Even in her latter years she was as beautiful to me as the first day I met her. Mind you, she always made the effort. You have to keep that spark alive, don't you, darling?'

'Yes, you're absolutely right, Arthur.'

I suspected Marge would put me to shame on that front. I remembered her well. She was a lovely woman, with kindly eyes and a fierce perm. She always looked beautifully turned out with nice clothes and manicured hands. I sighed, glancing down at my trackie bottoms and sweatshirt. Clearly there were lessons I could learn from Marge.

'Lovely seeing you, Arthur,' I called, determined then to make an effort that evening, after all, I couldn't remember the last time I'd worn anything that wasn't faded or had stains down the front of it. 'You must come down to the manor for tea very soon.'

'Will do, lovely.'

Instead of going straight home as I'd planned, I popped into Alfords, the village butchers, and picked up two of their juiciest fillet steaks, Max's favourite. Since the arrival of Noel, we'd barely had a night to ourselves, so this evening would be the perfect opportunity to have some one-on-one time with each other. Seeing Josie the other day had brought home to me how easy it was to lose sight of your partner when you were both so busy with your own lives and Arthur, bless his heart, had made me realise that I shouldn't take anything for granted.

'Okay, well don't go to any trouble,' Max had said on his way out.

It wasn't any trouble. Well, maybe a bit. But hopefully I'd have a few hours ahead where I could get everything just so in time for when Max arrived home later.

After I'd fed and changed Noel and put him down to sleep, I set to work, laying the table with a heavy red starched tablecloth, putting out the best china, polishing the silver cutlery, and placing red cloth napkins in crystal glasses. I found some tea lights and holders and placed them in the centre of the table in a heart shape. I peeled potatoes and boiled them ready for sautéing later, seasoned the steaks and topped and tailed the green beans. Max's favourite pudding was an old-fashioned English trifle so I hooked out a recipe book and made my very first trifle, complete with jelly and custard, which was cause for celebration in its own right.

With the kitchen cleared of the trail of devastation I'd left and the conservatory lit up with fairy lights, I rushed upstairs for a quick shower before changing in to a little black wrap jersey dress. I wriggled it over my head and confronted my image in the mirror. Not bad considering. The soft fabric was ruched to one side of the waist hiding all my lumps and bumps and offering a flattering fit. I tipped my head upside down and blasted my hair with the dryer, scrunching my fingers through to give it a tousled, just out of bed look. Then I reacquainted myself with the contents of my make-up bag and applied a light covering of foundation, dusted on some eyeshadow, lined my eyes with a kohl pencil, applied mascara, bronzer, blusher and a lick of lip gloss.

What a transformation! The woman who greeted me in the mirror was like an old friend, someone I hadn't seen in months. She'd changed a bit. She was a bit plumper around the middle and if you looked closely you could just see the start of some fine lines around her eyes, but she had a glow about her and a confidence in her smile. How lovely it was to see her again!

I slipped some shoes on, checked on Noel and then dashed down the stairs. Pulling out a frying pan, I melted some butter with some olive oil, and started sautéing the potatoes with some garlic, the delicious flavours mingling in the air. With everything under control, I poured myself a glass of wine and was just about to take a sip when I heard the sound I least wanted to hear, a noise that made my whole body tense. Noel's gentle whimpering, which I knew from my limited experience was likely to escalate quickly into a full-blown wail.

Ignore it. Perhaps that's where I was going wrong. Just the slightest murmur and I would be there, soothing him, trying to work out whether it was a feed, a change of nappy or just a cuddle he wanted. He might just be stirring, making himself heard, before falling gently back to sleep. That would be it.

Please Noel, I pleaded silently, *don't wake up!*

Keeping one ear out, I refreshed the water on the green beans and got the steaks out from the fridge to bring up to room temperature. I paused for a moment, taking a breather and a sip of wine to soothe my frazzled nerves, trying to ignore the cries which I couldn't dispute were getting louder and louder.

'Aargh!' Reluctantly I put down the barely touched wine, kicked off my heels and sprinted upstairs. Honestly, who would have thought such a small person could make such a racket.

'Come on, sweetie,' I soothed, scooping him out of his cot, and holding him to my chest. Both the men in my life always smelled so gorgeous. If only I could capture their sweet delicious scent and bottle it, I'd make myself a fortune. 'You need to be good for your mummy tonight because I'm making daddy a special meal.'

After giving Noel a quick top-up feed, I changed his nappy and jiggled him in my arms, watching gratefully as his eyes gradually fluttered close. I placed him safely back in his cot, keeping everything crossed that he wouldn't wake again until the morning, or at least until our special meal was over.

I glanced at my watch. It was a good job Max was running late too. Those extra minutes would give me a chance to catch up with what still needed doing.

Downstairs, greeted by the unmistakable whiff of burning, I turned over the potatoes, grimacing at their blackened bottoms. Never mind, I'd just have to arrange them carefully on the plates so that Max wouldn't notice and hope to goodness they didn't taste too charred. I lit the candles on the table, the softly flickering light instantly offering a romantic ambience. I took another much more relaxed sip of my wine and looked around me. The scene was set. All I needed now was for Max to put in an appearance and…

The steaks! My head whipped round to the worktop where I'd left them. I stared at the plate in disbelief. The now *empty* plate. I could have sworn I'd left them there, but maybe I'd put them back in the fridge by mistake. I rushed to look, yanking open the door with force, hoping against hope, that they'd be sitting there looking at me, but I knew it was futile. I went back across to the side and moved the kettle just in case they'd jumped behind there on their own, checked that they hadn't fallen on the floor and even pulled open the bin in case I'd thrown them away in a moment of madness. No, the empty plate was taunting me with its traces of meat juices, there could be only one possible explanation.

'DIGBY!'

That brought Holly and Bella padding in from the utility room where they'd been curled up in their beds. They looked up at me expectantly as though they might be in for a treat. Digby hovered beneath the kitchen table where he'd been lurking, unbeknown to me, for the last few minutes.

'Did you steal the steaks?'

He lowered his head, not daring to come out from his hiding place or look me in the eye, his sorrowful brown eyes an admittance of his guilt, not that it had ever been in question.

'Digby! How could you? Bad dog!'

He slunk off back beneath the table, no doubt ready to collapse after his sumptuous meal. Holly and Bella wandered off too when they realised they weren't getting anything after all.

What on earth was I going to do now? I rushed across to the freezer and riffled through the contents: frozen peas, pizzas, a green soup of who knows what flavour, soft scoop ice-cream and a bag of scallops. I'd not cooked scallops before but my options were severely limited and the instructions said they only took a couple of minutes. The blue cheese sauce I'd intended to go with the steak would have to do for the scallops. It wouldn't be the same, but unless Max fancied having fish fingers for dinner, then it would be the next best thing.

After settling on what I could throw together now for Max, I poured myself another glass of wine and sat down at the table, my limbs twitchy with anxiety.

Eight p.m. and waiting.

Where the hell was Max?

I expected him half an hour ago. His meeting couldn't have gone on this long and now I was worried that something may have happened. Perhaps his car had broken down or maybe he'd fallen ill or what if there'd been an accident?

I jumped up from my seat, grabbed my phone and called Max's number, but it just rang and rang. My heart was beating rapidly and I could feel the tell-tale blotches of anxiety growing on my chest and neck and my hands becoming clammy. I thought about going out to his office to see if I could find out who he was supposed to be meeting, but I didn't know his passwords or even where to find the keys. No, there was no need, there would be some logical explanation.

I rang his number again, but this time it went to voicemail.

'Max, where are you? Can you call me please?'

He didn't call me.

There was another half an hour of pacing up and down the kitchen, checking on Noel, and driving myself senseless with worry, convinced that something terrible must have happened to him, before I tried his phone again. This time he picked up immediately.

'Ellie darling!'

I startled, actually surprised to hear his voice, as warm and carefree as ever. I paused, waiting for his apologetic explanation, but it wasn't forthcoming. There were no sounds of sirens in the background, nothing to indicate that Max was in dire straits, just some very familiar noises I could easily make out.

'Where are you?' I said crossly, knowing full well the answer to that question. 'I've been worried sick, Max.' All the tensions and anxiety that had been building up in me for the last hour or so rushed out of my body replaced now with a bubbling anger. 'You knew I was cooking a special dinner for you. And you couldn't even be bothered to come home.'

'Oh, sorry, I kind of thought it was a loose arrangement. I was going to call and see if you wanted me to grab a takeaway.'

'When, Max? When were you going to call me? It's nine o'clock. I've not eaten a thing waiting for you and now you're down the pub, clearly having a whale of a time by the sounds of things.'

'Oh, come on, Ells, you don't begrudge me a pint, do you? It was meant to be just a quick one, but your Mum and Dad are here with Paul and Caroline, and they led me astray.' He chuckled, but I didn't find it funny in the remotest. 'I just lost track of the time. You know what it's like?'

I knew exactly what it was like. Over the years, I'd seen many men seduced by the idea of a quick pint only for it to turn into two, three or more, and for them to become all giggly and silly as the hours slipped away and they realised they'd have to face the wrath of their partner waiting at home. Is that what I'd become? The woman waiting at home?

'It's a shame you couldn't be here, it's a good night,' Max piped up.

Now I couldn't believe what I was hearing. 'Really? It is a bloody shame, Max, but we have a baby now, if you hadn't forgotten, and we can't all go out gallivanting when we want to.'

'Don't be like that, Ells. I'm coming home. Wait there. I'll be five minutes, I promise. Uh… maybe ten… I'll have to walk.'

I stabbed the call closed with my finger. *Wait here!* What other option did I have? I scrunched up the tea towel I'd been holding and flung it across the room in frustration. Digby gave me a worried glance from his hiding place before curling up tighter in a ball, closing his eyes.

I turned over the potatoes and put another pan on for the scallops. I'd completely lost heart in this wretched meal, but I was starving. I tossed the scallops in the pan and shooshed them about violently, as though it was entirely their fault my evening had gone to pot. I poured myself a glass of apple juice now, needing to keep a clear head if Noel woke again, as his daddy clearly wouldn't be up to the job, heated up the blue cheese sauce, put the beans on to boil and wondered why I'd ever thought this would be a good idea.

Ten minutes later, Max came bundling through the back door with a sheepish grin on his face and held his arms open wide.

'Hey you, don't you look gorgeous,' he said, sidling up to me and wrapping his arms around my waist. He smelled of booze and that distinctive oaky aroma that I always associated with the pub. It should have put me off him, but it didn't, the scent lingering on his body, strangely seductive.

I pushed him away determined not to be swayed by his apologies, smooth-talking charms or that sexy smell of his.

'Hmmm, something smells good,' he said, diverting his attentions to the hob. 'What is that exactly?'

'Scallops with a blue cheese sauce,' I said, unable to keep the annoyance from my voice.

'Ah right,' he paused, a smile playing on his lips. 'Interesting combination.'

'Yes, well, if you'd come home earlier, you would have had prime steak, but while I was running around preparing your dinner, setting the table, beautifying myself and seeing to our baby, Digby stole the steaks.'

'He did?' Max bent down to confront Digby, who had one eye open, looking up at us warily from beneath the table. 'You're in the dog house too, are you, boy?'

'It's not funny,' I snapped. 'I wanted this to be so special and now everything's been ruined.'

'No, it hasn't. Honestly. Don't be like this.' Max tried to run a soothing hand down my back as I slopped the sauce over the scallops, but I shook his touch away. 'Come on, Ells. Let's just sit down and eat. It'll be great.'

The potatoes were charred, the scallops were a gloopy white mess and the beans were curled up at the ends. I threw the plates down onto the table, not feeling in the least bit romantic and my appetite vanished into the air as soon as I sat down and contemplated my culinary creation. I glanced across at Max and was certain I caught him grimacing. He stirred his fork around the plate as if summoning up the courage to go in, and then bravely did so, his whole face contorting as he valiantly tried chewing his way through the first of his scallops.

'Ew, it's um a bit chewy… quite rubbery, I'd say… and that sauce, er, an acquired taste, I think. It's… it's… um…'

'The word you're searching for is 'inedible' I believe. It's all right, you don't have to eat it!' I scooped up the plates and marched over to the bin, depositing the contents inside. Max didn't even try to stop me. Tears were brimming in my eyes and exhaustion hung off my body. 'This was supposed to be lovely and it's a complete bloody disaster.'

I broke down, crying, not wanting Max's reassurances, cross at myself for getting upset over something as stupid as a dinner.

'I went to so much trouble, Max. And you didn't even give me a second thought. You were too busy enjoying yourself down at the pub.'

'You're being unreasonable, Ellie. I had a meeting and then went for a pint. You didn't seem to mind me doing that when you were down there.' He paused, his expression softening. 'Hey, look, I know it's disappointing when you go to a lot of trouble for someone, and those efforts are not appreciated, but you know, sometimes these things happen.'

His gaze locked onto mine and his words replayed in my head. The silence between us electrifying.

'You're not talking about New Year, are you? Your proposal? Is that what this is all about? You getting your own back? Tit for tat?'

'No, don't be stupid. I'm just saying I know what it's like to be disappointed.'

'Oh for goodness sake! It's not the same at all. If that's the way you feel, it's probably just as well we're not getting married after all!'

'Whatever you say, Ellie.' He shook his head. 'I've had enough of this. I'm going to bed.'

'Good!'

Max waltzed out of the kitchen, I blew out the candles on the table and just as I was about to climb the stairs to bed, Noel started wailing; loud, angry, demanding cries. My whole body crumpled inside. I knew exactly how he felt.

Ten

The morning following my disastrous attempt at wooing Max, he brought me a cup of tea and some toast in bed and it was as though our falling-out had never even happened. He presented me with a clean and scrumptious Noel, who was thankfully in a much happier mood than he'd been the night before. It hadn't seemed prudent to have a post-mortem about what had gone on as we would have only started bickering again. Least said, soonest mended and all that. I was just clear in my own mind that I would never cook scallops again, and made a note to myself to steer clear of the subject of marriage proposals.

Later that day, after a walk round the village with Noel and Digby, I let myself back into the kitchen, and Holly and Bella greeted us enthusiastically, running round my legs for attention. I bent down to hug them both and was rewarded with a flurry of thumping tails and wet noses. When I stood up again, I paused for a moment, my gaze distracted by the beautiful room which was flooded by the winter sun, casting patterns over the tiled floor. I was reminded of the very first time I'd visited the manor, recalling my sense of bewilderment at its scope and luxury.

Funny to think that this place was now my home. How crazy was that? Back then it was more a showcase of Max's design and building skills than a proper family home, but now it was filled with people, babies and dogs, and there were coats and hats and wellington boots of various sizes abandoned casually by the back door in a heap, and a real sense of warmth and love filling the eaves of the house that had been missing before.

With Noel sleeping in his buggy, I made myself a cup of coffee and sat at the round wrought-ironwork table in the conservatory overlooking the gardens. My mind flittered towards Josie, wondering how she was doing today. She, like Polly and Johnny, had been a friend for as long as I could remember and they were all hugely important to me. Sometimes in my head we were still those crazy teenagers who didn't have a care in the world, only big plans for the future. We'd chosen different paths, but we'd come a long way together, building up businesses, creating homes and making relationships and babies, and yet we'd all gravitated back to the village. There'd been a time when I couldn't wait to escape Little Leyton, feeling claustrophobic at seeing the same houses and faces and landscape every day, desperate for a change of scene, but having sampled living in Central

London, I'd been just as desperate to come home again. Now, looking out over the sweeping gardens with the rolling hills in the distance, I couldn't imagine a better place to live.

The back door opened, interrupting my daydreams, and I turned to look over my shoulder, smiling to see Max enter the kitchen. It was bitterly cold outside, but he didn't wear a coat, only a heavy red and black check lumberjack shirt, thick brown cords, and fingerless gloves on his hands. He deposited the bundle of logs he'd been carrying into the wicker basket in the utility room and came over to where I was sitting, putting his hands on my shoulders.

'Do you fancy a coffee?' I asked, getting up.

'No, don't worry,' he said, pushing me gently back into my seat. 'I've not long had one. Where is everybody?'

'Mum and Dad went into town, I think they've got a few things to sort out before they go back at the weekend. Katy's at college, and we've just got in from our walk. I was just thinking about Josie actually.'

'Oh, how's she doing?'

'Struggling at the moment. I didn't say, but things aren't great between her and Ethan, they're going through a bit of a rough patch at the moment. She told me he's moved out, just for a while, so they can try and decide what it is they want to do.'

Max's brow lifted in surprise and he shrugged, looking thoughtful. 'That's a shame. I really hope they can work it out.'

'Me too. They're the last people in the world I would expect to split, they've always seemed so strong together.'

'Yep, just goes to show you never can tell.'

I glanced at him. Just a throwaway comment, but I wondered if he was alluding to us. I shook the thought away, chiding myself for being ultra sensitive.

'Look, Max, I know it's been difficult these last few weeks with Mum and Dad here. I feel as though we haven't spent much time together, but things will get back to normal next week.'

'It's not a problem,' he shrugged. 'I've enjoyed having your parents around. I'll miss your mum's cooking that's for sure.' He stifled a smile. 'And it's great having another bloke about the house. Means there's always someone around to have a pint with.' I raised my eyes at that comment. 'Although admittedly it might be good to have some alone time with my…' he hesitated for a moment, his gaze scanning my face, choosing his words carefully, '…the woman I love, but, hey, I can be a patient man if I need to be.'

He pulled out a chair and came and sat beside me, putting an arm around my shoulder. He smelt of the great outdoors, the cold air still wrapped around him. There were stray pieces of wood and debris scattered over his shirt and through his hair. He reached across for my hand and I shivered at his touch, pushing him away playfully.

'Oh my goodness, your hands are so cold!'

He smiled, pulling off his gloves and threw them on the table, rubbing his hands vigorously. 'There, is that better,' he asked, holding them up to me.

I nodded, smiling, allowing myself to fall into the crook of his arm, relishing the scent of him, and the protectiveness of his embrace. At five foot seven, I wasn't exactly small, but up against Max's six foot plus height and the width of his broad shoulders, I always felt tiny in comparison, a sensation I was revelling in at the moment. I sighed, breathing in his delicious and reassuring scent.

'You know, Mum and Dad won't be back for ages,' I said, looking up into his dark eyes. I thought back to my conversation with Josie. If I'd learned anything it was that relationships had to be worked at. You couldn't take anything for granted. 'Noel probably won't wake for another thirty minutes or so if we're lucky. We could go upstairs and have a cuddle, that's if I wouldn't be distracting you from something more important.' I picked off some of the debris from his shirt, brushing his chest down with my hands, before cupping his face. Handsome, hungry, heavenly.

His eyebrows lifted, the smile breaking at the corner of his lips giving me my answer. Max went over to the buggy and I held my breath as he gently picked up Noel, holding him close to his chest, my heart melting at Max's tenderness. Would there ever come a time when I could see Noel wrapped in Max's embrace without it squeezing at my heart? I didn't think so. I followed Max upstairs where he put Noel down in the crib in the newly decorated nursery. He wasn't sleeping in here yet, but it was all ready for when he made the move into the big cot.

'Come on,' said Max, holding out his hand to me and leading me into the bedroom.

He spun me round, taking my face in his hands, before kissing me gently on the lips. His mouth lingered, my body reacting as it always had, recognising the familiarity of his touch, remembering past intimacies.

'We don't have to do this, not if it's too soon?'

'No, I want to,' I said, meaning it. I wanted to feel the intimacy of his touch, to experience the closeness of his body up against mine. To make up for the bad feeling of last night. He didn't need to know there was an element of me wanting to get this first time over and done with.

Max held my gaze as he unbuttoned his shirt and pulled it off his shoulders. I watched as he discarded his clothes on the floor and stood in front of me, the beauty of his toned body making me feel ridiculously shy as though I was seeing his nakedness for the first time. Max would never go to a gym to work out, he would see that as a waste of his time, but then he didn't need to, not when he spent hours working out in the extensive gardens of Braithwaite Manor. All that hard physical work had paid off. There wasn't an inch of fat on him, just defined and accentuated muscle. An elaborate tattoo of a raven, acquired when he was a teenager, marked his shoulder, delivering a frisson of danger, even more potent and compelling today.

I began to slip out of my clothes, taking off my jumper over my head and wriggling out of my jeans, but then I stopped. Standing in only my underwear under the scrutiny of Max's gaze, I suddenly felt self-conscious. My body had changed beyond recognition; it bore no resemblance to the slim and toned figure I had before I was pregnant. My breasts were big and soft with deep blue veins apparent through my pale skin, my tummy had a vivid pink stretch mark running from my belly button down to my groin and my skin settled in soft folds around my stomach and hips.

'Stop it, don't look,' I said, turning away, wrapping my arms around my chest. I jumped into bed, away from his prying gaze.

'What? Are you kidding? Why wouldn't I want to look at my gorgeous girlfriend?' He pulled the duvet down, which I'd been hanging onto grimly, his expression full of warm admiration. He slipped down my bra straps, his hands sweeping gently across my breasts.

'My stomach,' I said laughing, 'it's gross!'

'No, it's not, it's beautiful.' The flat of his hand caressed my tummy. 'It carried our baby for nine months, how could it be anything other than beautiful.'

He kissed me gently on the lips before depositing a trail of kisses along my collarbone, my body turning into his touch. My hands felt the firmness of his torso, and the desire that had been slowly burning inside of me grew stronger as he pulled me against him, our limbs wrapping around each other instinctively. His hands were gentle and exploratory, caressing every contour of my body, as though he was discovering it for the first time. He pulled away to look into my eyes and under the intensity of his gaze all my worries and self-consciousness fell away. When Max looked at me like that, his dark eyes full of longing and warmth, I couldn't feel anything but beautiful and strong.

'It's not too late to change your mind. Are you sure you want this?'

I nodded, never more sure of anything in my life.

'Tell me if I'm hurting you, I can stop.' Those dark, warm eyes were now flecked with concern.

I nodded again.

I hadn't known how my body might react after everything it had been through, how painful or uncomfortable it might be, but I needn't have worried. Max took his time, gauging my reaction to his every move, feeling his way slowly and gently until all my concerns were assuaged and everything was made right just by the mere act of being loved by Max. The intensity of emotion I felt wrapped in his arms was all-encompassing and afterwards, lying in the crook of his arm, my head snuggled onto his chest, tears gathered in my eyes.

'We're good together, aren't we, Max?'

'What a daft thing to say. Of course we are.' He pulled me closer. 'I didn't even know it was possible to love someone the way I love you,' he said, the rawness of his words tugging at my heart.

'I was worried after New Year, you know… that you might think I didn't feel the same way as you. I do. You know that. I think…'

'Too much thinking. Besides, I really don't want to talk about that.' Max held a finger to my lips to stop me from continuing, which was just as well because I was floundering, not having the foggiest idea where I was going with that thought or what I wanted to say. 'It's fine,' he said. He pulled his arm out from behind me and climbed out of bed, padding towards the bathroom. A dog barked, the baby cried and that moment, the brief magical moment of tenderness and togetherness we'd shared, was broken.

Eleven

Noel's soft cries coming from along the landing grew louder, more demanding and more insistent until they reached that ear-piercing 'you cannot possibly ignore me' pitch. I was just clambering out of bed trying to locate my hastily discarded clothes when I heard the back door open downstairs.

'Mum and Dad are here,' I hissed at Max, when he reappeared.

'Ellie? Are you up there?' Mum called, just about making herself heard above the din Noel was making.

'I'm coming. Won't be a moment,' I called, hopping around on one leg, trying to pull my knickers on.

Anxious to calm Noel's crying now, I rushed out onto the landing dressed only in my underwear running straight in to Mum who was halfway up the stairs with the same intention in mind.

'Oh dear, Ellie, what's the matter? Are you not feeling well?'

'No, everything's fine. I was just having a nap while Noel was sleeping and…'

'Hi Veronica.' Trust Max to take that moment to wander out onto the landing, half-dressed. Mum's gaze flittered to me, to Max and back to me again. I gulped and wrapped my arms around my chest.

'Oh Max! It's you!'

Who was she expecting, I wondered, the window cleaner? I glared at Max, wishing he would make himself scarce, but he wasn't picking up on my telepathic hints. Mum meanwhile had gone into something of a tizzy, probably at being confronted with Max's naked torso when she was least expecting it. She waved her hands in front of her face, which was flushed now with colour.

'Well you go and get yourself sorted, Ellie, and I'll see to Noel. Actually I'm glad you're both here. There's something your father and I want to talk to you about. Put some clothes on the pair of you and we'll see you downstairs. I'll pop the kettle on.'

'Oh my god!' I said, darting back into the bedroom and closing the door behind us. 'How embarrassing. There are some things you don't want your mother to see.'

'Why?' said Max, laughing. He pulled out a clean shirt from the wardrobe and put it on.

'Mum, catching us out like that! I feel like a teenager again!' I shuddered, replaying the whole scene over in my head, making myself blush. 'It was awful.'

'I don't see why. This is our house. We've got nothing to be ashamed of. You're a grown adult and mother to a baby now. I mean you could almost be a married woman, no less.' He flashed me a glance and I saw the devilish smile playing on his lips. 'Oh come on, Ellie, she must realise you've had sex before.'

'Yes, but I don't think either of us want to face that fact, full on, in broad daylight.'

Max chuckled, shaking his head. 'Ha, you see, Ellie, you're more of a traditionalist than you think. You know I would offer to make an honest woman of you, but... oh yeah, I already did that.'

'Oh stop it!'

He was teasing me, but I hated it, not wanting to revisit that whole subject. I picked up a pillow from the bed and threw it at him, but Max's reflexes were way too fast for me. He ducked, picked the pillow up and chucked it straight back at me. With his aim being much better than mine, it caught me, straight in the heart.

*

'Oh there you are!'

By the time Max and I made it back downstairs again, Noel was happily gurgling in Dad's arms, who was sat at the oak table which had been laid for afternoon tea. It was groaning with shortbread biscuits, rock cakes, a Victoria sponge, what was left of the Christmas cake and cheese straws, and two china teapots and dainty teacups and saucers, which I didn't even realise Max possessed. I wondered if I had overlooked a social engagement, and we had a dozen guests turning up at any moment. I was just thinking I might need to rush back upstairs and change into something more tea party appropriate when Max asked the question that had been puzzling me.

'Are we expecting visitors, Veronica?'

'Oh no, I just thought I'd do us a few treats. In Dubai, I don't really have the chance to bake, so I thought I'd take the opportunity here.'

'You should have said, Mum. I would have got Josie down, and Eric too. We could have made an occasion of it. A farewell party if you like.' Mum glanced at me and then at Dad, and I noticed the almost imperceptible shake of her head. 'Josie was saying how she must come and see you before you go back. The time has gone so quickly.'

Far too quickly for my liking. In some ways it seemed like only yesterday that Noel had arrived in such dramatic circumstances and in other ways I found it hard to remember a time when he hadn't been here. Normally, Mum would have been round to see Josie straight away, she adored little Stella, and Josie was like another daughter to her, but with everything that had been going on and the bad weather making getting around the village tricky, the weeks had slipped away from us.

It wasn't my place to tell Mum about Josie's problems because I knew she would only worry and Josie would want to tell Mum herself when she felt ready to. Besides, the news would be common knowledge soon enough.

'Come and sit down. I'll pour the tea,' said Mum, flapping around as though the Queen might knock at the door at any moment. Dad looked as bemused as we were. I pulled out a chair and sat down, taking Noel from my Dad and cradling my little boy in my arms, his little mouth searching out the bottle Mum had prepared. Now, she handed us each a small plate and instructed us to help ourselves.

'Well, this is very lovely,' said Max awkwardly, doing exactly as Mum had asked and helping himself to a sultana scone, which he cut in two and proceeded to dollop with strawberry jam and a big spoonful of clotted cream. It looked so tempting that I went to do the same, but pre-empting me, he offered his scone to me. Honestly, it was the little things. How could you ever resist a man who would voluntarily give you his cream scone.

'So, what was it you wanted to talk about then?' I asked.

I saw Dad glance over at Mum and wondered what these two were cooking up. One thing was for certain, they were acting very oddly.

'Well, we have some news,' Dad said.

'Okay,' I said, a feeling of disquiet stirring in my stomach.

'Good news. Don't look so worried,' said Mum. 'The thing is, we've decided, we're not going back to Dubai. We're moving back into the village.'

There was a moment of silence as we all looked at each other and I tried to make sense of Mum's words.

'What? But why? You're only partway through the contract, aren't you, Dad?'

'Yes, but I've managed to get myself out of it.' He smiled and shrugged as though this wasn't a big deal at all. 'It's fine. We've parted on good terms, but it's something your mother and I have been thinking about for some time now. We decided we wanted to come home.'

It didn't make any sense at all. 'But why?' I repeated. 'You love it out there. What about your gorgeous apartment, your friends and the yacht club!'

Max and I had paid a visit to them in the autumn and had an amazing time, soaking up the sunshine, lazing by the pool, going to relaxed and carefree brunches every day and just revelling in the ex-pat lifestyle. We'd even remarked how they would find it hard returning to the quiet of Little Leyton when the time finally came. But that was meant to be a few years down the line, not now.

Dad laughed. 'I think the yacht club is the least of our concerns.'

I flashed him a look, and so did Mum. Concerns? What possible concerns could they have? They were baby boomers, full of enthusiasm and energy, enjoying this part of their life, seemingly without a care in the world. Clearly I was wrong. Although I'd known something was amiss, I could never have imagined they would be turning their backs on their lives in Dubai to return to Little Leyton. Had something happened out there to make them want to come home? Was there anyone else involved? Whatever it was, there was definitely something they weren't telling me.

I looked across at Max to see if he had any answers, but he shook his head looking as bemused as I was feeling.

'We'll miss the lifestyle and the friends we've made, obviously, but it was only ever going to be a short-term thing. Besides, things have changed. We have a gorgeous grandson now and I didn't like the idea of missing out on any of his growing-up.' I'd passed Noel into Mum's arms so that I could drink my tea and she was looking down at him with a gamut of emotions flittering across her features.

'Is that what this is all about?' I asked, looking from Mum to Dad. 'You're coming back because of us. I'd hate to think you're changing your plans, giving up on an amazing opportunity, because of what's going on here. I know we have little Noel now, but we won't let you miss one single part of it. There's the phone and Skype. And the next three years will pass in a flash and you'll be home again and glad that you made the most of your time in Dubai.' I felt guilty that somehow I may have influenced their decision in some way.

'We've thought about this long and hard, Ellie. And it's the right thing for us to do now. Honestly. From your reaction, anyone would think you don't want to have us home again.'

'Oh, it's not that. I just want you to be sure that you're making the right decision.' On a purely selfish note, having them back in the village would be wonderful, but was it really the best thing for them right now?

'We are,' said Dad, firmly.

Their minds were made up and clearly anything I said wasn't going to have the slightest impact on their decision.

'That's what we've been doing today,' added Mum. 'I've spoken to George and he's happy for us to move back into the cottage this weekend. He's living with Polly already so he's said he'll just move his few remaining bits over in the next couple of days. I've organised with Sofia who manages our apartment in Dubai to pack up our remaining belongings and get them sent over by carrier.'

'Well, it sounds as though you have it all organised. But what I can't understand is why you didn't mention anything earlier? What about all your friends out there? Won't they be surprised that you've just upped sticks and moved back.'

'Well we're not going to lose touch completely and they can always come and visit us here if they'd like to,' Mum said, matter-of-factly. 'I wanted to make sure we had everything sorted before we said anything, just in case there were any problems. To be honest, I'm just relieved that the decision has been made. I can't wait to get back into my home now and settled into village life. I've missed the cottage, the gardens and the Aga. You are pleased, aren't you, love?'

'Of course. It's just so unexpected that's all.'

'Group hug?' offered Max with a smile, attempting to defuse the awkwardness, but possibly only adding to it. We stood in an uncomfortable huddle, with Noel at the centre in Mum's arms, rubbing each other's backs, going through the motions, but I wasn't really invested in the display of affection. It wasn't that I wasn't pleased, just that my head was still having trouble computing the news. Mum had always confided in me, so why not this time?

I pulled away feeling strangely unsettled by their announcement. I hated being kept out of the picture. Firstly, Josie, my so-called best friend had kept from me that she'd separated from her husband and now my parents, who'd been staying in my house for several weeks now, hadn't thought to tell me they were moving back to Little Leyton. I turned away and busied myself collecting the dirty plates from the table, stacking them haphazardly in the dishwasher, their clattering resounding around the kitchen.

'Oh Ellie, whatever's the matter?' asked Mum.

'Nothing.' I turned to look at her, surprised even by my own anger. 'I just don't know why you had to be secretive. There was me thinking you were going back to Dubai in a couple of days and all the time you had this planned.'

'I thought you'd be pleased,' said Mum, bristling.

'I am, but…'

Max interrupted. 'It's no big deal, is it, Ellie? In fact, it's great news. We'll be spoilt for choice for babysitters.'

'Well I wouldn't expect you to understand!' I snapped.

He raised his eyebrows at me, his expression darkening.

Noel, as though picking up on the tension, started grizzling.

'What's up, Ellie?' I could hear the puzzlement in Max's words as he laid a hand on my arm. 'Are you tired or something?'

'Yes, I am bloody tired actually.' I snatched my arm away. 'But that's got nothing to do with this.'

'Aw, what's the matter little man,' said Mum, jogging Noel up and down in her arms as his cries became much louder and more insistent now.

'Here, give him to me,' I snapped again, taking Noel from her. My mood had plummeted in a matter of a few minutes, and still I wasn't sure why. A little while ago I'd been wrapped in Max's arms and now I felt like throttling him. Mum and Dad had wound me up with all the cloak and dagger stuff. There was no need for it. Max had only made matters worse by not seeing how that might have upset me.

'I'll make some more tea then,' offered Mum.

Dad found a newspaper to bury his head in and started contemplating the crossword puzzle. Max sat down at the table observing me curiously.

I took a deep breath and sank down into the window seat, counting slowly to ten in an attempt to get my temper under control. I soothed Noel in my arms, tears brimming in my eyes unbidden.

'Here you go, darling.' A few moments later, Mum handed me another cup of tea and I smiled, determined to shake off my bad mood. We chatted about how she'd be able to look after Noel when I went back to work and how I could pop in for afternoon tea after a lunchtime shift – she had it all planned out – and I was genuinely pleased that they were coming back to the village. That had never been the issue. I wasn't sure now what it was exactly. I was just mulling over that when the back door opened and Katy flew in.

'Ooh, cakes! Is it someone's birthday?' She swooped on the table and descended on the shortbread biscuits, before eating one greedily and then helping herself to a rock cake. 'Oh my god, these are so good!'

'We're celebrating,' said Max. 'Veronica and Malc are staying in the village, they're not going back to Dubai, after all. Isn't that good news?' He raised his eyebrows at me questioningly as he addressed Katy.

'Really?' she said, with a mouth full of cake crumbs. 'That's great.' She swallowed hard, clearing her mouth. 'Are you going to be living here permanently then?'

We all laughed, as Katy struggled to hide the awful realisation that she might be sharing her home with my mum and dad indefinitely.

'Don't worry,' said Dad, laughing. 'You'll be rid of us soon enough. We're moving back into our home at the weekend.'

'That's cool,' she said. 'Although I wouldn't have minded you staying. Honestly, I love having lots of people around. All the cakes and meals have been amazing too,' she said, deftly recovering the situation.

'Yes, I'm afraid it'll be back to my ropey offerings from now on,' I said, with a sigh, recognising the awful truth of that statement.

Katy headed off out of the kitchen, stopping for a little chat with Noel on the way, who gazed up at his aunty adoringly, with big wide eyes. She called out to Max, as an aside, 'I'm just going to get changed and then I'm popping out for a while. That's okay, isn't it?' she said, employing the same wide-eyed expression that Noel had mastered at only a couple of weeks old, a look so hard to refuse in teenagers and babies alike. Unless you were Max, that was.

'Where are you going?' he asked.

'Just to meet a friend.'

'Haven't you got homework to do?' he said, gruffly.

Katy snorted, and glanced at me, an expression of disbelief on her face. 'I'm not at school, Max.'

'No, I know that, but they must give you some work to do from college.'

'They do!' She rolled her eyes and shook her head despairingly. 'I have study periods during the day and I try to get it all done then so I don't have to do it at home. You know, I am on top of everything.'

'Well, I'm glad to hear it,' he said, begrudgingly.

Max was great at dealing with his subbies, suppliers, clients, old folks, randomers down at the pub, small children and dogs, but he never seemed quite sure how to handle his little sister, turning into a cantankerous old curmudgeon in her company. He adored her, but because they shared so many similar traits it didn't take much for the sparks to fly. Also, I suspected he felt a huge sense of responsibility caring for Katy, as his mum had come to him, at her wits' end, not knowing how to cope with her wayward daughter when she was intent at the time in causing as much trouble as she possibly could. Thankfully Katy had settled down since she'd first arrived from Spain, and the huge rows and bust-ups weren't so prevalent these days.

'Well make sure you're not late. I don't like you coming home in the dark. Who are you meeting? Ryan?'

'Um…' I heard the hesitation in her voice. 'Yeah. Don't worry, I'll get a lift home,' she said, quickly disappearing upstairs.

'Make sure you've got your phone with you.'
'Will do!'

'And make sure you pick up if I call you.'

'Yep! Just chill, Max, I'll be fine.'

Max shrugged, blowing his cheeks out in exasperation. Mum and Dad shared a knowing glance. Somehow I suspected they couldn't wait to get back to the peaceful tranquillity of their cosy cottage.

Twelve

In the following weeks it was as though half the village was involved in an elaborate game of musical houses. Ethan was living at home with his parents, Eric was settled back into the pub and looking as though he'd never been away, George had moved into Polly's home where he'd commandeered the spare room as his writing den and Mum and Dad were living happily back at Ivy Lane Cottage and seemingly not regretting their decision for one moment. Not that life at the manor was any more peaceful. No sooner had Mum and Dad returned home than Max's mum, Rose, and her partner, Alan, had arrived to stay with us for a few days, to meet their new grandson.

Rose was just as besotted with Noel as my mum had been and it was wonderful to think how much joy our little baby had brought, not only to our lives but to those of our families as well. I'd met Rose once before but I hadn't known her that well and Alan was fairly reserved, so while I was pleased to welcome them into our home, I wasn't as relaxed having them around as I'd been when my own parents had stayed. Max's relationship with his mum hadn't always been easy either, but they'd been working on their differences over recent months. Today, with Alan off visiting family, Rose and I had headed out for a walk with Digby, Holly and Bella in tow. The air was sharp and it was bitterly cold, but we were wrapped up warm against the elements and the bareness of the trees and bushes offered a stark beauty to our surroundings. I'd just been explaining to Rose about Mum and Dad's decision to come home.

'It came as a total surprise and all seemed to be decided upon very quickly. One moment I was getting ready to say goodbye to them and the next they were back in the village to stay.'

'It's understandable,' said Rose, digging her hands deeper into the pockets of her coat. 'They want to be near to their family to see their grandson grow up. The sort of lifestyle they were living sounds lovely, but really, at the end of the day, you want to have your nearest and dearest around you.'

'I suppose so. I mean, you'll know what's it like? Can you imagine giving up your life in sunny Spain to come back and live in the UK?'

'Not really. I'm not sure Alan would want to.' There was a tinge of sadness to Rose's words. 'We left because Alan and I wanted to put everything behind us and make a new start. We thought by moving to a different country we'd be able to do that. Although you can never really escape your past, can you?' she said, wistfully and I suspected I knew exactly what she was referring to.

I glanced to my side to catch her expression and was struck by the strong resemblance to Max. They shared the same defined jawline and set of the mouth which wasn't noticeable face on, but in profile the similarity couldn't be denied. Cold whispers of breath gathered in front of her as she spoke.

'Katy was very young when we moved away and I think that's why she's always held a romantic attachment to the UK. She's wanted to move back for years and said as soon as she was old enough, she would come on her own if she had to.' Rose gave a rueful laugh. 'I hoped it was a passing phase, that once she'd settled in Spain and made friends she wouldn't want to come back, but I was wrong. You do things for what you think are the right reasons, but it doesn't always work out for the best. I think Katy still resents me for moving her abroad.' I could hear the note of regret in her voice.

'Well, at least Spain isn't on the other side of the world. She seems happily settled now though. She's enjoying her new college course.'

'Oh yes, she loves it here, as she keeps on reminding me. I miss her though. I thought I'd have her for a few more years yet, but now she's made the break I can't see her coming back to Spain again. It feels like I've lost her.' The sadness clouded around her body, her words hanging starkly in the cold air.

'I'm sure that's not the case,' I said, uncertain of what to say to comfort her. 'Katy is probably just enjoying her independence.'

'Yes, and I don't begrudge her that, but I wish she would let me in a bit more. There was a time when we were really close, but not anymore. She hardly ever texts or calls me and I don't know how we can come back from this. She still hasn't forgiven me for all that hoo-ha last year.'

Hoo-ha? That wasn't what I would have called it. Katy had found out that the man she always thought was her father, Rose's first husband and Max's Dad, who had died when Katy was only four, wasn't her father after all. From what I understood, Katy was the result of a brief affair Rose had while married. Her husband had known the truth but had agreed to bring up Katy as his own and doted on the little girl. The secret might have been kept forever had it not been for Alan, Rose's new husband and Katy's stepfather, who had blurted out the truth in the middle of an explosive row. The revelation had caused a devastating rift between Katy, her mum and Alan, and had heralded Katy's arrival in Little Leyton.

'I realise now that it was the worst possible thing to do and how shocking it must have been for Katy to find out the truth. I wish I'd been honest with her from the start, but I honestly thought at the time I was doing the right thing. She hasn't forgiven me and I'm not sure she ever will.'

Rose was pushing the buggy with an increased determination now, Digby walked at my side and Holly and Bella galloped ahead, darting off into the undergrowth to investigate what was hiding in the bushes before emerging further along the lane, their tales wagging excitedly.

'She's been looking forward to you coming over.'

'Has she? Perhaps I'm oversensitive, but she seems very distant and distracted to me. As though she finds it hard to be around me now. Sometimes I catch her looking at me and I can see hatred in her eyes.'

'No, I'm sure it's not that,' I said, only just realising myself that Katy *had* seemed preoccupied these last few days, but I hadn't attributed that to Rose and Alan's visit. 'She has a busy life what with her college course, working shifts at the pub and seeing her friends and Ryan, of course. She's always dashing in and out.'

'Hmmm. I just wish I could turn back the clock and do it all differently,' Rose said. 'I had no idea at the time that it would all blow up in my face like this, but I suppose it's nothing less than I deserve. It was a stupid thing to do,' she said, the despair evident on her face.

'I'm sure it will all work out eventually.' It was a platitude I knew, but I was struggling to find a way of offering comfort to Rose. Her hurt and regret were palpable, but she couldn't undo what she'd done. At least now the truth was out in the open and they could hopefully move on in their relationship.

'I hope you're right,' she said, stopping for a moment to take a deep breath of air. The cold had coloured her cheeks and the tip of her nose red. She leant forward to check on Noel beneath all the woolly blankets, pulling back the almost impenetrable cover of the buggy. 'Hello you!' she said, her voice lifting, sounding so much brighter than she had done up until now. Her face broke out in a big smile at the sight of Noel's little face peeping out at her. 'He's so scrumptious, isn't he? Just like Max when he was a baby. I'll have to show you some photos when we get home, the likeness is uncanny.'

'I'd love to see the pictures. Do you have the naked shot of baby Max on the fur rug that was all the rage back then? We could embarrass him with that.'

'Do you know, I might have somewhere,' she said, laughing. 'It's super for Katy too. She just adores the baby and is a natural with him, don't you think?'

'Yes. She's been such a great help to me. She's always volunteering to babysit or to take him out for a walk. I'm just hoping the novelty won't wear off.'

'I don't suppose it will. We've never had a big family and I've always been slightly envious of those people who have, so it's lovely to add to our small clan with Noel, and you, of course.' She looked across at me with warm affection in her eyes. 'Look, Ellie, I just wanted to say thank you for listening, for being so caring. I've found the last year particularly difficult and what's made it worse is that I've not had anyone I can really confide in. Alan doesn't like to talk about it, he just gets angry with me. Max is very tight-lipped on the subject, but I can tell that's he disappointed in me and my actions. And, as for Katy, some days she can barely look me in the eye. What I'm trying to say is that I'm just so pleased you're here, somehow it makes it easier. Knowing that you're looking out for them both and that I can talk to you, at least, even if they might not want to talk to me, it means a lot. You've been very kind.'

I took hold of Rose's gloved hand and squeezed it tight, touched by her words. 'It might take some time, but it will come right in the end. I know both Max and Katy love you and that's the most important thing.'

'Yes, of course. And I can see how Max has changed. He's a different man since you came into his life, do you know that? And now with the baby here, I've never seen him happier.'

'Yes, we are very happy,' I said, as if I'd only just realised it for myself.

We carried on walking until we reached the top of the lane, where we stopped to look down over the sweeping valley to see the imposing buildings of Braithwaite Manor nestling in the countryside in the distance.

'What a beautiful view,' said Rose as we stood and gazed in awe at the stunning winter landscape. Through someone else's eyes I could appreciate just how much I had to be grateful for, a beautiful home in a stunning village with my beautiful family.

I took a deep breath, the cold air stinging at my cheeks as a sharp reminder of Rose's experiences. I didn't want to get to her age and have any regrets about the things I hadn't done. Another reminder that I shouldn't take any of this for granted.

Thirteen

'Noel's milk is in the fridge. There's a change of clothes by his changing mat and everything else too; nappies, cream et cetera. If there are any problems, you'll ring me, won't you? I can be back in five minutes. I'd be happier if Dad was here. Why didn't he come?' I said, trying to quash the panic rising inside of me.

'I told you,' said Mum, laughing, 'I left him watching the football on the telly. He's got some beers in and a pork casserole in the slow cooker. He'll be happy as Larry to have some time to himself. I've got George's latest book to read if I have a spare moment, so you get off and have a good time. There's no need to fret, I have done this before, you know?'

I'd been looking forward to tonight for ages, our first night out as a couple since the baby had arrived, but now it was here I was reluctant to leave Noel behind.

'I wonder if I should go,' I said aloud. 'They won't need me there. Perhaps I'll stay…'

'No, you won't. There's nothing to worry about here. Noel's fast asleep and when he does wake up,

I'll see to him. You and Max deserve a night out together. Where is he by the way?'

'He's out in his office. He's always working that man,' I said, glancing at my watch. 'Let's have a glass of Prosecco while we're waiting.' I pulled out two flutes from the glass-fronted cabinet and found a chilled bottle of fizzy in the fridge. Just seeing the bubbles filling the glasses lifted my mood for the night ahead.

Everything was in place for the Valentine's Night event at The Dog and Duck and we were expecting a decent turnout. I'd popped in earlier in the day to check we had everything we needed and to put up a few decorations. Red and white heart-shaped bunting had been hung from the eaves, posters of moody Paris street scenes with couples held in embraces adorned the snug walls and small blackboards with romantic phrases inscribed in French lined the bar tops. Katy had put together a playlist of some suitably romantic background music and there was a selection of heart-shaped cheeses and different breads available, country pates, smooth French wines, plates of colourful French fancies and macarons, and, of course, a huge selection of beers. I knew once I got there I'd enjoy myself, it was just leaving Noel behind that was tugging at my heart.

I lit a tea light placing it in the filigree holder and put it in the centre of the table. 'Rose and Alan will be back later,' I told Mum. They'd taken the opportunity to be tourists for a day and had gone into London to see a show.

'So,' said Mum, lowering her voice to a whisper. 'What did Max get you for Valentine's Day?'

'Just a card,' I said, breezily.

'Really?' She couldn't hide her disappointment. 'No flowers, chocolates or jewellery?'

'No,' I laughed. 'I think Max sees Valentine's Day as being a bit of a con. He's not the type to buy me a soppy card and a bunch of flowers just because that's what he's expected to do.'

Mum let out a low murmur, one that told me she wasn't remotely impressed by my explanation. 'Well, call me old-fashioned, but I was half-expecting Max to take the opportunity to propose to you.'

I shrugged and took another glug of the happiness-inducing fizz. I had no desire to be pursuing this particular line of conversation.

'Why ever not?' she went on. 'It would be lovely, and seems like the natural next step to me. It would give you and Noel a bit more security too.'

'We're happy as we are, Mum. Really.' I hoped my tone might indicate I didn't want to talk about this subject any more, but Mum didn't take the hint.

'Young men today, eh? They don't want to make that commitment anymore. It might not be important to you now, but one day it could be. Who knows what will happen a few years down the line.' She fell silent for a moment, mulling over her thoughts. 'Well, I suppose the night is still young,' she said wistfully, glancing at her watch.

'Mum! Stop it. It's not going to happen, not after last time.'

No sooner had the words left my lips than I realised my huge mistake. Mum did a double-take. I jumped up clearing away my empty glass and grabbing the bottle to refill Mum's glass, hoping that she might have missed it, but no such luck.

'What do you mean last time? Ellie?'

My silence gave the game away.

'Max has already proposed, hasn't he? Oh, Ellie, how lovely! And there was me wittering on. Why didn't you say anything?'

Oh Lord!

Now I was worried that Max would wander into the middle of this conversation with my mother and get completely the wrong idea.

'Mum, please don't say anything. Max has proposed, yes, but…'

'But what?' she blurted out, looking suitably outraged.

'Well, it's something we've talked about, but for the moment we don't have any firm plans. I'm sure we'll get around to it one day.'

'Ellie, please don't tell me you turned Max down?' She peered into my face, much like she'd done when I was a little girl and she suspected I might not be telling her the whole story. 'Why would you do that? It doesn't make any sense. Max is a real catch. You have a family together now. Why wouldn't you want to get married?'

'Mum, please don't! This is something for Max and I to sort out when we're good and ready. For the moment we're happy as we are,' I told her brightly, reaching out to pat her on the hand.

She shook her head despairingly and a palpable whiff of disappointment wafted across the table at me. A part of me wanted to reassure her that it would be okay, that of course Max and I would marry and we would have our happy ending, but I was old and wise enough to realise I couldn't base my decisions on what my mum wanted for me.

'Well, I just hope you don't come to regret this, young lady.'

I grimaced, feeling like a teenager again, imagining that this must be how Katy felt when we were all telling her what was best for her.

'What you don't realise at your age is that life is short. You think you've got all the time in the world when really you haven't. The years whizz by and before you know it you're facing your autumn years and looking back over all those things you didn't do.' Mum's face had taken on a wistful quality.

'Are you trying to depress me? Come on, let's have another glass of fizz.' I went over to the worktops and refilled our glasses, before collecting my handbag. Nothing, not even my mum telling me what was best for me, was going to spoil this evening. 'Look, Mum, please don't worry. I'm fine, we're fine. We have our gorgeous baby; my wonderful parents are living back in the village and I'm going out tonight for an evening of fun and romance with Max and my friends in what has to be the best pub in the country. What more could I want? Life is good.'

'Well, I'm very pleased to hear that,' said Max, arriving in the kitchen, smiling. He was already changed, wearing chocolate brown cords, a white twill shirt and brown brogues, managing to look super sexy and every inch the country squire, the *Max effect* working to its full potential tonight. He came across and slipped an arm around my waist, his newly showered scent mingling with his favourite aftershave to tease at my senses. 'Hello Veronica,' he said, going over to welcome Mum.

'Oh, Max, look at you. Doesn't he look dashing, Ellie?'

I giggled. Those bubbles must have gone straight to her head.

'Well, you two go off and enjoy yourselves. It's the night for love and romance and who knows what else!' She raised her brow, a mischievous glint in her eyes, and I didn't trust her one iota not to say something she shouldn't say.

'Come on, Max,' I said laughing, literally dragging him out the back door, before Mum had the chance to propose to him herself.

Down at the pub we walked through the old oak door of The Dog and Duck and that familiar welcome of chatter, laughter and warmth, from the customers enjoying themselves and the blaze of the fires, greeted us.

'Here they are, the two lovebirds,' said Arthur, who was propped up on a stool by the bar, a pint of beer in his hand. 'How's that little lad of yours?' he asked, planting a wet and whiskery kiss on my cheek. 'I was so pleased you decided to call him Noel after my old pal.'

'There wasn't anything else we could call him really,' laughed Max. 'Let me buy you a pint, Arthur.'

Arthur was one of our most long-standing customers, and was one of Noel senior's old drinking buddies. I loved the links our older customers provided to the history of the pub, with their memories and anecdotes from days gone past. Now, to think that our little Noel might be bringing his own dad down here one day, in the future, for a pint, warmed my heart.

I left Max chatting to Arthur and went round the back to see who was in and if anything needed doing. A habit of old. Being in the pub, I couldn't help rolling up my sleeves and getting involved. I found Dan, Silke and Gemma working behind the bar. Rich was down in the cellar changing over a barrel and Eric was out in the kitchen, having a sneaky cuppa. In the snug bar were Polly and George, Paul and Caroline, Mum and Dad's neighbours from Ivy Lane, and Johnny had put in an appearance too.

'You made it,' I said, when I got him to one side. 'Thanks, Johnny, I'm so pleased you came, it means a lot. And it's not so bad, is it? Just a few friends coming together for a good time, with some wine and cheese thrown in for good measure. I promise I won't mention the "L" word if you don't.'

'Ha, don't worry, it's cool. I don't want you thinking I've become old and embittered, destined to remain a grumpy old sod on my own for the rest of my life. I'm really pleased you and Polly are both so settled and happy now. It's made me realise that I'm probably ready for a similar sort of thing.'

My eyebrows shot up involuntarily, hardly believing this was Johnny Tay speaking.

'I know,' he said, laughing at his own admission, 'I've had a few false starts along the way, romantically speaking, but now, if the right person were to come along, then who knows.'

'Crikey. My Valentine's Day event is working its magic already. You're feeling the love, aren't you, Johnny?' My gaze drifted around the bar. There were some loved-up couples in and some women on their own, but I suspected they were all over-65. 'Although to be fair, I'm not sure you'll meet the love of your life in here tonight, but just knowing that you're ready to meet that special person is a step in the right direction. I reckon it will happen for you soon.'

Johnny smiled, looking doubtful. 'I hope so, Ells. I really hope so.'

I laid a hand on Johnny's sleeve. 'I'm just going to check in the other bar. You haven't seen Katy, have you?'

'She was here earlier, said something about needing to pop out, but that she'd be back'

'That sounds like Katy,' I said, laughing. 'I can never keep up with that girl, she's always dashing from one thing to another.' A bit like her big brother.

Out in the front bar, Josie and Sasha were just arriving.

'Hey, well this is a lovely surprise. I wasn't expecting to see you two tonight.'

'Well, it was a bit of a last-minute thing. We're only here for the red wine and cheese, I might add. I mean, a night out is a night out, right?' It was so good to see Josie smiling again.

'Too true. Come on.' I led them over to the bar and put in their drink orders with Dan. 'Any news from Ethan?' I said quietly. I didn't want to spoil Josie's mood tonight, but thought it would be rude not to mention it at all.

'Not really. He's still living at his parents. He pops round to see Stella one night a week and has her one day at the weekends, but all our conversations revolve around her. It's as if we can't find anything to say to one another anymore.' She gave a rueful shrug. 'He didn't send me a Valentine's card.'

'Don't worry,' said Sasha. 'I didn't receive a card from Peter, and I've never felt more relieved. It's the sort of thing he would do, just to keep that contact between us, but hopefully, this is a sign that he's got the message now, that our relationship is well and truly over.'

'Listen to us two,' said Josie, laughing. 'We're putting a real dampener on your night of love and romance, aren't we? How's things with Max? Do you have any news to share with us?' she asked, picking up my left hand playfully in search of something sparkly.

'No, don't be silly.' I patted her hand away, not wanting to draw attention to myself. 'Come on, let's go through to the back. There's plenty of food.' I ushered them through, desperate to escape another awkward conversation.

We sat down with Johnny and Max and were just tucking into some bread and cheese, with Edith Piaf warbling away in the background, when Ryan wandered into the room. Dispensing with all friendly greetings, his gaze cast round the room.

'Have you seen, Katy?'

'No, but apparently she was in earlier. I just assumed she'd be with you?'

'She's meant to be,' he said, crossly. 'Don't worry, I'll find her.'

I hadn't been worried until Ryan had swept in bringing his black mood with him. Rose was right, Katy had been in a funny frame of mind recently, but I suspected it had more to do with whatever was going on with Ryan than anything else. Thankfully, Max had gone to the bar to order more drinks and had missed Ryan's broody appearance or else he'd now be scouring the streets in search of his little sister, and the last thing we needed tonight was any drama.

'Here, Mary, do you fancy a dance? Someone's got to get this party started!' With the help of his walking stick, Arthur who'd been sitting at a table with some of our regular customers, eased himself up, wriggling his shoulders to ward off all his aches and pains, I suspected.

'If my knee will hold out.' Mary was well known in the village, she was on every committee going and a great supporter of most village events. She stood up, laughing, and blushed like a teenager.

'Oh, don't worry, we can hold each other up.'

The two pensioners swayed in time to the music. Frank Sinatra was now doing his thing, his warm and mellow voice crooning through the speakers about strangers in the night exchanging glances. It was one of my favourite songs and sent goosebumps along the length of my arms. When Max came and sat down beside me and slipped his hand on my thigh, the fluttering sensations reached every other part of my body too.

'Do you want to dance?' I asked, in my very best French accent.

'Er no, Ellie. I really do not want to dance.'

'Ah, and who said romance was dead,' said Josie, laughing.

In fairness it was only Mary and Arthur who were in the mood for dancing, everyone else was happy with the food and the beer and the wine and the conversation so I wasn't too disappointed.

Polly was keen to talk about her wedding preparations and no one was going to begrudge her that, tonight of all nights although I felt a bit uncomfortable with Max sat right next to me.

'Now, we've booked St Cuthbert's it all seems very real. It's only a couple of months away and I bet that time will just whizz by. It's so exciting.' She clapped her hands excitedly in front of her face. 'The best thing of all will be getting married in the village with all our friends and family around us. You're going to be my maid of honour, aren't you, Ellie?'

'Am I?' It was the first I'd heard of it.

'Yes, of course, you are!'

'Well, I'd be delighted to, as long as I don't have to wear a flouncy floral dress and a straw boater. Erm, one of my first outings as a bridesmaid,' I explained to the questioning faces. 'There have been several better experiences since then.'

'No, we'll find something suitably simple and classic. Cream and flowing, I'm thinking with daisy garlands for our hair. To go with our theme of a typically English country wedding.'

'That sounds lovely,' said Sasha.

Josie glanced at me, and I saw the devilment flickering in her eyes. I knew she was clamping her lips tight shut not to say anything suitably acerbic about the joys of marriage.

'In my day, they used to say *three times a bridesmaid, never a bride*,' said Mary helpfully.

'Oh well, there's absolutely no hope for me then,' I joked, feeling the weight of Max's imposing presence.

176

Thankfully, Katy had turned up and joined us then at the table. There was no sign of Ryan and I thought it probably best if I didn't mention his name if they were going through some difficulties. I knew from experience that young love didn't always run smoothly.

She was just making us laugh with a story about a friend of hers from college who'd been dumped this morning, receiving the bad news inside a naff valentine's card. We were all agreeing that the poor girl was better off without the hapless lothario when someone else skidded into the room.

'Sasha! There you are.'

Peter, Sasha's ex, and father of baby Ruby, was standing on the threshold to the snug, holding a decidedly lacklustre bunch of flowers.

'What are you doing here?' asked Sasha, curtly.

'I went to the house. I've been desperate to see you. It's Valentine's Day and I couldn't ignore that. I want you to know how much you mean to me. I've got a card for you. And flowers,' he said, thrusting his sorrowful blooms in her direction.

'What does he want, a round of applause?' whispered Josie.

Polly tutted quietly and muttered beneath her breath, 'Honestly, he should have come to me. Those flowers look as though they're beyond reviving, if they were ever alive in the first place.'

'A bit like our relationship,' said Sasha ruefully.

Max, who was a business acquaintance of Peter's, sidled up to him, recognising this wasn't going to plan, and attempted to take him into the other bar, offering him a beer, but Peter wasn't for budging.

'No, I need to speak to Sasha. I'm sorry to have to do this in front of everyone, but I want you to know I still love you. I don't think I'll ever stop loving you.'

Josie made a gagging motion by pretending to put her fingers down a throat. 'Oh, I do hate public displays of affection,' she grumbled.

'Oh for goodness sake,' said Sasha, dropping her head in her hands. 'We've been through this and I'm not going through it again. You made the decision to go back to your wife. That's the end of it. Our relationship is over.'

'But I made the wrong decision,' he said mournfully. 'I realise that now. Can't we give it one more try?'

Peter had been vacillating between Sasha and his wife for months now, and Sasha had understandably got fed up with his antics. I'd seen her hurt and disappointed more times than I cared to remember and I just hoped she wouldn't be swayed by Peter's latest declaration of love.

The whole of the snug was now agog at the drama being played out and I gestured at Katy across the table to put the music back on again, in the hope that it might drown out their conversation.

'No,' said Sasha, pulling herself up by the table. 'Go, just go!'

Quick as a flash, Josie and I turned to each other, out of earshot of the others.

'*Just turn around now, cos you're not welcome anymore!*' we mouthed at one another.

'Don't do this, Sasha,' said Peter, a pleading tone to his voice now. 'Let's talk about it. Come on,' he said, holding out his hand to her. 'Let's go home, we can't do this here, we need some time alone together.'

'NO!' said Johnny, from out of nowhere, which caught us all by surprise, not least Peter.

He turned to stare, as though he'd only just realised he had an entire audience hanging on to his every word. 'What's it got do with you, fella?'

'Sasha's told you she wants you to go, but you don't seem to be getting the message. Why don't you just do one?'

Josie and I exchanged a look, and a little swirl of pride gathered in my chest. Johnny Tay to the rescue! He could be so masterful when he wanted to be.

'Is that what you really want?' Peter asked Sasha, bashful now after Johnny's intervention.

She nodded, dropping her gaze, and Peter shook his head disbelievingly, turning to walk out the room, taking his wilting flowers with him.

'I'll be back,' he called with none of the conviction of The Terminator and bumped straight into Ryan in the process.

'Oi, watch where you're going, mate?'

Peter span round and bustled his way out, not stopping to apologise to Ryan. Sasha ran her hands through her hair, looking totally deflated. She sighed and sat back down again.

'I might have known he'd try something like that.'

'Look, are you all right?' asked Johnny. 'I hope I wasn't overstepping the mark there, but you looked as though you could do with some help.'

'No. Honestly, I was really grateful. If I never see that man again, it'll be a day too soon. He may be Ruby's father and I know I have to have some kind of relationship with him, but I just wish he'd understand that it's over between us.'

'Look let me get you a drink,' said Johnny. 'You look as though you could do with one.'

'Please,' said Sasha, her cheeks flushed pink by the fracas with Peter. She went across to the bar with Johnny, their heads close in conversation. I breathed a sigh of relief, grateful that the drama had passed, but meanwhile, trouble was brewing in another corner.

'What's up with you, Katy?' Ryan's voice was loud enough so that everyone else in the room could hear.

'Nothing, don't go spoiling everything.' She turned to glare at him, shifting in her seat to use her body as a barrier against him.

'Me! We were meant to meet up half an hour ago. I came here looking for you and you were nowhere to be seen. You wanna tell me where you've been?'

'Ugh…' she shook her head, exasperated. 'I don't know, I was probably out the back or something.'

'Katy!' said Ryan, forcibly now. 'Don't mess me about. I know you're up to something.'

'What? Why would you even think that?'

'Ryan!' Max interrupted from across the table. 'Don't speak to Katy like that.'

'I saw you,' Ryan accused her, totally ignoring Max's warning. 'With some guy down at the bottom of the High Street. What's been going on?'

What on earth could Ryan be talking about? Katy idolised Ryan, she would never cheat on him, I felt sure.

'Oh for Christ's sake, have you been following me? What sort of relationship do we have if you can't even trust me?'

'I'm wondering the same, Katy.' He paused, the tension bristling off his body and filling the room. While next to me I could tell Max was straining to go over and put Ryan in his place. I had to put my hand on his arm to stop him. 'So come on then, who was he?' Ryan demanded to know.

'Just some guy. It's not important.' She folded her arms crossly, dropping her chin to her chest, Katy speak for *I don't want to be having this conversation anymore*. 'You don't own me, Ryan, and I don't have to tell you every single thing I do every minute of the day. You're a control freak, do you know that?'

'Right, well if that's the way you feel.' He picked up his beer and downed it in one.

'I think it's best if you go, Ryan.' Max stated.

'Fine, I'll leave you to it, then Katy.' She glared at him accusingly, a swirl of emotions brewing in her eyes. 'You clearly don't want me here and I'm not hanging around while you decide what it is you do want. Go and be with that other guy if that's what you want. I'm out of here.'

'Good,' said Katy, petulantly.

'Great,' said Josie, beneath her breath. 'That's two relationships down tonight. The whole Valentine's thing is working a treat. Let's hope there won't be any other casualties.'

'Oh gawd,' I sighed, picking up my glass of wine, looking for comfort there. 'Why did I ever think this would be a good idea.'

'Well to be honest with you,' said Josie with a wry smile, 'I've always thought romance is very much overrated.'

Fourteen

Thankfully, with Peter and Ryan gone, the mood inside the pub lifted and everyone seemed to enter into the spirit of the night and enjoy themselves.

Apart from Katy that was. She sat in the corner, nursing her Diet Coke and crouching over her phone. I'd known her long enough by now to know when she wanted to be left alone and this was one of those occasions. When she was ready to talk she would come and find either me or Max.

'Well, this is just like old times,' said Max when we found ourselves alone together for a quiet moment. 'It's as if you've never been away.'

'I know and it's lovely to be back. This was always one of the things I loved most about running the pub, the special events, bringing the village together, although maybe in hindsight, I think perhaps the residents of Little Leyton weren't ready for a night of love and passion.' I kicked off my shoes and tucked my feet up to the side of me on the cushioned oak pew, dropping my head on Max's shoulder. 'It would have been nice if we could have done a bit of matchmaking tonight, but maybe that was wishful thinking on my part.'

'Oh, I don't know. Arthur and Mary had a dance, and Johnny stepped in as Sasha's knight in shining armour. What more could you want?'

I interlocked my hand with Max's, gazing up at his handsome profile, a myriad of thoughts filling my head. This was romantic enough being curled up next to Max and, after the epic disaster of my planned romantic meal, we needed to take our moments where we could find them. Looking up into his deep brown eyes which had always held the power to enthrall me, I recognised the uneasy feeling in my chest as one of disappointment. The realisation surprised me. That I'd actually hoped Max might propose again today. I suppressed a sigh. It wasn't Max's style to do it on a day like today, I told myself. Too easy. Too cheesy. But now, in the crook of his embrace, I wondered if he might ever ask me again. He'd said not and that thought suddenly made me feel inexplicably sad.

*

'So how did it go?'

Much later that night, back at the manor, Mum was eager to hear all the news from The Dog and Duck.

'Just one moment.' I held up a finger to her, before dashing upstairs to see Noel who was sleeping peacefully in his cot looking so adorable in his green and white hippo-printed sleep-suit, his little rosebud mouth moving in his dreams. My arms ached to pick him up and to hold his face to mine, to catch a whiff of his sweet and milky scent, but I knew he would only wake up if I did so I reluctantly tiptoed downstairs again, where mum was waiting to hear all about our night.

'Well, let's put it this way,' I told her. 'There wasn't a lot of love in the room! There was plenty of argy-bargy however. At least it didn't come to fisticuffs, but it did get very close at one point.'

'Really, do tell me more?'

Katy wandered into the kitchen at that precise moment, so I shook my head at Mum, who thankfully guessed the situation. Rose and Alan were back from their trip to London and we all sat around in the kitchen drinking hot chocolates and eating heart-shaped cookies that Mum had baked earlier. Max sipped on a whisky, with his dogs resting at his feet, and Digby was curled up next to me, not that I'd entirely forgiven him yet for sabotaging my special meal.

Rose and Alan's visit had passed so quickly and they were due to travel home tomorrow. I'd got to know Rose much better, and I'd enjoyed the time I'd spent with her, especially seeing the way her entire being lit up spending time with Noel. I glanced across at Katy who was scowling into her mug of hot chocolate. I suspected, beneath her bravado and 'couldn't care less' attitude, she was struggling with the thought of having to see her mum off again. Goodbyes were always difficult, but when you were still a teenager and you'd gone through a tricky patch with your mum, it must be doubly hard.

'So, when will your next visit be?' Mum asked Rose. The pair of them had grown closer during this latest visit, bonding over their new found status as grandmothers.

'Soon hopefully. I want to come back and see my little grandson before he gets too big. And, of course, I need to keep an eye on Katy too.' There was only warmth and affection in her voice, but Katy pounced on her words.

'You don't need to worry about me!'

'Oh, but I do, Katy.' Rose remained calm at Katy's outburst, but I saw the hurt flicker in her eyes. 'I'm your mum and I miss not seeing you every day. You might not want to believe it, but I'm always here for you whenever you need me.'

'Huh.' Katy slumped forward on the table, cradling her head in her arms, and Rose gave me a questioning look. I shrugged and looked to Max.

'It's not you, Mum,' said Max appeasingly. 'Katy had a falling-out with Ryan tonight, she's just upset.'

'Oh dear,' said Rose. 'What's happened?'

'Nothing.' She snapped. She paused, her gaze scanning around the table warily. Then to my surprise the floodgates opened. 'It's just Ryan being an idiot. And on Valentine's Day too. I should have known. He always jumps to the wrong conclusions. Instead of talking to me he makes his mind up and that's it, there's no budging him. I'm not sure I can be dealing with him at the moment.'

'What a shame,' said Rose, seemingly bolstered by Katy's openness. 'He seems so very fond of you. Why don't you sit down and have an honest chat with him? If you get everything out in the open, I'm sure you'll both feel differently about the situation.'

'Right, and you would know everything about honesty, wouldn't you, Mum?'

'Katy!' Alan, Max and I all chastised her together. My mum looked horrified and Rose appeared as though she might burst into tears.

'What? I'm sick of people telling me what I can and can't do when they're no better themselves.'

'Don't speak to your mother like that,' said Alan crossly, jumping up from his chair.

'You can't tell me what to do.' Katy's gaze was defiant. 'This isn't your house and you're not my father. You're nothing to me.'

'KATY!' Max bellowed this time. 'Apologise! Mum and Alan are guests in our house and I won't tolerate rudeness to anybody here. There's no need for it.'

'Sorry,' she mumbled, barely perceptibly, pushing back her chair. 'I'm going to bed.'

'No, don't go,' said Rose. 'Not like this. We're going home first thing in the morning and I would hate for us to leave under a cloud. Please!'

Katy sighed and sat back down again.

'Well, if you don't mind, I will go to bed, I've got an early start.' Alan attempted a smile, but he wasn't fooling anyone, not with his face turning into an ugly grimace. He swept out of the room, the tension dissipating somewhat as soon as he left.

'He finds all this very hard,' said Rose, by way of explanation. 'I understand how you feel, Katy, really I do, but if we want to have any hope of moving on in our relationship then you have to forgive me for what I did. You can't throw it back in my face every time we have a row or else we'll never get over this. And you can't take it out on Alan either, he loves you very much, as do I.'

'You know, I should be going too,' said Mum, looking increasingly uncomfortable.

'No don't, please stay.' Rose laid a hand on my mum's arm, as though she needed her there for moral support. 'Besides, you're staying here tonight, aren't you?'

'Yes, of course,' mum said, as though she'd only just remembered. She was clearly desperate to get out of the way of this particular family conflab, but Katy and Rose didn't seem to have any such qualms about discussing their differences in front of us all.

Katy wandered over to the sink, pulling out a glass from the cupboard above and filling it with water. She turned to face her mum.

'Mum, this isn't like a small disagreement over a borrowed handbag or a pair of shoes, this was a major secret you kept from me for all of my childhood. Sometimes, when I think about it, when it all comes rushing back to me, I still can't believe that you actually did that. The hurt hits me again as though I'm experiencing it for the first time.' Katy's voice was tremulous, the pain evident to see in her eyes, and my heart twisted for her. 'You kept the identity of my real father a secret and denied me a relationship with him. And you didn't tell him either. It's unforgivable.'

Rose's shoulders slumped, her exasperation almost tangible. 'I know. I can't believe I did it either. But I did. And nothing I can say or do can change that in any way. I hope you'll find it within yourself to forgive me one day. I'll do whatever I can to make it up to you, Katy, but you have to meet me halfway. It breaks my heart that our relationship has been so damaged by this. We can make it work again, I know we can, but you have to want to do that.'

'Your mum's right,' I offered tentatively. 'We all makes mistakes, some bigger than others, but if you can't find it in yourself to forgive your mum, then it's just going to eat you up inside. It will make you more and more bitter to the point where it will affect everything else in your life, your job, your friends, your relationship with Ryan. You don't want that, do you, Katy?'

Katy shook her head, her chest rising exaggeratedly until she couldn't contain her emotions any longer and it all came rushing out in a torrent of ugly sobs.

'Oh Katy!' Rose rushed over to her daughter, wrapping her in her arms. 'I'm sorry. I never meant to cause you all this hurt and pain. I wish I could turn the clock back and do things differently, but I can't and all I want to do is make it up to you. I love you, Katy, more than you'll ever know.'

'We all do,' said Max. 'You've got a loving family around you, good friends, Ryan, and a little nephew who's going to grow up adoring his funny aunty. When you think about it, you've got lots to be grateful for.'

'I know,' she sighed, looking desperately sad as she glanced up at Rose. 'I'm sorry, Mum, but I just find it so hard at times.'

'You don't need to apologise to me,' said Rose, still cradling her daughter, emotion written all over her face.

'Oh, but I do. I must have ruined your holiday.'

'No you haven't.' Rose waved the thought away. 'It's been lovely spending time with you and little Noel, and Max and Ellie, and getting to know you too, Veronica. As I get older my family becomes even more important to me. And if things between us are good, Katy, then that's all that matters. I can go back to Spain tomorrow with a happy heart. We are okay now, aren't we?' Rose pulled away from Katy, to look into her eyes, smoothing her hair down at the same time.

'Yeah Mum, we're good,' she said, looking relieved to have cleared the air. She kissed her on the cheek. 'I'll try harder not to get so wound up about things.' She fell silent, thoughtful for a moment. 'There's someone else I need to try harder with too.' Her face clouded pensively. 'Ryan. I think I have some making up to do there, as well.'

Fifteen

'What do you think?'

Polly came out of the dressing room, the slim sheath dress she was wearing pushing her knees together so that she waddled like a most becoming penguin, the big flouncy flower on the neckline tickling her chin.

I couldn't help myself, I burst out laughing, much to the disdain of the snooty shop assistant.

'It's one of our most popular designs. Sophisticated, elegant and classy.'

Polly wobbled precariously, waving her arms at her side in an attempt to stay upright. 'It is a lovely dress, I know, and it is all of those things you mentioned, but sadly I'm not,' she giggled. 'I'll have to keep on looking I'm afraid.'

After leaving the shop, we gave up on the idea of finding the perfect bridal dress and ran through the streets, trying to avoid the pouring rain before decamping to a wine bar, giggling as we fell through the door, where we ordered two large glasses of Sauvignon Blanc instead. Noel was at home with his dad so there was no rush for me to get home and I was determined to enjoy this first girly time out I'd had since becoming a mum.

'Who would have thought that finding a dress could be so hard? They were all lovely, but much too formal and grown-up for me. I know exactly what I want. Something ethereal and summery and flowing. Imagine Kate Moss running through a corn field.'

'Isn't she a bit old for that sort of thing?'

'Yes.' Polly spluttered. 'But you get the idea. Look.' She grabbed a pen from her handbag and proceeded to draw a sketch on the back of an old envelope. Polly's drawing skills were about as good as mine so her design looked like a fancy oblong with a squiggly flower on it, but I nodded my approval anyway.

'Why don't you go and see Caroline in the village. She was a dressmaker for many years. She doesn't do it as a business anymore, but I bet she'd jump at the chance to make your wedding dress.'

'Do you think so?'

'I'm sure she'd love to.'

'That's such a good idea. I'll ask her. Then it will be a proper village affair. Honestly, Ellie, I don't think I've ever felt so excited in my whole life. I know some people might think it's a bit soon, I mean we haven't known each other that long, but we're both absolutely certain that we want to spend the rest of our lives together so what's the point in waiting?'

I nodded.

'I mean, you must feel the same way about Max?'

'Oh yes I do.' Max was the centre of my world and I couldn't imagine a time when he wouldn't be in my life. It was just that the whole marriage thing had become a bit of a sensitive subject between us recently.

'It's all I think about,' said Polly dreamily. 'When I'm at work preparing the bridal bouquets, I imagine how I'll be feeling when it comes round to the morning of my special day. I spend all my spare time looking at wedding favours, wondering whether key rings or scented candles or sugared almonds are the way to go. You will tell me if I turn into Bridezilla, won't you? I catch myself talking about the wedding all the time, to George, to my customers, to you and the girls, to anyone who will listen really. I'm sure I must be boring everyone half to death. I really hope I don't send George running in the opposite direction.'

'Well you've every right to be excited. You only get married once in your life.' I paused, realising that wasn't necessarily so. 'Well hopefully!' I added. 'And everyone loves a wedding. I'm just as excited as you are.'

'Well, it's not too late to make it a double wedding, Ellie. That's probably the only thing now that could make it even more special.'

I laughed and took a sip of my wine, buying myself some time. 'Stop it! This is your special day we're talking about here, it should all be about you. I would hate to steal any of your thunder even if I could persuade Max round to the idea.' I joked.

'Ha Max wouldn't need any persuading at all. You know, I could have a word with him if you like?'

'No!' I told her firmly.

'Anyway, you wouldn't be stealing my spotlight. We'd be sharing it. Wouldn't you love to get married in the village with all your friends and family around you? With little Noel in your arms?'

It could be so easy to get swept away by Polly's enthusiasm. An image of Max dressed in a morning suit flashed into my mind, causing my heart to flutter in my chest. Undeniably, he would make *the* most handsome groom. Starting to make plans for Polly's nuptials these last few weeks had meant she wasn't the only one who had been focussed on all things bridal. We'd discussed menus, welcoming drinks, table arrangements, dresses, shoes, posies and perfumes; it was only natural to wonder about the choices I'd make if I was in Polly's shoes. Still, as I kept reminding her, this wasn't about me. It was all about Polly and George, and I was determined that her day would be as magical as it could possibly be.

'Of course, I would,' surprising myself by saying it aloud for the first time. 'But who knows when that might happen. This year it's your wedding that's going to be the society event of the Little Leyton social calendar.'

Polly laughed and went all swoony again. 'Yes, and I can't wait! I still don't understand though why you didn't say yes to Max in the first place. Organising a wedding is just the best thing. You're mad not to want to do it.'

Very probably, I thought ruefully, especially if both Polly and Mum thought it to be true.

'It just took me by surprise that was all. Every single time… I'm the sort of person who has to think about these things, to get it straight in my own head how I feel. There was so much going on when he asked me the last time, I'd just had Noel and was leaking milk everywhere, feeling fat and frumpy and not at all like how a blushing bride-to-be should feel. It just wasn't the right moment. I think Max is pretty pissed with me, he can't understand it either, but honestly it had nothing to do with the way I feel about him. It was more about how I was feeling about myself. Does that make any sense?'

Polly nodded and I continued.

'Now I can't even talk to him about it because it feels like it will just turn into a row.'

'Oh, really?' Polly reached her hand across the table to find mine, scrunching up her face sympathetically. 'Why didn't you say? There's me banging on about my wedding and all the time you've been feeling like this. What's been going on?'

'Honestly, it's nothing serious. Just a passing phase, I'm sure. We're both really tired, Noel is having us up two or three times in the night at the moment, and Max is really busy with work so we're not getting to see each other much and when we do, well... we're not always at our best. I'd hoped that the Valentine's event would bring us back together but somehow we still seem to be like ships in the night.'

I gave a rueful smile, my mind flitting towards Josie. Hadn't she told me exactly the same thing about her and Ethan? Wasn't this the same way that all their problems had started?

'Oh dear.' Polly's face crumpled and I could see genuine concern in her eyes.

'Look I don't want you getting the wrong idea.' I was quick to reassure her. 'We're still good together. I guess it's just one of those things you go through as a couple, especially when there's a baby on the scene.'

'Maybe. Anyway, one thing I do know is that Max adores you. You only have to look at him when he's with you to see how much he cares for you.'

I smiled, glad for her reassurance. 'And I love him too, Polly, with all my heart and who knows maybe one day we will make it up the aisle,' I said brightly.

'Well, in that case,' said Polly, with a big smile on her face, 'you've got absolutely nothing to worry about.' Lost in thought for a moment, she played with her engagement ring, the light flooding through the window of the wine bar and bouncing off the huge sparkly diamond. 'Hey, you know what you should say to Max, "About that marriage proposal, I've been thinking, and my answer is yes!" Or you have to hope that he asks you again. If not, you'll have to ask him yourself. That's what I'd do!'

'Well you never know, I might just do that, but not yet.' To be honest, it was something I'd been thinking about, telling him I would marry him after all, but finding the right moment, that was another matter. 'Anyway, we shouldn't be talking about me, we need to put all our energies into your big day first and then once you're happily married, I might start thinking about my own marriage plans then. How does that sound?'

'Is that a promise?' asked Polly, holding up her pinky finger.

'Definitely,' I said, grinning, holding mine up to seal the deal.

After a delicious lunch of fried calamari with garlic bread and a green salad, we left the wine bar and mooched around the old town, gazing in the shop windows, and chattering aimlessly in that way old friends do, jumping from one random subject to another, revelling in each other's company. The sun was peeping through the clouds, teasing us with its promise of better days ahead, and bright tulips and daffodils in wooden planters provided a lovely splash of colour to the High Street. A little later, just as we were about to cross the road, something caught Polly's eye up ahead.

'Look, isn't that your mum and dad there.'

'Oh yes. Mum!' I called, as both Polly and I waved frantically, trying to get their attention, but they didn't see us and quickly they'd gone, climbing the steps to one of the Georgian terraces at the bottom of the road. 'Where are they going?'

Curious now, we wandered down and stood in front of the building Mum and Dad had disappeared into, staring up at the wooden plaque on the wall.

I read the sign aloud, 'Shaw and Rogers Solicitors – Family Law. That's odd,' I said, 'they didn't mention anything about going to see the solicitors.'

Funny thing was, when I'd asked Mum if she could look after Noel today, she'd been apologetic, explaining they'd already arranged to meet some friends for lunch and could we do it some other day. Why wouldn't she have mentioned they were going to the solicitors too?

Or perhaps there never was a date with their friends in the first place.

'Well, they don't have to tell you everything, do they? Come on,' said Polly, grabbing my arm and leading me away. 'Do you fancy a cup of tea and a slice of cake? I shouldn't really, or else I might never fit into my non-existent wedding dress, but it's not often we have the opportunity to spend a proper girly day together.'

'Go on then,' I said, needing no persuasion whatsoever, although my mind was still puzzling over what my parents were up to, and what was with all of the secrets lately. I shook the thoughts away. 'Hey, but if I can't fit into my maid of honour dress either, then you'll only have yourself to blame.'

'Don't worry, I'll make sure Caroline tailors in some cake eating room in those dresses,' she joked.

On our way home, I texted Max to let him know that I was just going to call in at the pub to run through some orders with Dan. Max said he'd meet me there as he was about to take Noel and Digby for a walk.

Back in the village, I hugged Polly and thanked her for a lovely, if unproductive day, before waving her goodbye, watching as she dashed off in the direction of Caroline's house. There was no time like the present when you had weddings outfits to organise.

At The Dog and Duck, I sat down with Dan in the kitchen and discussed stock levels and staffing for the coming weeks. It didn't take us long, and when I heard some familiar voices coming from the snug bar, I wandered through to find Digby already asleep in his favourite spot in front of the fire, and Max walking up and down with a grizzling Noel in his arms.

'Hey!' Max greeted me with a wide smile and a kiss, pulling me in for a hug with my two main men. 'Am I glad to see you?'

Apparently, Noel had been crying for most of the day. Poor Max, I thought fleetingly. It had been a proper treat going out for the day with Polly, to get dressed up and not to have to worry about seeing to Noel. Max had volunteered to look after him when Mum had said she couldn't and I could tell his nerves were frayed to pieces. I stifled a smile, only too happy to relieve Max of his duties. Only a few hours away, but I'd missed my fellas so much.

We hadn't intended to stay at the pub, but Eric and Gemma were both in for the start of the next shift and we all got talking and soon Eric had persuaded us to have just one drink. Max opted for a gin and tonic, and I settled for a small glass of wine. We took our drinks and sat on the old church pews that were covered in an assortment of tapestry-covered cushions.

'You missed all the drama here, earlier,' Eric said.

'What was that then?' I asked.

'Well, Arthur was on the way to the loos, took a tumble and banged his head on the edge of the table as he fell down.'

'Crikey no! Is he all right?'

Eric shrugged. 'I think so. He said his leg just gave way beneath him, but then he's not terribly steady on his feet at the best of times. He'd only had a pint as well, so he couldn't even blame the booze. We called the paramedics because he was a bit dazed and they wanted to take him off to the hospital but he wasn't having any of it. He was asking for you. "Get Ellie, get Ellie, she'll know what to do." In the end he refused to go to the hospital. You know what he's like, he can be a stubborn old so-and-so when he wants to be.'

'How did he get home?' I asked, worried sick.

'I put him in the car and drove him back. He said he was going to have a nap, but I'm not sure how much longer he's going to be able to manage in that house on his own. He's had a few bouts of ill health recently.'

'Oh dear,' I said, looking at Max. 'I hope he's okay.'

'We can pop in on the way home if you'd like,' said Max, reading my mind.

'I think we should.' Arthur had lived alone since he lost his wife, Marge, a few years ago. He'd always managed perfectly well, but in recent months he'd become frailer and he seemed much more vulnerable these days. He used to come into the pub a few times each week, but his visits were becoming less frequent and I suspected that was to do with the difficulty he had in actually getting here.

'And then that chap came in, the one who turned up here on Christmas Day and stayed for lunch. His name's Andy apparently. He ordered a pint and went over and sat by the window there. Ryan came in a few minutes later and they picked up where they left off on Christmas Day, trading insults at each other. All over Katy, I think.'

'For goodness sake! What's that all about then? I saw him in the village a few weeks ago and wondered what he was doing here.'

'Did you?' said Max, seeming surprised.

'Yeah, I didn't think too much of it then,' I said, trying to play it down, wondering if I should have mentioned it at all. There was something about the man that unsettled me, but I couldn't quite put my finger on what it was. 'Maybe he just likes it round here and wants to explore the area. I'll have a word with Katy. See if she knows what's going on. We can't have our customers being driven out by the locals.'

'Well, you know what Ryan can be like when he gets a bee in his bonnet. Do you want me to have a word?'

'No!' I said, far too sharply. 'Leave it to me.' Max might go in heavy-handed, only making things worse. 'I'm sure it's something and nothing.'

Sometimes running the pub felt like being at the head of an extended dysfunctional family. People were forever falling out with each other, having rows and misunderstandings, making accusations, even coming to fisticuffs at times too, but they made friends here as well, fell in love sometimes – you only had to look at Polly and George to see that – and shared happy, sad and intimate times. It could be frustrating and challenging, but ultimately incredibly rewarding too. I'd sort Katy out, and I'd sort Arthur out too. It was all part of the job, a part I didn't have any intention of turning my back on even if I was still on maternity leave.

Sixteen

Later that afternoon we arrived at the row of four cottages where Arthur lived and I clicked open the white picket fence gate. It was such a long time since I'd been here but I was immediately transported back to when I was a little girl and visited during the long summer holidays. I would run down the long path shouting hello, taking a break from my adventures around the village, often bringing friends with me. Marge would make a jug of lemonade and a batch of raspberry buns and we would sit outside on the front lawn, chatting and laughing. Then we might have a game of Swingball with Arthur, before rushing off again, on to our next stop, usually taking a stash of goodies with us, like some cooking apples or a batch of scones. Back then, the sun always shone, the wooden fence was a brilliant white, the wide lawn lush and green, and the roses rambling around the door frame, the most vivid of pinks and yellows. Like a faded photo, the scene had lost its vibrancy and was tatty and worn around the edges, but still it filled me with a sense of nostalgia for that lost time.

I rang on the doorbell of Arthur's cottage, but there was no answer. We peered through the letter box and called his name, but there wasn't any sign of life inside. Eventually I tried the door handle. To my surprise it eased open.

'Arthur,' I called out, trying to ignore the feeling of dread growing in my chest.

We wandered down the darkened hallway and to my relief we found Arthur in the small living room, fast asleep in his chair. He stirred as we approached him, his eyes flickering open to greet us.

'Hello, Arthur,' I said, putting an arm on his shoulder so as not to alarm him. 'Sorry for just wandering in like this, but we heard about your fall and wanted to check you were okay. How are you feeling now?'

'Oh, all right, love.' He grimaced as he pushed himself up in his chair. 'A bit sore, but nothing that won't sort itself out.'

'You should have gone to the hospital, Arthur.' Here, wrapped up in a blanket in his chair, in the quietness and emptiness of his front room, he seemed that much smaller and older than when he was at the pub. 'They could have checked you over to make sure you don't have any broken bones. You probably need your blood pressure measuring and some tests to see if there's anything else going on?'

'Nah, I don't need anything like that. You've got to expect a few problems when you get to my age. I'll be all right.'

I noticed Max taking in the scene around us. They were books and papers everywhere, a couple of dirty mugs and plates on the side and some washing hanging over the radiators. It was a sweet old cottage, but could do with a good clean. I was guessing it was some time since it had been vacuumed or dusted because there was no family to speak of and obviously it was more than Arthur could manage. On the walls were several photos of Arthur and Marge, from years gone by. A silver framed picture of the couple on their wedding day, one when they were in their forties, I guessed, looking glamorous, all dressed up ready for a night out and another one, taken more recently, not long before Marge passed. All the photos were brimming with happiness, the love and affection they shared for each other clear to see in their eyes. It saddened me to think how difficult it must have been for Arthur to carry on without his lovely wife who'd been by his side for over half a century.

'Have you had anything to eat?' I said, bringing myself back to the moment.

'Not yet, I was going to do that in a while.' He shuffled in his chair looking uncomfortable.

'Would you like me to make you a cup of tea?'

'Oh yes please, Ellie. You are a sweet girl. And you Max. And you've bought that lovely little baby of yours along. I don't get a lot of visitors these days so this is a proper treat.'

My eyes met with Arthur's rheumy eyes and I felt a pang of regret that I hadn't visited sooner. I hadn't stopped to think about his life outside the realms of the pub. I knew he always ordered a pint of Bass beer, that he was a keen gardener and had an allotment on the council ground at the back of the church, although I wasn't sure how often he'd been able to get up there recently. Last year he'd brought me some of his home-grown rhubarb, runner beans and courgettes and I'd always been delighted to receive his special bundles of produce, making him his favourite puddings of a rhubarb or apple crumble by way of a thank you. But other than that, I didn't give much thought to his day-to-day life, how he managed at home alone, whether he was lonely. Now, I could see that Arthur needed help.

In the kitchen, I filled the kettle and flicked the switch on. While waiting for it to boil, and with Max chatting to Arthur, I had a quick tidy-up. I put away the pots and pans on the draining board and ran some hot water in the sink, washing up the dishes on the side. I swooshed a damp cloth around the sink and the worktops and soon it looked a bit better.

Inspecting Arthur's fridge, I found half a carton of milk, corned beef, some spread, yoghurts and a partly eaten ready meal. Not a lot to keep him going and it made me wonder how well he was eating and looking after himself these days.

Back in the living room, his eyes lit up at the sight of the mug tea.

'Ooh lovely, although I shall need to go to the loo first. Give me a hand, Max.'

Max supported Arthur around his waist, helping him to stand, but the effort was clearly too much for the old man and the pain it caused was evident to see across his features. He winced as he steadied himself and he grabbed onto his walking stick, although it was Max's support that was keeping Arthur upright.

'Always takes me a while to find my legs. I'll be fine when I get going.'

Despite Arthur's assurances, Max cast me a worried glance. As soon as Arthur attempted to move, his legs seemed to want to buckle beneath him and every movement was punctuated by a wince of pain.

'Where is your bathroom?' I asked, concerned.

'Upstairs. You'll see me up there, won't you Max?'

'You could really do with a downstairs loo,' I said, thinking aloud, 'or a stairlift at least.'

'I can manage,' he said, through gritted teeth. 'There's ways and means for all these things, you know.'

But it was apparent that Arthur could barely cope. With every movement so slow, purposeful and painful too by the looks of things, it took an age for Arthur to even reach the bottom of the stairs. I dreaded to think how he would have got on if he hadn't had Max practically carrying him. He had to heave himself up each step in a crab-like fashion with both hands hanging onto the banister. Max was behind him all the way, supporting him and taking the weight of his body in his ungainly climb, but my heart was in my mouth the entire time. He could so easily lose his footing and fall. How on earth did he manage when he was alone? It didn't bear thinking about. Finally, after several minutes and several attempts, Arthur completed the treacherous climb to the bathroom and then the equally dangerous descent and was safely ensconced back downstairs in his chair, supping on his tea, looking mightily relieved, as we all were. Thankfully, Max put into words exactly what I had been feeling.

'Look, Arthur, you can't stay here, it isn't safe.'

'What you talking about? A good night's sleep tonight and I'll be as right as rain tomorrow. I've got my cup of tea. If you can just get me a slice of bread and butter, that'll do me for today.'

My heart twisted to see Arthur's bravery, but there was no way we could leave him here alone. Anything could happen. Would I need to stay with him, I considered, just until we could get him to the doctor's tomorrow? Then again, I would never be able to get him up the stairs on my own. And while I was happy to leave Noel for a few hours, I wasn't really ready to leave him overnight.

'I think we should run you up to the hospital just so that they can give you the once-over,' Max said. 'It shouldn't take too long. And if they're happy for you to come home again, then we'll be happy too.'

'Max is right,' I said, trying a softer approach. 'We're worried about you. If anything were to happen tonight we'd never forgive ourselves.'

'There's no way I'm going to hospital, so you can get that idea out of your head.'

'But, Arthur, you can't support yourself on your legs. You could easily have another fall and you might not be so lucky next time.' Max's voice was firm, but I was beginning to think he may have met his match in Arthur.

'I'm not going to hospital and that's the end of it. I'll see our doctor tomorrow if they can fit me in. My Marge went in to hospital for a check-over and she didn't come out again. I won't do it.'

Max and I exchanged a knowing glance. I could completely understand where Arthur was coming from. He probably felt frightened and vulnerable, and begrudged us waltzing into his house telling him what he should do. We couldn't make him go if he really didn't want to.

'Okay, fair enough. In that case, you'll have to come home with us,' Max said.

'What?' Arthur blustered.

'Come and stay with us for a few days, just until you've got over this little hiccup. We've got an en-suite guest room on the ground floor where you'll be able to manage a bit better. I think I still have the walking frame in the garage that Granddad used. It will make getting around a bit easier for you, even if it's just until your leg is better. Tomorrow we'll get you into the doctor's and we'll see what they have to say,' Max said. I nodded in complete agreement with him, touched once more by the lovely man that he was.

'What you need is a bit of TLC at the moment, Arthur,' I added. 'We can look after you, feed you up, make you cups of tea, just until you're well enough to come home again.'

'No,' he shook his head. 'You won't want me down at your place. I'd feel like I was in the way and I don't want to be a burden to anyone.'

'You won't be. And I'm not taking no for an answer. Ellie can put together a bag of your bits and pieces while I go and pick up the car.'

Arthur's mouth fell open as he looked from me to Max and I half expected him to tell Max what he could go and do with his idea, but he didn't. Instead, his shoulders slumped in his chair and his eyes filled with tears. He fumbled around in his trouser pocket and pulled out a handkerchief, blowing his nose noisily.

'This blimming cold!' he complained, sneakily drying his eyes at the same time.

I found myself welling up too at his obvious relief and gratitude.

'If you're absolutely sure,' he said, through his sniffles, 'then it might be a good idea. Only for a day or two, mind.'

*

With some effort, we managed to get Arthur home and I was thankful that I'd had the foresight to put a beef casserole in the slow cooker before I'd left that morning. He didn't eat a full bowl, but what he did have he seemed to thoroughly enjoy, although the events of the day had clearly caught up with him. When we showed him where he'd be sleeping, his face lit up in disbelief.

'Oh my, this is lovely. Like a posh hotel.' His gaze travelled around the room which was decorated in shades of cream and yellow. There was a double bed, with a bedside table, a wardrobe and a comfy high-backed armchair, in which Arthur could sit and overlook the garden. And the bathroom's there,' he said, craning his head to look. 'And my own telly too.

Well, that's everything I need.' He chuckled. 'I won't want to go home at this rate.'

'You're welcome to stay as long as you like,' I told him truthfully. I was still feeling wretched thinking about Arthur struggling at home by himself and what could have happened to him there.

Digby had taken it upon himself to be Arthur's new best friend and was slumped on the rug next to Arthur's bed, snoring happily.

'You can't sleep in here, Digby,' I said.

'It's all right with me if he stays. That's if you don't mind,' said Arthur, reaching a hand down to give Digby an affectionate stroke 'He's a lovely boy. I miss having a dog about the place.'

'Oh I remember your little dog. Tinker?' A little brown and white scruffy mite who lived up to his name? 'He was always taking himself off around the village for a walk, everyone knew him.' Arthur looked wistful at the memory. 'All right then, Digby. You can stay, just until Arthur gets fed up with you.'

'Thanks for everything, Ellie. You've been so very kind.'

'Not at all, what are friends for! Good night, Arthur.'

I left him to settle in to his new room and went to join Max who was sitting on the sofa in the cosy TV room, where he was deep in conversation with baby Noel, who was all smiles now.

'Well, Arthur seems okay for the moment,' I told him, sighing with relief. 'I've left him watching the telly and I've given him that little bell that was in the back of the cupboard in the kitchen. I've told him to ring it if he needs anything.'

'Good idea. I'm just pleased that we managed to get him down here. I would have been concerned if he'd stayed on his own tonight.'

I nodded my agreement and nestled into Max's side as he put an arm around my shoulder. Max had the biggest heart and most generous spirit of anyone I knew. A lot of people would put the offer out there and say something like 'give me a call if you need anything' or 'you only have to ask', but Max always went that step further. That's how it had been from the very first time I met him. Then I'd been due to go on a charity run to France with Eric, but at the last moment he had broken his leg. Max, who I barely knew at the time, had stepped in to take his place. I'd been horrified at first, knowing that I was going to be holed up in a van with a very attractive and distracting stranger, but Max's mind had been solely on getting the job done.

Then, last year, when his pregnant ex-girlfriend Sasha had come to him for advice on finding a property, he'd gone the extra mile and offered her one of his cottages in the village to rent. That had caused me some sleepless nights. I'd thought the reason he'd done it was because he must be the father of Sasha's baby, but that turned out not to be the case. It was purely another instance of Max reaching out and helping someone when they most needed it.

Seeing him today with Arthur had reminded me, if I'd needed any reminding, just what a lovely man he was. I gazed up at him, a warm shiver running through my body.

'It was so lovely how you looked after Arthur today. Not everyone would have done that.'

'Well, you did it too, and when you think about it, it's the least we can do. Arthur was one of Grandpa's closest friends. We've got the space here and he needs our help. It's not as though he's got any family around to help him out.'

'No, we can be his family now.'

'Exactly,' said Max, looking down at me fondly and stroking my ear. 'It took me back to when I first came to the village to look after Gramps. I'd like to think if I hadn't been around to take care of him then, some kindly person might have stepped in to do the same.'

I nodded. It was a nice thought, but honestly I didn't think there were too many other people around like Max. He was definitely one in a million.

Seventeen

In the following days we managed to persuade Arthur along to the doctors who arranged a series of blood tests and X-rays for him. He was also given a steroid injection in his knee, which helped with his pain and enabled him to get around a bit better. An occupational therapist made a visit to Arthur's house and plans were put into place to install grab rails, high seats and lots of other support items to make his life easier in his home, although I was still worried about how he would ever manage those stairs.

'Do you know,' said Katy, one morning at breakfast, when she'd already been in to Arthur's room to deliver him a cup of tea and her thought for the day, which had become a bit of a routine ever since he arrived. 'I love having Arthur here. He's a lovely man and it's brilliant to come home and know someone will be here. When I was little I always dreamt of living in a big house with lots of brothers and sisters and my nanna and grandad. I was always envious of those kids who had big families. With Max being that much older than me, I can't even remember living with him. And then when we moved to Spain, just Mum, Alan and me, it was as though I was an only child. I hated it. I always felt left out and as though I was in the way.'

'Oh Katy, that's sad. Your mum would hate to hear you talk like that.' Katy's mood hadn't improved any since her mum and Alan had gone back to Spain.

She shrugged, combing her hair behind her ears with her fingers. 'She knows how I feel. And don't get me wrong, I love her to pieces, but I always yearned to be a part of something else, something bigger, to get away, to come back to the UK. I feel much more at home here.' She fell silent, thoughtful for a moment. 'When I'm older I'm going to have a huge family.'

'Are you?'

'Definitely,' she said. 'Will you have more babies?' she asked, taking me off guard with her question.

'Yes, I'm sure we will. At some point. I wouldn't like Noel to be an only child. And we've got all these bedrooms in this house. We have to fill them up somehow,' I laughed. 'First though, we'll probably get another dog. I've been on at Max for ages about getting an English Pointer, I've always wanted one, and I think I could be winning him round. I do miss all the doggy clients I used to have when I ran the daycare business.' Max and I hadn't discussed having more babies, but I knew it was something we both wanted for our future. But right now we had enough on our plates and I wanted to properly sort things out between us before we even thought about having any more children. 'Anyway, you should be off, young lady,' I chided her, glancing at my watch, 'or else you'll miss your bus. What time will you be back tonight?'

'About four. Ryan's picking me up.'

In all the kerfuffle around Arthur, I'd completely forgotten about the altercation Eric had told us about between Ryan and that man in the pub. I glanced across at her, she was in a reasonable mood this morning and as she could be prickly as far as Ryan was concerned I decided not to say anything. There'd been no more fallings-out with Ryan, as far as I knew, so why upset the applecart when there was no need.

'What are you up to today?' she asked.

'I'm going into the village. Mum and Dad are looking after Noel for an hour or two while I pop in to see Caroline. She's making Polly's wedding dress and my bridesmaid dress too, so I'm going to get measured.'

'Oh my goodness, that's so exciting. Can I come?'

'No, you can't,' I laughed. 'You need to be at college.'

'I can't wait for the wedding. I will have to get a new dress and shoes and a bag too. It's going to be amazing, isn't it? And the fact that it will be in the barn at the pub will be brilliant. First a birth, then a marriage, then… oh!'

'Katy stop! Please. We're only in the business of happy occasions, but you're right it will be brilliant.'

'Will you have your wedding there too?' she asked wide-eyed, her face full of mischievous delight.

'Er, I'm not getting married.'

'Not now, but you will do soon, won't you? You should have a word with Max and get it sorted. I'm still down to be a bridesmaid, aren't I? You promised, remember?'

I'm sure I did no such thing, but I wasn't going to get into a conversation now with Katy about my non-existent wedding. Although if such an event were to take place, then of course she would be one of my bridesmaids.

My gaze drifted out of the window, the sun casting a warm and golden glow over the lawns, the white and pink blossom on the trees providing such a pretty outlook. The perfect day for a wedding in fact. The perfect place too. Unbidden, an image appeared in my head, Max in a morning suit looking impossibly handsome, me in a flowing white dress, standing together beneath the wrought-iron archway in the grounds, the splendour of the house in the background.

I gave myself a mental shake, trying to rid myself of the fanciful thoughts which were becoming increasingly more frequent, although we were no further on in sitting down to talk things over.

'Go,' I said to Katy who was waiting expectantly, as if she knew exactly what I was thinking and that I might say, *oh yes, I forgot to tell you, the wedding's next weekend.* When she didn't budge and gave me an innocent wide smile, I pointed in the direction of the door. 'Go now, Katy!'

After I'd seen her off, fed and changed Noel and got myself ready, I popped my head round Arthur's door. He was sat in the tartan fireside chair overlooking the garden, a newspaper in his lap, looking completely at home.

'How are you today, Arthur?'

'Very good,' he said, with a warm smile. 'That Katy of yours is a lovely girl, isn't she? She's so kind and caring, and always makes me laugh with her funny stories. She's a real tonic.'

'Yes she's a good kid, although she can have her moments.'

Arthur chuckled. 'Yes, I don't doubt that for a moment, but she could be a lot worse.'

'I'm going out now, Arthur, but Max is here if you need anything. He'll poke his head round the door later and make you a cuppa.'

'Oh don't you worry about me, I'm fine. Sometimes when I'm at home I don't see anyone all day long. And I like sitting here looking at the garden. There's so much going on. All the squirrels and the birds out there keep me entertained for hours.'

'Good, well you'll have Digby for company if you don't mind. I'm going to see Caroline in the village to be measured up for my dress for Polly's wedding and I don't want Digby's short black hairs getting over any fabric she might have to show me.'

'Don't worry. I'll look after him. You go and enjoy yourself, lovely.'

Since Arthur had taken up temporary residence at Braithwaite Manor there'd been a steady stream of visitors from the village, bringing with them magazines, bunches of grapes and boxes of chocolates, which had done wonders to lift the spirits of the patient.

'Honestly, love, I didn't know people cared so much,' he'd told me the other day. While Arthur might still have had some physical problems that were now being addressed by the doctors, I wondered if part of his problem hadn't actually been that he'd become lonely and depressed spending so much time on his own. I was glad that he was getting back to top form, and I was happy to leave him knowing that he wouldn't be alone for long.

Later, with Noel safely deposited at Mum and Dad's I slipped next door to see Caroline.

'Ooh hello, gorgeous. Come in, come in. It's lovely to see you.' She gave me a big squeeze and kissed me on the cheek. 'I was hoping you'd bring that lovely little baby of yours,' she said, looking disappointed.

'I was going to but I thought it would be easier if Mum had him. That way we won't get distracted.'

Caroline made coffees and we sat at her little kitchen table while she showed me the designs she and Polly had come up with. Caroline's sketches were romantic and whimsical, full of long flowing lines, capturing perfectly the essence of an English country wedding.

'Polly knows exactly what she wants, in her mind, she just had a bit of trouble explaining that to me. She even gave me a little drawing…' Caroline's brow rose.

'Oh, yes, I think I may have seen that drawing,' I laughed.

'Well, we got there in the end. We went through lots of photos in bridal magazines and finally came up with a design that matches exactly what she wants.'

'These sketches are amazing.'

'This is your dress here,' she said, pointing to one of the drawings. 'Very similar to Polly's, but with a halterneck instead of a strapless bodice and yours will be in a taupe colour, which will complement the off-white of Polly's dress perfectly. The material is chiffon, look I've got a swatch here.'

I turned over the soft silky fabric in my fingers. 'It feels amazing.'

'It will be beautiful and this colour will look stunning with your skin tone and the lovely auburn highlights in your hair. It's a very simple design. There's a ruched high waistline and then it falls in soft swishy pleats to the ground. Polly has chosen flower crowns for your hair, so the whole look will be very natural and bohemian.'

'It's gorgeous,' I said, taken aback by the prettiness of the dresses. Up until now it had all been speculation, some of it wild and far out there, but with definite plans in place for Polly's forthcoming nuptials it was becoming very much a reality and I recognised something stirring deep inside me. Excitement, anticipation and a longing that I wasn't sure was entirely reserved for Polly's wedding alone.

'Come on then, let me take some measurements, and then I can make a start on your dress.'

Caroline grabbed her notebook and tape measure and jotted down my details, working quickly and efficiently.

'It's good that I'm taking these now, then I'll have them ready for when I come to design your own wedding dress.'

I tilted my head to look at her, bewildered. 'Do you know something I don't?'

Caroline laughed. 'Oh, sorry, love. It was just something your mum said. I must have got the wrong idea.'

I shook my head disparagingly. 'No, I don't suppose you have at all. That'll be Mum and wishful thinking on her part.'

'Hmmm, well it's not such a bad idea, is it? Now you have little Noel and you're living up at the manor and your mum and dad are home again, well I suppose there's no reason for you not to get married.' She said it matter-of-factly as though it was just a mere formality. Not that I minded. I'd known Caroline since I was a little girl and she was like a second mum to me. One of the dubious joys of living in a village was that everyone knew your business, thought they knew what was best for you and weren't afraid to tell you so. Some people would hate living in that goldfish bowl environment, but it was all I'd ever known and I enjoyed that sense of belonging that came with part of being a community.

'Well you know, once the date is saved, you will be the first to know and I'll be along here to put my order in.'

'I should jolly well hope so,' she laughed. 'What about your mum and dad coming home early from Dubai? That was a bit unexpected, wasn't it?'

'I know, it took me completely by surprise. I thought they were enjoying the ex-pat lifestyle too much to want to come home; wining and dining, sailing at the weekends, living a life of luxury and they'd made so many new friends too. Just goes to show, eh?' Mum and Dad had settled happily back into village life and hadn't shown any regrets at their decision to come home.

'Yes, well it's lovely to have my best friends living back next door, I did miss them, although I won't mind admitting that George made a very good neighbour in their absence. I used to go round saying to all my friends, "oh yes, the bestselling author GG Williamson, he's my next door neighbour, you know!"' She flicked her hair off her collar theatrically. 'He's such a lovely, man. I'm so pleased that Polly managed to nab him.'

'Me too, and he'll be a proper Little Leytoner now. I always say that once the village has worked its magic on you, you'll never want to leave, or if you do, it will always bring you back into the fold.'

'Definitely. I can't imagine living anywhere else. That's obviously what happened to your mum and dad. They missed home too much. Especially now they have a gorgeous little grandchild to dote on. I've seen a lot of your mum, but your dad's been keeping a low profile. Normally I would see him out on his bike or pottering about in the garden, but your mum says he's sorting out a few loose ends before deciding what it is he wants to do; he might look for some part-time consultancy work, she says.'

'Yes, I can't imagine him giving up work completely. He's always given his all to his job, working flat-out, fourteen-hour days often, and sometimes not coming home for weeks on end when's he been in the middle of a big project. Mind you, he couldn't continue at that pace indefinitely. There has to be some point where you start to take things a bit more easily.'

I paused, thoughtful for a moment. Dad had always been defined by his work, it was his reason for getting up in the mornings, his drive and passion for what he did were plain to see. He was still a few years away from retirement age so it was curious why he'd suddenly decided to take a backwards step now.

My mind flashed back to the day when we'd spotted them at the solicitors. Mum had never mentioned anything about that visit, which was strange in itself. Normally she would tell me everything about the minutiae of their day. I also thought back to when they were staying with us at the manor over New Year when Dad had been subdued, somehow less than his normal self. And what about when mum was chiding me about not accepting Max's marriage proposal, saying I would be grateful for the security it might bring me one day.

A cold shiver ran through my body. Perhaps Mum and Dad's reasons for coming home weren't as straightforward as they were claiming.

'I should go,' I said, sounding far more abrupt than I'd intended. 'Noel will probably be ready for a feed.'

'Okay, lovely. I've got everything I need here,' she said, tapping her notebook to her chest. 'I can make a start on your dress now. When I've got something to show you, I'll give you a call and you can come along for a first fitting.'

'I can't wait to see it.'

'Let me come with you,' said Caroline, grabbing her cardigan from off the back of a kitchen chair. 'I haven't seen that baby of yours in far too long and I'm in desperate need of a cuddle.'

With Caroline at my side I wouldn't be able to quiz Mum and Dad about what they'd been doing at the solicitors that day, although that was probably a good thing. What would I have said? 'What's going on?' 'Why have you been acting strangely?' 'Are you getting divorced?' Please God, no. Maybe either one of them had embarked on an affair in Dubai and that's why they'd returned home unexpectedly. A last-ditch attempt to save their marriage? None of the scenarios currently buzzing around my mind were filling me with optimism.

*

'How are you doing, Dad?' I asked a little later, leaning over his computer, while Mum and Caroline were cooing over Noel.

He took off his glasses and rubbed at his eyes. 'Very well, thank you, darling' he said smiling. 'Although I sat down here this morning thinking I'd get my accounts straight for the tax man and I haven't done half of what I wanted to do. My little grandson is such a time-waster. How am I expected to work when he's smiling and laughing away at us all morning?'

'I know exactly what you mean,' I agreed.

What had I been worrying about? Dad didn't seem in the remotest bit subdued, distracted or upset. Certainly not like a man who was trying to save his marriage. Maybe he had financial difficulties and that was why he was poring over his figures, but that couldn't be right either. His contract in Dubai had been extremely lucrative and he wouldn't have given up on it if he had any money problems. I was clearly over-thinking things.

'Do you miss being at work?' I asked him, trying to sound as nonchalant as possible.

'Well, there's a funny thing,' he said, shaking his head, 'I don't miss it at all. I thought I would, that the empty hours of the day would roll out in front of me and I wouldn't know what to do with myself, but it hasn't happened, although I suppose it's still early days yet.'

'Oh don't worry, love, I've got a whole long list of jobs for you if there's any risk of you becoming bored,' Mum piped up from the other side of the room.

Dad rolled his eyes. 'Maybe I'll take up golf,' he whispered to me as an aside. 'Or find myself a mistress?'

'Dad!' My reaction chastised him and he looked at me alarmed.

'It was a joke, sweetheart,' he said, lifting his palms to the air.

Either way they weren't acting like a couple who were at odds with each other. Unless this little display of domestic unity was for my benefit.

'So, how did the measuring up for the dress go?' asked Mum excitedly. 'A wedding in the village is always exciting. Isn't that right, Caroline?' she said, nodding, wide-eyed, in my direction.

Subtlety was not my mother's strong suit. Thinking about it, I wouldn't have been surprised if my parents had come back from Dubai with the sole intention of harrying me into making some wedding plans.

Eighteen

'A question for you?'

Later that day, back at home, Max made us a pot of tea and we sat in the conservatory, eating chocolate biscuits and gazing adoringly at our son. Dad was right about one thing, Noel was a proper little time-waster. The minutes of the day would slip away as we watched him, marvelling at every sound and movement he made. All the more special because he wasn't wailing his head off for once. It was lovely to snatch some rare quiet time alone with Max too. Arthur was taking an afternoon nap, and the dogs were of the same mind, slumped on their beds in the utility room.

'What?' Max asked through a mouthful of crumbs.

'This is a bit random, but do you think Mum and Dad have been acting oddly since they came back from Dubai?'

'No.' Max's brow furrowed. 'Why?'

'Oh, it's probably just me being oversensitive then, but I thought Dad wasn't himself over New Year and it still doesn't make any sense to me that they decided to come home from Dubai when they'd been enjoying it so much out there. Then, I didn't mention it to you before, but I saw Mum and Dad the other day in town. They were going into the solicitors. Mum hadn't told me they were going and she didn't say anything about it afterwards either. It's not like her at all. It just made me wonder if there was something going on with the pair of them.'

Max gave me a doubtful look. 'Like what?'

'Well, I don't know, maybe money problems or perhaps something happened out in Dubai. All those good-looking and wealthy people and all those fabulous dos! Who knows what went on out there? I wondered if they might be thinking of a separation or something.'

'Are you kidding?' said Max genuinely amused by the idea. 'They're one of the most solid couples I know. Maybe they've just got to that stage in their lives where they want to take things easier. To relax a bit and spend more time with each other and their family. Especially now they have this little man in their lives.'

'Yes, you're right, of course.'

Now I felt silly for even thinking such ridiculous thoughts.

'If you're really intrigued about that solicitor's visit, then you should ask your mum. It was probably something so mundane that she didn't think to tell you about it.'

'Yes, I will.' Talking to Max always gave me some perspective. He was much more level-headed than me and not prone to wild flights of fancy. 'Oh, did I tell you I saw Caroline today for the measuring up of my bridesmaid dress. She's come up with something really special, it's going to be so beautiful.' I paused for the briefest moment before deciding that now was a good a time as ever to have that long overdue conversation. I took a deep breath. 'She was teasing me that she would keep my measurements on file for when I need a wedding dress of my own.'

'Really?' said Max, sounding distinctly disinterested and much more enamoured by his biscuit.

'Yes. It was quite exciting really. It made me think about… well you know… if we were ever to get married,' I said it casually to gauge his reaction, but he cast me a fierce glance through narrowed eyes. I ploughed on regardless. 'Well, I couldn't help it really. Everyone I bump into these days asks me when our wedding is. I'm sure the whole village are involved in a conspiracy to get us to the altar.'

Max swallowed hard. 'What do you tell them?'

'Oh, that we'll probably get round to it one of these days.'

'How very romantic,' he said drily. 'You know what you should tell them? To mind their own bloody business.'

'Oh Max, don't be like that.' I shifted my body to look up at him. 'I mean, we will get married one day, won't we?

'I didn't think you wanted to,' he said, gruffly, giving all his attention to Noel who was staring up at his daddy raptly, completely oblivious to the fact that his parents were in the middle of one of those awkward and delicate conversations.

'I never said that! I suppose I just wasn't in a good place to even consider it.'

'Right.' Max sounded decidedly unimpressed by my explanation. 'And now, with your best friend Polly getting married, you've come round to the idea with all the talk of dresses and flowers and parties going on.'

I let his words sink in.

'Yes,' I nodded, 'that's not such a bad thing, is it?'

'Hmmm,' he made a low rumbling sound. 'I don't think deciding to get married on a whim just because you fancy wearing a white frock and having a big bash is the best reason for signing on the dotted line, do you?'

'No, I know that and that isn't what I meant. You're twisting my words. I…' My thoughts trailed away. Was that why I was suddenly more amenable to the idea? Because I'd been caught up in Polly's excitement for her wedding and I wanted to experience that for myself. Thinking about it in those terms made me seem shallow and fickle, and that wasn't how it was at all.

'What *do* you mean then, Ellie?' He said sharply. I took a deep breath not wanting to get into an argument.

'Just that it would be nice to get married. At some point.' I paused. 'And get a Pointer puppy too,' I added, trying and failing to raise a smile from Max.

Instead, he simply raised his eyebrows. 'Nice…?'

'Well it would be more than nice, obviously.' I sighed inwardly with frustration. 'Oh Max, you're being deliberately awkward. Why can't we talk about this sensibly?'

'We are. Nothing's changed though since I last asked you to marry me and you didn't want to then. You said we were happy as we are. What's so different now?'

'Nothing. Maybe just my perception of what married life will be like, that's all.'

'Right,' Max nodded as though that was a totally understandable response. 'So what, is this your bungling attempt at proposing to me?'

'No! I was just saying, that's all.' I had the distinct impression Max was trying deliberately to provoke me. 'Although…' I hesitated, a feeling of devilment filling my bones, 'supposing I were to ask you to marry me, would you say yes?'

A silly question, I knew, because Max had made it clear how much he wanted me to be his wife. He'd made no secret of that, but now, right at this moment, I just wanted to make things better between us, to see the longing in his eyes and to hear him say yes. To say the words 'that of course he wanted to marry me.' Instead, he looked me squarely in the eyes.

'No.'

'What?' I startled, jumping up on the sofa, looking at him accusingly. 'What do you mean?'

The faintest of smiles appeared on his lips and I hoped he was teasing me, but deep down I still experienced a pang of disappointment. I picked up the cushion to the side of me, just about to whack him round the head, when the back door flew open and Katy breezed in discarding her jacket, scarf and gloves, depositing them in a heap in the utility room. She threw the empty can and chocolate wrapper she'd been holding into the bin and dropped her bag in the middle of the floor.

'Hey, you two are not in the middle of a domestic, are you?' she asked, seeing the cushion poised above Max's head.

'No, of course not!' Frustration and confusion seeped through my bones. Max was still clearly miffed with me, although he would never admit to it. I so wanted to have a proper and serious conversation about our marriage plans, but it was as though Max was still punishing me for saying no previously and all my attempts now only resulted in silly bickering.

At that moment a heavy knock sounded on the front door, Noel started to cry and the dogs barked fiercely before rushing through the hall in a mad frenzy.

'If that's Ryan, I'm not here,' said Katy, darting up the stairs.

Max and I exchanged a look and I wondered what could possibly have gone wrong this time. Max picked up Noel and wandered off to change his nappy so I jumped up and followed the dogs to answer the door.

'Hello?' It took me only the briefest moment to recognise the person standing at the manor entrance. 'Oh, it's you. Can I help?'

'Yes, I wanted to see Katy.' It was the man from the pub who had shown an unhealthy interest in Katy on Christmas Day, the same one I'd caught skulking around the lanes and now he was here on our doorstep. A cold shudder ran down my spine. What on earth could he want?

'Is she expecting you?' I asked warily, trying to make sense of what he was doing here.

'No, just tell her Andy is here.' He adopted a wide-legged, crossed-armed stance, as though staking his position. He clearly wasn't going anywhere.

'Katy!' I called up the stairs. 'There's someone here to see you. He says his name is Andy.'

'Oh my god!' There was a lot of banging and cursing coming from up above us before Katy stomped down the stairs, pulling a sweatshirt over her head. She pushed past me to meet the man at the front door. 'What are you doing here? I told you not to come.'

'What did you expect me to do? You've not been picking up my calls or replying to my texts. I thought we'd been getting on okay. Tell me what I did wrong? I don't want anything from you, Katy. Just for us to be friends.'

'Everything okay out there?' called Max.

'Yes, yes, it's all fine,' I said. The last thing I wanted was Max getting involved, not in the mood he was in. However curious I was about this man's intentions, Max would be asking much more demanding questions of them both.

'Look,' I said, lowering my voice, feeling very uncomfortable about this whole situation. 'Katy has made it clear that she doesn't want to speak to you. You should go before her brother realises you're here. And I suggest you stay away.' Katy had her head in her hands.

'With all due respect, Ellie, I think that should be Katy's decision and not yours.'

'What…?' I could feel my hackles rise. How dare he?

'Oh no, that's just what we need!' Katy sighed, peering over the man's shoulder to the main gates of the estate where the throaty roar of a motorbike scrunched along the gravel driveway. 'Quick, you'd better come in. Ryan's here now and if he sees you, he's bound to kick off.' She physically manhandled Andy, pulling him into the hallway, slamming the front door shut and pushing him into the library. I wasn't entirely happy about him being in the house but obviously Katy had come to know this man much better than either Max or I had done in our brief introduction to him over Christmas lunch. 'Just stay there and don't move,' she told him. 'I'll go and get rid of Ryan.'

Back in the hallway Katy ran straight into Arthur. If he'd been hoping to have a quiet siesta this afternoon then he'd just had a very rude awakening.

'Ah hello, Katy, I thought I heard you out here.' Arthur shuffled forward with the help of the metal frame, peering round the door into the library. 'Is this your young man?'

'No!' I said firmly.

'Just a… friend,' added Katy What exactly was going on between these two? Friends? It seemed unlikely. What would they possibly have in common? He had to be at least twenty years older than her. I just hoped to god it wasn't a romantic attachment. Was that why Ryan had been on her case?

'Max,' she called through the house, 'can you tell Ryan I'm not home yet.'

There wasn't any response from Max. Just as well really, if he got any whiff of this he'd go absolutely ballistic.

'Ah, that's nice,' said Arthur, calling to Andy, who had no option but to come out into the hallway again so he could speak to Arthur. 'Lovely people to be friends with. They've looked after me a treat. I live in the village, you know, but I had a fall recently and they got me moved in here.'

Arthur proceeded to tell Andy all about his recent troubles and, in fairness, Andy listened intently, nodding and replying in all the right places. I was just hovering awkwardly in the hallway hoping that we would soon hear the roar of the motorbike disappearing back down the drive. Then we might be able to discreetly get rid of Andy too, who seemed to like turning up uninvited on people's doorsteps. Katy was upstairs on the landing dashing from one window to the next keeping a tab on Ryan's movements.

'What's he doing?' I could hear her mumbling, as she padded up and down. 'Hasn't Max told him I'm not here? Oh, I just wish he would hurry up and go. I can't be doing with all this stress.'

She wasn't the only one.

Moments later, she came tiptoeing down the stairs, in a semi-crouched position as though she was on manoeuvres.

'Katy!' The familiar gruff tones of Ryan came wafting through from the kitchen. He'd clearly invited himself in. And where the hell was Max? He was supposed to have intercepted him. Honestly in recent days the manor had become as busy as Piccadilly station in the rush hour. 'I know you're in. Come and talk to me now or I swear to you, I will walk out of this house and you'll never see or hear from me again.'

Katy grimaced exaggeratedly, lifting her shoulders around her ears and putting a finger to her lips. We all stood stock still, not daring to move for fear of making a sound and even Arthur cottoned on to what was going on. I just hoped Ryan would do exactly what he threatened and leave. It was only the dogs, overexcited by unexpected visitors in the hall and kitchen, running frantically between the two rooms, who gave the game away.

'There you are!' Ryan said triumphantly, waltzing into the hallway. Katy's attempt at making herself invisible by dodging behind Arthur clearly failed to work. She pushed Andy back into the library before Ryan saw him. 'What are you playing at, Katy? You're not taking my calls, you're deliberately avoiding me. Will you please tell me, what's going on?'

'Glad I'm not the only one,' piped up Andy, who took a tentative step back into the hallway, clearly intent on being part of this showdown.

Katy and I glared at him for his audacity.

'I thought I told you to stay out of the way,' hissed Katy.

'You!' said Ryan. 'Well, I might have known you'd have something to do with all this.' A vein in his forehead stood proud and Ryan's eyes grew large as I thought for one awful moment we were in for a repeat of the scuffle they'd had on Christmas Day.

'Look, look, look,' said Andy, holding up his hands in a defensive gesture. 'I'm not here to cause trouble. I just wanted to see Katy, to talk to her, to get to know her a bit better. That's not a lot to ask, is it?'

'Actually, mate, it is. I'm her boyfriend and if you don't want a bloody nose, I suggest you crawl back under the rock where you came from.'

'Ryan! Don't talk to him like that,' Katy protested, but now he'd found his stride he wasn't about to stop.

'I know what your game is,' he said, stabbing a finger aggressively in Andy's direction. 'Don't think I haven't seen you, waiting for her outside college, putting your arm around her, god knows what else? I mean it, just leave her alone or else I won't be responsible for my actions.'

'Really? Well from what I know of Katy, she's a level-headed, sensible girl quite capable of making up her own mind about who she wants to spend time with. I'm sure she doesn't need the likes of some Neanderthal monkey to fight her battles for her.' *Oh no!* Where on earth was Max? How could he not hear this racket?

'Er... what did you call me?' Ryan took a step forward in Andy's direction. Arthur looked on wide-eyed, his head whipping left and right to each of the men in turn, trying to make sense of what was going on.

'Oh for goodness sake, would you please just stop it,' Katy pleaded, holding her arms up to stop them from killing each other. 'Both of you!'

Ryan backed away from a physical confrontation, but he turned on Andy angrily. 'You're a perv, do you know that. Preying on young girls. It isn't normal.'

'Ryan, please! Just stop it.'

'No I won't. Someone has to tell him. Look at him, for Christ's sake, he's old enough to be your father.'

'Oh Ryan!' Katy slumped against the wall, cradling her head in her arms, sighing loudly. 'Don't you get it?' She paused. 'That's exactly who Andy is. He *is* my father.'

We all fell silent as the enormity of that snippet of information filled the air, the utter shock on Ryan and Arthur's faces reflecting the torrent of emotions swirling inside me.

'WHAT?' It was all Ryan could manage to say.

'Everything okay?' Better late than never Max wandered in with a newly changed and freshly scented Noel in his arms, completely oblivious to the drama that had been unfolding in his home.

'Do you think it might be time for a cuppa?' Arthur piped up.

'That's the best thing anyone's suggested for a long time,' I agreed.

Nineteen

Having taken Max to one side and filled him in on Katy's revelation, I popped the kettle on and made some tea. I decided to use the best china teapot and cups and saucers in a pink rose and trailing ivy design in recognition of the importance of the occasion, although now, with the delicate china sat in the middle of the kitchen table and four shell-shocked grown men sat around it, I wondered if I shouldn't have opted for something more manly.

'Well that was a real surprise,' I said, for want of something better to say.

'Yes, sorry, I should have told you all sooner, but, well…' Katy faltered over his name, '…Andy and I have just been getting to know each other. I've been trying to make sense of it myself.'

'This is all my fault.' The stranger wasn't a stranger at all, but Katy's father. I studied his features more closely, readjusting my mental image of him. Not a burglar or a crazed stalker, but part of the family. That idea might take some getting used to. 'I never had any intention of coming to Little Leyton and causing all this trouble, upsetting everyone's lives, but when I found out that I had a grown-up daughter, well you can imagine, it came as a shock.'

'Did you not know about Katy then?' Max asked. I glanced across at him wondering what he must be thinking coming face to face with the man who had an affair with his mum when she was still married to his dad.

'No, didn't have a clue.' Andy scratched his head as though he was still trying to make sense of it all. 'Rose got in touch with me out of the blue late last year, said she had something to tell me and then dropped that little bombshell. I couldn't believe it. Thought it must be some kind of joke. I asked her why she was telling me now and she told me that she had to, that Katy had found out the truth and she was worried you might turn up on my doorstep and give me a heart attack.'

'To think that you never knew about your daughter for all those years,' said Arthur, who seemed to be the only one vaguely enjoying this get-together.

'I know. It's crazy!' Andy shook his head. 'But the more I thought about it the more curious I became. To think that I had my own flesh and blood out there somewhere, well, it was a wonderful feeling. Up until last year I didn't believe I had any family of my own, my partner Jill has two children, Luke and Tessa, and they're great kids, we've always got on really well, but to suddenly find out I had a child of my own, well it changes everything, doesn't it?'

'Marge and I were never blessed with children,' said Arthur sadly, still the only one to answer as the rest of us took in the enormity of the news. 'We would have liked some, but it never happened. Still we were very happy together.'

I picked up the teapot and topped up everyone's cup, and handed around the plate of biscuits. The china set had definitely been a bad idea. Not only did the men look slightly ridiculous, trying to get their big fingers in the china handles, but a couple of sips and the cups were empty.

'Let me get some mugs,' I said, unable to bear it any longer. Jaw-dropping news of the type we'd received today needed proper sustenance. Settled back at the table with freshly made tea for everyone in mugs, Andy continued his story.

'Jill told me to leave it for a while. To maybe write you a letter in the new year once you'd had time to come to terms with the news, but I couldn't. The more I thought about it, the more I wanted to see you. I was still thinking that there might be some mistake, that it couldn't really be true. That when I saw you I'd realise you weren't really my daughter after all. I had this urgency inside me, that it had to be done straight away. What if something happened to me and I missed out on the opportunity completely? I'd missed out on eighteen years of your life as it was and I didn't want to miss a day longer.

And then when Christmas came around, I couldn't wait anymore. It's all about family, isn't it – Christmas? I just had to see you. My plan was to come to the village and bump into you, but I hadn't thought what I would do beyond that. With the snow and the bad roads, it gave me the perfect excuse to gatecrash your Christmas party at the pub. I'm sorry about that.' Andy turned to look at me remorsefully.

'No, don't worry, it was fine,' I said, thinking back to that day in the barn. It would definitely go down as a Christmas to remember. I'd been far too wrapped up in my own forthcoming miracle to realise that there were others going on right beneath my nose.

'Hey look, mate, I'm sorry I punched you on the nose.' Ryan looked as shell-shocked as the rest of us were feeling. 'I had no idea.'

'No worries. How could you have possibly known? You were only looking out for your girlfriend and in a way I respected that. I wanted to stand up that day and tell everyone who I was, but I couldn't. I got to see you though, Katy, and talk to you and that was all that mattered to me.' He chuckled. 'I had no idea what I was walking into that day though, what with me meeting my daughter for the first time and then an engagement and then the arrival of your little baby. Best Christmas I've had in a long time.'

I'd become aware that Katy hadn't said a word. She'd had her head bowed the entire time, listening to Andy, occasionally glancing up to take in our reactions. What must she be going through? Poor love. No wonder she'd been so up and down these last few weeks. All I wanted to do was to hold her in my arms and to tell her that everything would be okay.

'So when did you find out who Andy really was?' I asked her gently.

'Just after Christmas. We bumped into each other in the High Street…'

'Not entirely accidentally, I will admit,' said Andy sheepishly.

'We went for a coffee and Andy told me what he's told you today. It was a shock.'

Max nodded, his shock evident too, and laid a hand on Katy's arm.

'I bet.'

'Right,' said Ryan, nodding. 'So that explains everything, the times I saw you together, the secret meetings, the reason you've been upset recently. I just wished you'd told me, Katy, and then I would have understood. I like to think I could have helped you with this in some way. Instead I acted like a complete dick, hassling you all the time, wanting to know what you were doing and where you were going? I'm sorry, Katy. Really, I am. If I'd known, I would have given you the space you needed.'

She looked up at him, emotion brimming in her eyes. 'It's okay, Ryan, you must have wondered what was going on. I didn't say anything because I didn't know what to make of it myself. This man turned up claiming to be my father, but how could I know for certain that what he was telling me was true. For seventeen years I'd believed one thing and then when I found out that the man who I thought was my real father wasn't, after all, it was devastating. It made me question everything. I was going to tell you, and you Max and Ellie, but I wanted to get things straight in my head first of all.'

'I'm sorry, Katy,' Andy said. 'I probably handled things in the wrong way. I wanted to see you and talk to you and maybe have some tests arranged to confirm for certain what Rose had told me. I mean, this all happened eighteen years ago. I wasn't sure it could be true either. But do you know that all paled into insignificance when I saw you for the first time. I looked across at you and I just knew. Deep down in my heart here.' He banged his fist on his chest. 'I was looking at my daughter. My beautiful baby girl.'

'There's definitely no denying the family resemblance,' I said, looking from Katy to Andy. They shared the same shaped eyes and their mouths twisted in the same way when they smiled. They had other similar mannerisms too. No wonder Andy seemed familiar that first time that I'd met him.

'It's weird though,' said Katy. 'I know you're my father, there's definitely a connection, but we don't know each other at all. We've missed out on so much and it's like you're a stranger to me.'

'I know that, Katy, but it doesn't have to be that way. There's nothing we can do to change what's happened in the past, but I'm here now and I'd like to think that somehow we can forge some kind of relationship together. I just want to be in your life, if you'll have me. I'm not asking you to call me dad or anything like that. You can call me Andy. I mean, what do I know about being a dad? Nothing. So I'll have to pick it up as I go along, that's only if you want me to though.'

'Well, I suppose it's a good thing that it's all out in the open now. Shall we just see how it goes?'

'I'm happy with that,' said Andy, smiling, looking relieved. 'Look, I ought to go. I've taken up too much of your time as it. Thank you, Ellie and Max, for listening and for not throwing me out on my ear. You've got my number, Katy, give me a call whenever you need to. I'll always be here for you.'

'I should go too,' said Ryan. 'And sorry, Katy, for being a rubbish boyfriend recently. I'll make it up to you, I promise. And Andy,' he said, holding out his hand, 'I'd like to apologise to you for what happened before. Can I take you for a quick beer to make up for all that madness?'

'Well,' said Andy, a sense of relief washing over his features, 'I wouldn't say no to that. Anyone else fancy a pint?'

Max, Katy and I made our excuses. I sensed Katy needed some time alone to get her thoughts together.

'Ah, The Dog and Duck is the best pub around for miles,' said Arthur, his face lighting up. 'It's my local, you know. Been going there for years. It's always been a great little boozer, but this young lady here has injected some new life into the place. It's had a real spruce up recently and it serves some lovely beers.' Arthur went all dewy-eyed, probably thinking about all those ales. 'Of course, I've been out of action recently so I've not had the chance to get down there. Maybe one of these days though.'

'Come with us now,' said Ryan, and Andy nodded his agreement.

'Ooh, I'd never get on that bike of yours, I wouldn't be able to get my leg over.'

Katy looked at Ryan and giggled, and I think we were all glad of the light-hearted relief.

'You can come in the car with me,' offered Andy.

'Yes, and I can come and collect you when you're done,' said Max.

After they'd left, taking a very chipper Arthur with them, we sat down on the sofa with Katy in between Max and me, and with Noel in my arms, sucking contentedly from his bottle.

'Oh Katy, you have been through it this last year, haven't you? I'm so proud of the way you've handled it all.' I squeezed her closer to me. 'I can't imagine how difficult it must have been for you when Andy turned up out of the blue like that.'

Katy shrugged. 'Well, it's not something that happens to you every day. I didn't know how I was supposed to feel. This man turned up, just some randomer who also happened to be my father. I felt numb really.'

'I can imagine.'

'He seems like a genuine sort,' said Max, voicing his opinion for the first time. 'And at least you have something to build on now. You can do that at your own pace, or if you decide you don't want to have a relationship with Andy, then that's okay too. It's whatever you want, Katy.' There was a tenderness in Max's voice that tugged at my heart. This was clearly strange for him too, yet he'd handled it so calmly. 'When you think about it, he's only just found out that he has a daughter. That must take some getting used to as well.'

'I guess so.' Katy dropped her head onto Max's shoulder. 'I'm so glad I have you two in my life though, and little Noel as well. This feels like how a proper family should be. I love it. I've got everything

I need here. Anything else, well I suppose that will just be a bonus.'

Katy's words warmed me. That's what we were now, a proper family and with Arthur in the fold, we covered all the generations. Perhaps because both Max and Katy had experienced unhappy times growing up, they valued so much more being part of a loving and relaxed household, without the spectre of drama and tears and secrets hanging over them.

The doorbell rang then and we all looked at each other, I so hoped it wasn't Ryan and Andy back again. I'd seen another side to them both this afternoon, a softer more understanding side, but I wasn't ready for any more high emotions today. I put Noel into his bouncer and went to answer the door.

'Hi Ellie!' Sasha was standing on the doorstep with Ruby in the buggy, a big grin on her face and my heart lifted to see her. 'I was just passing and thought I'd pop in. It's not a bad time, is it?'

I gave a rueful smile. How could she have possibly known?

'No, not at all. Come in, I'll pop the kettle on.'

'Hi Sasha.' Max got up and came to kiss me lightly on the forehead. 'I ought to go and do some work. I've got some emails to see to. Give me a buzz if you need anything.'

'I'm going upstairs,' said Katy, after she'd said hello and given Ruby the mandatory cuddle. 'I'm going to chill on my bed, I'm totally knackered after all that.'

'Oh dear, was it something I said?' asked Sasha, picking up on the emotionally charged atmosphere wafting around the kitchen.

'Absolutely nothing to do with you, I promise. Just family stuff. I'll tell you about it sometime,' I said, with a carefree wave, not wanting to break Katy's confidence until I knew she was happy to share the news.

Sasha peeled off her leather jacket before putting Ruby down on a Peter Rabbit activity play mat, the little girl settling happily, playing with some plastic bricks.

'It's so lovely to see you both,' I said. Noel must have thought so too, as he was kicking his legs in his bouncer watching Ruby at play.

'Well actually there was something, or should I say someone, I wanted to ask you about,' she said rather intriguingly. She paused, before adding, 'Johnny.'

'Johnny? What it is you want to know.'

'Well you've known him for years, haven't you? What's he like, really like?'

I smiled, conjuring up an image of my old friend. 'Um... where do I start? He's funny, outrageous, stubborn, a bit of a pisshead at times, but a really lovely, sweet guy.'

My reply obviously pleased her as her face lit up.

'Why?' I asked, suspecting I already knew the answer.

'Well, over these last couple of weeks we've been texting each other and I've met him for lunch a couple of times. Now, well he's asked me out on a proper date.'

'Ooh! Well that's good, isn't it?'

'I don't know,' she shrugged. 'I really like Johnny, he's great company, but I don't know whether we'd be better off staying friends. After everything that happened with Peter, I don't want to jump into a relationship that's going to end badly. Now I've got Ruby, the stakes are so much higher. If I start seeing someone, then I need to know that they will be honest with me and won't mess me around and that there is at least some chance of it leading to something more serious. The thing is, I know that you had a brief romance with Johnny and Polly did too. Is he a player or something, afraid of commitment?'

'Oh Sasha, Johnny is the loveliest guy you could ever meet. Polly and I went to school with him so we were friends first and I think that's probably why it didn't work out romantically for us. I know he broke Polly's heart when he went off travelling, but I think that was just because Johnny needed some time alone, away from the village, to get his head straight and to decide what it was he really wanted from his life. I think he got that whole wanderlust thing out of his system and came back with a renewed attitude. From what Johnny's told me, I think he's ready for something serious now.'

Sasha's full mouth widened into a hopeful smile. Even when she was troubled, she still managed to remain so impossibly cool and elegant. At first I'd been intimidated by her beauty, assuming she was remote and judgemental, but beneath the long luscious hair and the perfect complexion, she was such a down-to-earth and lovely woman. Now I considered her to be a real friend. Thinking of Sasha and Johnny together filled me with excitement. Why hadn't I considered it sooner? They'd make such a gorgeous couple.

'I'm so frightened of getting hurt again,' Sasha continued. 'Being with Johnny is exciting, but it scares the wits out of me too.'

'I can understand that, but sometimes if you want to find love then you have to take a risk.' *Wasn't that the truth?* 'I don't think Johnny would ever go out of his way to deliberately mislead or hurt you, but none of us can never know for sure how things will work out. There are no guarantees.'

Sasha was thoughtful for a moment.

'No, I suppose not. So, you think I should, you know, give it a go with Johnny.'

'I do,' I said, without any hesitation. 'You've got nothing to lose and everything to gain.'

It was so easy to give advice on matters of the heart to other people. Maybe, one of these days, I should start taking some of my own advice too.

Twenty

A few days later, Mum rang me to fix a date for Sunday lunch. She suggested we go down to the pub for drinks before going back to the cottage for one of her legendary roast dinners. Eric, Josie and little Stella would be going too, and my mouth began to water just at the thought of the culinary delights my mum would have in store for us. I couldn't wait, it would be just like old times.

Then I made the mistake of asking after Dad. She took a sharp intake of breath and I braced myself.

'Oh your father, he's absolutely impossible. He's been out in the garden with a chainsaw chopping down trees. Who does he think he is? Bear Grylls? He worries the life out of me. I'd rather pay for Katy's young man, Ryan, to come and do it, but Malc won't hear of it. He's out there now making a godawful noise. I'm half expecting him to chop off his nose, or something worse.'

I chuckled to myself. 'He'll be fine. He's got all the safety gear on, hasn't he?'

'Yes, but why does he put me through the stress? Honestly, he doesn't give me a second thought at times. He just goes ahead and does things his own sweet way. I thought now we were home we might find some more time to spend together, but it doesn't seem that way.'

This was so unlike Mum. Her anxiety was making me twitchy. Normally she would have left him to it and gone off and done her own thing, made some biscuits or planted some bulbs or settled down with a good book. Maybe she was struggling with adjusting to life back in the UK.

'Mum, are you sure everything is all right?'

'What do you mean?' she snapped.

'It's just that you seem a bit uptight recently and I just wondered if there was anything worrying you. You know you can always talk to me if you need to.'

'It's nothing, just…'

'Mum?' I didn't like the way she'd fallen silent as though she couldn't bring herself to tell me whatever it was that was troubling her. 'You and Dad are okay, aren't you? I wasn't going to mention it, but I saw you both the other week going into the solicitors.'

'Oh good grief, did you?'

'Yes. What's going on, Mum? You're worrying me. There's something you haven't told me, isn't there?'

'Bother, I knew this would happen. I told Malc that we should have told you from the start, but he was insistent that we didn't. You know what he's like when he gets a bee in his bonnet.'

Now I was worrying all the more. 'Tell me what? You're not getting divorced, are you?'

'What? No! Whatever gave you that idea. Oh dear, your father's here now. I shall have to go.'

'Mum! You can't go. You have to tell me what's going on?'

'It's Ellie,' I heard my mum whisper to Dad. 'I think you need to talk to her.'

There was a pause, followed by some rustling and then, 'Hello sweetheart.'

'Dad! Would you please tell me what's going on? Mum's not making any sense at all.'

'Well, no change there then. I've been chopping down the overhanging branches on those trees. I've been meaning to do it ever since we came home, but your mother doesn't trust me not to do some serious damage to myself or the garden. Sometimes that woman has little faith in me.'

Dad's warm and familiar voice wafting down the line reassured me that whatever it was that they weren't telling me couldn't be that bad. Could it?

'No, I didn't mean what you were doing now! Something's going on, I know it is, and Mum mentioned you might have something to tell me.'

'Did she now?' I heard his big exhalation of breath. 'Look, why don't you pop down. We can have a cuppa and a chat together.'

Why were they being so mysterious? Couldn't they have told me over the phone? I'd known instinctively as soon as they'd come home from Dubai that something wasn't quite right. I should have been more insistent about finding out what it was, but I'd been far too preoccupied with Noel.

Whatever it was, the uncertainty was driving me to distraction so I hurried down to their cottage, relieved to find them both seeming relatively normal, even if I thought they might throttle each other at any moment.

Dad took Noel from my arms and whisked him indoors, while Mum busied herself in the kitchen making the tea.

'So, what's this all about then?' I asked. 'I knew there was something up.'

'Well you see, this is exactly why I didn't want to say anything. I didn't want you worrying, getting the wrong end of the stick. I know what you're like. You're as bad as your mother.' Mum looked at me and we both bristled. 'Really, all of this… it's something and nothing.'

Dad's reassurances were not helping in the slightest.

'Okay, good. So…?'

'Would you just bloody tell her, Malc.'

He took a breath, fixed his gaze on me and adopted an expression that I'd only seen a couple of times in my life before. I recognised it now as his bad news face.

'I've got cancer.'

Three little words.

'What?'

The air whooshed out of my lungs and the room closed in on me.

I looked from Mum to Dad, the gentle nods of their heads confirming that I hadn't misheard or misunderstood.

'Oh god!' My hand flew to my neck and I dropped down on to a chair, hoping they would explain, tell me it was a big mistake, but I knew, deep down, it couldn't be. The words had been said, they were hanging there like a big black brooding storm filling the room, and they couldn't be unsaid now.

'Why didn't you tell me?' I couldn't feel anger, just disbelief and denial. In the matter of a few moments everything in my world had shifted and Mum promptly burst into tears.

'Oh Veronica,' sighed Dad heavily, 'what are you like?' He went across to her and put his arm around her shoulder.

'No, it's fine. I'm fine,' said Mum, sniffing. 'It's just a relief to get it out in the open. It's been such a burden keeping it from you Ellie.'

Dad shook his head resignedly. 'That was down to me, I'm afraid. I'm sorry, but it was my way of dealing with it. I wanted to know what I was facing and to come to terms with it before letting everyone else know. I know you're my daughter and everything – Veronica told me you had every right to know – but it was coming up to Christmas and you were expecting your little one, I didn't want to put a dampener on everything.'

'But Dad,' I said, reaching up for his hand, 'you wouldn't have done. Don't you realise how much I love you. I wish you'd told me, I knew something was wrong.' Somehow I was holding it all together, but my body was quivering inside. I was determined not to cry. Mum's tears had unsettled Dad and I needed to be strong for them both. 'So please, tell me now, tell me everything that's happened? Oh god, you're not going to die, are you?' So much for me being strong, but I hadn't been able to stop myself. It was the one thing that had been buzzing around my head ever since I'd heard those three little words.

Dad had the audacity to chuckle. 'We're all going to die, sweetheart.'

'Malc! Don't say that.'

'No!' I glared at Dad too. I couldn't consider it. My parents were still young. The thought that there would come a day when they wouldn't be in my life was inconceivable.

'No. I've been very lucky. I had a routine medical check out in Dubai and that flagged up a problem with my prostate. They sent me for further tests and that's when I was diagnosed with the cancer. I've had some treatment and I might need some more, but they're monitoring me regularly, checking my bloods et cetera. It's all under control, as well as these things can ever be. It was a shock when we first found out, but now we know more about it, it seems manageable. Really, there's no need for you to worry.'

'Your dad's right. It's just that when something like this comes out of the blue it rocks your entire world. Just hearing the word cancer is frightening enough and it's only natural you think the worse. Even when we talk about it now, it makes me tearful.'

'Oh Mum, I wish I could have helped you through this.'

'Well you did in a way. Having little Noel come along gave us something positive to focus on. He's brought such a lot of joy into our lives in such a short space of time. It's made us realise how much we have to be grateful for.'

I looked across at Noel held in my dad's arms and my heart almost broke.

I sniffed away the gathering tears. 'So that's why you decided to come home? It all makes sense now.'

Dad nodded. 'As soon as I got the diagnosis I knew what we had to do. We'd had a wonderful time out in Dubai, made some great friends, but when something like this happens, you want to be in the place that means the most to you. Home, where all your friends and family are. I quickly realised I didn't want to be working twelve-hour days anymore. That's precious time. Time I could be spending with Veronica, and with you and Noel. It takes something like this to make you realise what's important in life. We have to cherish every day, that's what this experience has taught me. You can't take any of it for granted.'

I had shivers listening to Dad's words. Mum and Dad were telling me that everything would be okay, that Dad's prognosis was good and how lucky he'd been to catch it so early, but it didn't feel that way to me. It felt desperately unlucky.

'So, when I saw you at the solicitors that day?'

'We were just updating our wills. Nothing like a scare to focus your mind on the practicalities of life.'

It was a sobering thought that Mum and Dad had been making plans for a time when they wouldn't be around. I shook my head to get rid of the worries clouding my mind. If Dad was being positive then I ought to be too.

'Right, and there was me thinking you might be getting divorced.'

'Ha! Well if your mother doesn't stop fussing over me and thinking I'm going to keel over every time I leave the house then we just might.' He looked across the table at her fondly, genuine warmth and affection in his eyes, and reached out for her hand. 'I'm joking, she's been absolutely marvellous your mum. My rock.' I looked down at my clasped hands in my lap, biting on my lip to ward off the tears. 'I really don't know how I would have got through this without her. When something like this happens, I think it's worse for the people around you because it's so awful watching a loved one go through something you have no control over.'

I nodded, feeling desperately sad for them both, although I felt certain Dad wouldn't welcome my sympathy. He'd dealt with it in his own way, and if that meant keeping it from his own daughter for a couple of months because that was easier for him, then I could respect and understand that.

'I don't mind other people knowing about it now, although I'm not about to shout it from the rooftops. Dealing with other people's sympathy, seeing the pity in their eyes isn't always easy. But your mum and I have come to terms with what's happened and that's the main thing and now we want to get on with the rest of our lives. It's the here and now that's important, isn't that right, Veronica?'

Mum nodded and smiled, but she couldn't hide the hurt and anxiety flickering in her eyes. I suspected it wouldn't be quite so easy for Mum as Dad made it out to be.

'Thanks for telling me,' I said.

'It's a relief to get it out in the open,' said Dad. 'And I promise I'll keep you in the loop from now on. Any changes or hospital appointments, you'll be the first to know.'

Dad gave that small tilt of his head and wonky smile that I remembered from when I was little and I'd been upset over something. He would try to make me laugh, his persuasive tone reassuring me that everything would work out in the end. He'd always been right in the past, I just hoped he was right this time too.

Walking home through the lanes of Little Leyton I couldn't help going over what Dad had told me, there was still a part of me that could hardly believe it to be true. Everything around me was so familiar, the rich honey-coloured stone cottages, the quaint old independent shops, the old-fashioned post box, the spire of St Cuthbert's Church standing high above the buildings and the welcoming sight of The Dog and Duck in the distance. It was as though I was seeing it for the first time, my whole personal landscape having shifted to an awkward angle in the space of a morning.

I pulled out my phone, just wanting to hear one person's voice.

'Max?'

'Hey you, everything okay?'

And that's when I cried, great big heavy, heaving sobs.

*

Back home, Max was waiting for me with a cup of tea and a warm welcoming hug. He got Noel out from his buggy, pausing to kiss him on the forehead, before putting him into the travel cot in the conservatory. Then he turned to me, compassion evident across his features. 'Come here.' He pulled me into his arms and cradled my head in his hands. We didn't speak, his strong and protective embrace saying everything I needed to hear. My whole body crumpled into his and I cried some more. It felt such a relief to be able to let go, releasing all that pent-up emotion I'd held onto in front of Mum and Dad, as Max rubbed my back soothingly. The dogs, alarmed by my crying, nudged at my legs, just as eager to make things better for me as Max was.

'Look,' Max said, when finally my sobs subsided. He brushed my hair away from face and mopped up my tears with his thumb. 'I know this is a huge shock, but it sounds as though your dad's going to be okay. He's got a firm treatment plan in place and he'll be monitored regularly from now on.'

'I know, but I'm so worried that he'll get worse. We just don't know, do we? Dad's so brave and matter-of-fact about it all. Mum's a mess, but I think that's because she had to relive it all when they told me about it. It changes everything, doesn't it? It makes you realise that your parents aren't invincible and they're not always going to be around.'

Max nodded, his eyes full of understanding. 'You can't think like that. You have to put it to one side and enjoy all the moments you do have with them. And there'll be plenty of them now they're back in the village.'

Max was right, of course, but it was a good few days before I could actually think about the whole situation without coming out in a cold panic. Having Mum and Dad living nearby meant that I could pop in to see them whenever I wanted, and I'd be doing that every day from now on, and that reassured me that life went on as normal. To see Dad now, more energetic and positive than he'd been over Christmas, it was hard to believe that he wasn't anything but totally fit and healthy. I think he felt wholly relieved too now that the news was out in the open.

When we all gathered at The Dog and Duck for drinks before the Sunday roast Mum had organised it was just like old times. It seemed as though the entire village was in for their lunchtime pint. Paul and Caroline were deep in conversation with Mum and

Dad. As I went past, Caroline grabbed me by the arm.

'Guess what I've been doing this morning?' she whispered excitedly. 'Just putting the finishing touches to your dress. It's so beautiful. I can't wait to see the pair of you in them together. You must come round this week for a fitting. I think you're going to love it.'

'I will.' Caroline's enthusiasm was infectious. 'Maybe make it towards the end of the week though. After today's roast, I'm sure I'll be sporting a very nice food belly for a few days.'

Arthur had joined us for the outing and was perched on a stool in his usual position by the bar. It was heart-warming to see him with his friends, laughing and joking, as though he didn't have a care in the world. There was no denying that he was still struggling physically, finding it hard to move around, but his mood was so much brighter than when we'd visited him at home after his fall. He'd fitted into our household as though he'd always been there, keeping us entertained with his funny stories and asides, and he was no trouble whatsoever to look after. I was beginning to realise that I would miss having him around when he eventually returned home, although we were all ignoring the inevitability of that prospect.

Out of the corner of my eye, I spotted Katy. Earlier she'd been chatting to George, no doubt

grilling him for details about the characters in his
latest book, but now she was bent over, clutching at
her chest, crying. My heart sank, what on earth could
have gone wrong now? She'd been so looking
forward to lunch at Mum's today, but I was really
hoping it was going to be drama-free. I stood on
tiptoes to see above the sea of heads and spotted
Andy with her, waving his arms around animatedly. I
might have known he'd have something to do with it.
I was all for them getting to know each other, but if
his visits only caused her upset and heartache then I
had to wonder if she was ready for a relationship
with him. I didn't mind telling him so either. I
wound my way through the crowds to find out what
was going on.

'Katy, what's wrong?'

She looked at me, her eyes moist, but she couldn't
speak. She was still crying, tears rolling down her
cheeks.

'Oh god, Ellie,' she finally spluttered. 'You'll never
believe this.'

My stomach twisted, hoping to goodness that she
hadn't received more shocking news, but when I
looked more closely into her face I realised she wasn't
crying after all. She was laughing. Uncontrollably.
And so was Andy.

'Look at his feet,' she giggled.

To be fair, I'd had much better offers in my time, but as Katy was so insistent I peered down to see Andy's left foot, which was surprisingly shoeless and sockless.

'What am I looking at?' I said, at something of a loss.

'Andy's toes. He's got webbed toes. Just like me,' she said, wiggling her left foot in the air. 'I've never met anyone with webbed toes before. It's hysterical. Now I know where I get it from. My dad!' she cried.

'It's a very exclusive club,' said Andy, clearly chuffed at being called dad by his new-found daughter.

'Well, that's… that's great. Great…but a bit weird too,' I said, deciding to leave them to their mutual foot comparing activities, glad they'd found something to bond over.

Sat a table in the bay window Polly and George had their heads together and were busy jotting down something in a notepad. Polly looked up and beckoned me over.

'Hi, darling,' she said, greeting me with a hug. 'You know we're off tomorrow on George's book tour for his latest novel? I don't know, it's such a busy schedule for an internationally bestselling author and his soon-to-be wife with book signings, interviews and appearances. So terribly glamorous, darling!' Polly flicked her hair off her shoulders dramatically. 'It's going to be so exciting. I'm acting as George's PA for a couple of weeks to make sure those adoring fans don't become too touchy-feely in their adoration.'

George shook his head and smiled indulgently, looking like a man very much in love.

'Then when we get back it'll only be a couple of weeks to the wedding. Squeee.' Polly turned to George. 'Shall we have another drink, George, there's a couple of things I need to chat to Ellie about. You know, girly-weddingy things.'

When George obediently wandered off to the bar, Polly squealed.

'Have you seen the dresses yet?'

'No, but Caroline's just told me I need to go and have a fitting this week. Have you seen them then?'

'Yes, mine is all done. It's beautiful, just how I imagined it to be. I'm so glad you suggested Caroline. She was putting the finishing touches to your dress when I visited her yesterday. Oh my…' Her eyes grew ever wider. 'I'll tell you what, we are going to be the most stunning bride and maid-of-honour ever to grace the aisle of St Cuthbert's, or the pages of any of those bridal magazines come to that.'

I giggled. It was hard not to get caught up in Polly's excitement.

'Ooh, I meant to say, you know we're booked into the cocktail bar in town for my hen do. I've been thinking about that. We'll have to get taxis there and back, and it's probably going to be packed out. Wouldn't it be easier if we just had the hen do here in the snug bar? You know how much I love this place, everyone does, and as we're having the wedding here too, it makes sense. If the wine's flowing then it will be just as much fun and we'll be able to stagger home afterwards too.'

I thought about it for a moment. As maid-of-honour, I was in charge of organising the hen do and Polly had specifically requested cocktails and canapés for a night of sophisticated fun. There weren't to be any crass or rude accessories, strippergrams, chocolate willies, or any other willies come to that.

'The trouble with having it in the snug bar is that we'll have all the fellas gatecrashing us, wanting to join in the fun. And we can't have that. It should definitely be a girls' night only. Why don't I book out the barn and we can transform it into a swanky cocktail bar for the night? You know the kind of thing, neon lighting, some sophisticated and sexy cocktails, a few posh bites, and some of your favourite Northern soul tunes so that we can dance away until the early hours of the morning.'

'Are you sure, Ellie?' Polly hunched her shoulders and screwed up her face. Honestly, the way this girl was going, she might expire in front of me at any moment from excitement.

'Of course I'm sure.'

She leapt across the table and gave me another huge hug. 'It's going to be brilliant!' Just then Josie wandered past on her way to the bar. 'Josie!' Polly beckoned her over and proceeded to tell her about the new arrangements for the night.

'I remember my hen night,' said Josie wistfully. 'I got paralytically drunk, much to my deep shame. I had a bit of a moment with a very good-looking groom who was out on his stag night.'

'What? I don't remember that!' My mouth fell open.

'No, I never said anything at the time. It was funny how it happened, I'd gone outside for some fresh air and he'd had the same idea. We shared a couple of deep meaningful looks, and there was a bit of a frisson between us, you know what I mean?'

Not really, but I nodded as if I did.

'We got talking, or probably the booze got us talking, and we were saying that maybe if we'd met under different circumstances, it could have been him and me getting married instead. And then we joked about doing a midnight flit and running off together.' Josie looked wistful for a moment. 'Hmmm, I wonder where he is now and whether he had better luck in the marriage stakes.'

I kicked Josie under the table, glaring at her. Now wasn't the time to be discussing her youthful regrets and marriage woes.

'Oh dear, is it still not looking good for you and Ethan?' asked Polly, genuinely sad.

'Not at the moment, but you never know. Perhaps all the love wafting around the village at the moment will work its magic on me and Ethan somehow. Anyway, that doesn't mean I'm not really looking forward to the hen night and the wedding too! I do love a good wedding. And I promise I will behave myself and not got completely sozzled.'

'I'll be disappointed if you don't,' laughed Polly.

It was lovely to have something positive to focus on, especially in the light of Dad's news, something to look forward to that most of the village would be involved in, one way or another.

When George came back with the drinks, Polly quickly dispatched him to the bar again to get one for Josie, while I declined the offer, and made my excuses, wanting to go and see how Noel was doing.

As I stood up my gaze drifted across the room to Dad who was now rocking Noel in his arms, gazing down at him, the love and pride in his face evident to see. I swallowed hard, tears brimming in my eyes. Everyone was telling me that Dad was going to be okay, and I wanted to believe that more than anything, but what if he wasn't? The thought that he might not get to see his grandson grow up tore at my heart. All those important milestones and birthdays and Christmases he might miss. To think that Noel might not know what it was like to go tadpoling with his grandpa or to play football in the park with him or to listen to him reading a bedtime story in those funny voices that always had me enraptured as a little girl.

I looked around me, overcome with emotion, not knowing which way to turn, running straight into Max's gaze from across the room. He raised a questioning eyebrow at me before making his way over.

'What's up Ellie?' he asked, pulling me to one side.

'I'm okay,' I said, desperately trying to get a handle on my feelings. This was supposed to be a happy occasion. I couldn't break down in tears here, in front of everyone.

'Why are you looking at me like that?' he probed.

'Oh just admiring my boyfriend, that is okay, isn't it?'

He slipped his arm around my waist and pulled me closer to his side, kissing me lightly on the nose, teasing my senses with the firmness of his body up against mine. In Max's warm embrace everything seemed much better, much safer.

'That's totally okay,' he nodded, his gaze scanning my features, a warm smile now on those eminently kissable lips.

'I was just thinking how lovely it is to be surrounded by all our family and friends, about to go and have a delicious Sunday roast with Mum and Dad, you and Noel. Life doesn't get much better than this, does it? It's days like these that shape our happy memories.'

'Blimey, Ells, you've gone all philosophical on me.'

I chuckled. 'Well, just taking a moment to smell the roses, that's all.'

Max narrowed his eyes at me, looking distrustful, as though I'd completely lost the plot.

'I do love you, you know that?' I told him.

Max nodded, that familiar warm smile on his lips. Our eyes locked for a lingering long moment.

'That's good because I love you too, Ells.'

And then, in the busy Dog and Duck on a Sunday lunchtime, I had a bit of an epiphany. I wasn't sure why it had taken me so long. Now I knew exactly what it was I had to do.

Twenty-One

The following day after I'd walked the dogs, seen to Arthur and delivered him with the daily newspaper and his mug of milky coffee, then got Noel ready for the day ahead, we ventured outside and made our way down the windy back lanes. The sun was attempting to break through the cloud, lending a soft dappled light through the trees, picking out the delicate scent of the bluebells carpeting the ground. It really was a magical sight, the beauty of the fragile blooms sweeping around us and winding their way into the distance. There was still a cold nip in the air, but the promise of better days ahead danced all around.

When we reached Bluebell Cottages, I parked the buggy under the wooden porch, unclipped Noel from his harness and lifted him out and into my arms, taking the opportunity for a sneaky kiss. I rapped on the door of Number One.

'Ellie! And Noel. What a lovely surprise this is. Come on in.' Sasha greeted us warmly. 'Look who's here, Ruby!'

Little Ruby was on all fours on a brightly coloured rug in the middle of the floor, looking as though she was on the starting line for a 100-metre sprint.

'Oh, it won't be long before she's off, by the looks of things,' I said, laughing.

'No, she's almost there. I've moved everything up high and put the stair gates up. I can't believe how quickly she's growing up.'

'Well, I hope you don't mind us turning up unexpectedly. I just wanted to ask your advice on something, if that's okay?'

'I don't mind at all. We were just going to have a drink and a biscuit, so I'll go and stick the kettle on. You can put Noel in the baby bouncer if you think he'll be happy in there.' I did as Sasha suggested, knowing Noel would be easily entertained by Ruby.

'So, how's it going with Johnny?' I asked when I followed Sasha out to the kitchen.

She spooned coffee into mugs and turned round to face me, a smile on her lips.

'Good. He took me out for dinner the other night. We went to that new Italian place in town and it was really lovely. It had been so long since I'd been out on a date and I was worried that it might be awkward and that we would run out of things to say, but we didn't. We talked and laughed, and I just found him really easy to be with. He's a nice guy, isn't he?' she said, a coy half-smile on her lips.

'Johnny's great. So, the big question is, are you going to see him again?'

'Yes, he's coming round here later this week. I thought I'd just do some pasta, something simple. We're taking it slowly and seeing how it goes. For the time being I'm happy just dating and getting to know each other. Anyway,' she said, handing me my coffee, 'what sort of advice are you after? You can't be needing my interior design skills already; the manor and the pub have only recently been refurbished. I am an expert on babies though, you know.' She went across to Noel who was happily reclined in the baby bouncer and ran her finger around his little chin, his eyes widening at her attention.

'No, not design or baby advice. It's Max advice actually.'

'Really?' She looked surprised. 'Well I'll try and help, if you think I can.'

When we sat down in the living room, Sasha was all ears.

'So, come on then, what's this all about?'

'Well, I've decided, and this is all top secret at the moment, but I'm going to ask Max to marry me!' A little frisson of excitement ran down my body as I said the words aloud.

'You are? Well, that's amazing. Congratulations.' She jumped up to hug me.

'Hang on,' I told her. 'I haven't asked him yet. He might say no!'

Sasha pushed that idea away with a dismissive wave of her hand. 'Just a mere formality, you know that. Max is champing at the bit to march you down that aisle.'

I smiled, hoping that was true, but after our previous conversations around the subject, I couldn't be sure.

'It's just that with everything that's happened recently, moving in with Max and having Noel, Dad being poorly, well it's been a bit of a wake-up call. It's made me realise what's important. I don't want to get to sixty or seventy and have any regrets about the things I didn't do. None of us know what's round the corner. I love Max and want to spend the rest of my life with him, but I realise now I can't take any of it for granted.'

'I get that,' said Sasha, nodding intently. 'But why do you need my advice?'

'Well, I thought you might have some ideas on how I might do the deed? I tried dropping it into the conversation casually the other day, thinking it might prompt him to propose to me, but he didn't take the hint at all. He just turned it round on me and said, "oh well, we're happy as we are, why change things." All the things I'd previously told him. I'm worried now that he's really not bothered one way or the other if we get married. That's why I want to propose to him formally so he can see just how much it means to me.'

Sasha looked woefully out of her depth. 'Well I think the best thing is for you to go straight ahead and tell him what you've told me. Do it tonight! Perhaps make him a romantic meal with candles and wines and then at the end, over dessert, you can pop the question.'

'Hmmm, last time I made him a romantic meal it was a total disaster. The food was inedible and ended up in the bin and we had a huge row.'

'Okay, scrub that idea. What about an intimate restaurant then?'

'No, I don't think Max would appreciate that either. You know what he's like with public displays of affection.' Sasha nodded keenly. Funnily enough there was no awkwardness talking about Max so openly with his ex, as I'd known there wouldn't be. 'And it could be embarrassing in front of the other diners if Max ends up saying no.'

'That's never going to happen,' said Sasha, shaking her head.

I smiled, wishing I shared her confidence. 'I want it to seem as if it's totally natural and spontaneous, but something memorable too.'

Sasha's brow furrowed as she gave serious consideration to my dilemma. 'Well, you know Max loves being outdoors. Why don't you go for a romantic walk in the countryside and when you come to a special spot, say at the kissing gate at the top of Bluebell Lane, overlooking the valley, you could pop the question then.'

It wasn't a bad idea...

'Trouble is we're bound to bump into someone we know and then the moment would be lost. But you're right, being outside could be very special. I might need to go further afield though.'

'What about the stepping stones over the river at Chullingham? It's only about fifteen minutes away from here and it's such a beautiful spot. Peter took me there once and it was very picturesque, we sat on the bank and drank Prosecco from plastic glasses and ate chocolate-dipped strawberries. It was a beautifully sunny day and so very romantic.' She sighed, transported to another place and time. 'Fat lot of good it did me, though.'

'Oh Sasha, you're much better off without Peter. You were far too good for him, and he just took advantage of you. There's someone much more suitable for you out there.' We locked eyes together, and I wondered if her mind had sprung to Johnny too. 'Anyway, what you were saying about Chullingham, that's not a bad idea. I haven't been there in years and I'm not sure Max has ever been. It could be the perfect spot.'

I looked across at Sasha and smiled. My fingers tingled, eager to get going on making things happen, and my whole body buzzed with anticipation at the thought of becoming Max's wife. I don't know why I hadn't agreed sooner. Deep down it was what I'd wanted all along, but my fears and anxieties had prevented me from saying yes and had threatened to ruin everything. Now I didn't want to waste another moment and I was impatient to make everything right. I just wanted it to be official now, to be able to say I was Mrs Golding. Hmmm, *Ellie Golding!* Didn't that have a very agreeable ring to it.

*

'Where are we going?'

Honestly, I hadn't anticipated just how difficult it would be to get Max out of the house. The way he was looking at me, through narrowed distrustful eyes, anyone would think I was up to something.

Mum was looking after Noel, on the pretext that Max and I needed to go into town to do some shopping, the dogs had been taken for a long run over the fields earlier, Katy was at college and Arthur was being visited by Betty Masters who had arrived with a batch of freshly baked rock cakes from her teashop. I'd even made sure that there was nothing in Max's diary to divert his attention today.

'I thought we could go into town and maybe have a spot of lunch, but on the way I wanted to stop off at Chullingham. I can't believe you've never seen it before. It's right on our doorstep and such a beautiful, peaceful spot. With our busy lives it's nice to take some time out to spend alone together, don't you think?' Max looked at me oddly, but I carried on regardless. 'Peacefulness, being at one with nature, treasuring the moment. What do they call it? Mindfulness. It's all the rage at the moment.'

I glanced across at Max as we drove out of the village and I'm sure I saw his mouth curl dubiously. He wasn't really one for new-age lifestyles or holistic practices.

He ducked his head to look out through the windscreen at the blackening sky. 'It's going to chuck it down, you do realise that, don't you?'

'It's just a passing cloud, it will clear in a while. I checked the weather forecast and there's not going to be any rain at all today apparently.'

'Ah, well that's good to know you've got it all organised,' he said, giving me a doubtful smile.

I'd tried to prepare for every eventuality. Sunny spells were forecast, it was the middle of a school day so hopefully there wouldn't be too many other people around and we were approaching one of the most picturesque spots in the county. The perfect place for a marriage proposal! Excitement rushed

287

around my veins and I could feel a heat of anticipation flushing in my cheeks. Although if I'd thought about it more carefully I should have somehow filched his phone while we were back at the manor and squirrelled it away for a few hours if it was going to keep on interrupting us every two minutes.

Max responded to its insistent demands. 'Hi Gary. Yep, yep… Can do. Leave it with me. I've got the most recent drawings in the office. I'm just out on an errand with Ellie. I'll get them sent over to you as soon as I get back.'

An errand? No, no, no. Didn't he get that this wasn't some rushed shopping excursion. This was a day for us to spend together at our leisure. That was the whole point. That we could take our time revelling in each other's company on what would be, in years to come, a memorable occasion. The last thing we needed was distractions from every other quarter. The phone buzzed again.

'Hi Martin, no, now's a good time. Ellie's driving. What is it?'

I smiled tightly focussing my attentions on the road, silently cursing Martin. *Actually, love, if you must know, it's the worst possible time. Why don't you just jog on and leave Max alone, just for today, it's not a lot to ask for, is it?* I hoped Martin might have extrasensory perception and would pick up on the evil thoughts I was transmitting his way, but it seemed Martin wasn't that intuitive.

'I'll put together a few options for the fourth-floor proposal. I'll get them sent over to you by the end of business today. How does that sound?'

It sounded bloody diabolical to me. I knew what Max was like, it would mean he'd be distracted now, wanting to get back to the office as soon as he could to do whatever it was he needed to do. I sighed. Maybe this wasn't such a good idea after all, but we were almost there now.

'Can't you turn that thing off?' I said to Max as we pulled into the car park of the beauty spot, glaring at his phone accusingly. Thankfully it looked fairly quiet, with only one other car and a minibus parked there. It would be fine just as soon as we got down to the river and Max appreciated for himself the significance of the area and the occasion.

'If you'd like me to,' said Max, looking totally bemused. 'There!' He turned his phone off with a flourish. 'I'm all yours now. You have my undivided attention.'

'Good, come on,' I said, taking hold of his hand, hopeful there'd be no more distractions and we'd just be able to concentrate on each other now.

We walked across the car park to the path that led through the woods and down to the river. I shivered and snuggled into Max's side, as he pulled me in closer, his broadness offering some shelter from the gathering breeze. It was much cooler than it had been of late and I was beginning to suspect that my light wind cheater and plimsolls might have been the wrong choice of clothes for this expedition.

'We should have brought Noel with us and the dogs. They'd love it here,' said Max, striding ahead.

'Yes, maybe next time.'

Ordinarily, I would have loved to bring them along, but I hadn't wanted to get to the serious moment of the proposal, only to have the dogs bombing off in chase of a passing squirrel, or Noel screaming blue murder. No, some things needed to be done alone, just the two of us. And after today this would become our special place and there would be plenty of return visits when we would reminisce and tell Noel how his mum had proposed to his dad that day.

As we walked on further it began to rain, hardly noticeable at first but with each passing step the rain grew heavier and heavier until we reached the shores of the river, where we huddled beneath the nearest tree, watching as the rain pelted down, ricocheting off the surface of the water like bullets.

'So much for your weather forecast,' chuckled Max. 'Look, shall we just make a run back for the car.'

'No, we can't!' I said, rather too vehemently, and Max gave me a puzzled look. Well, we were here now. Okay so I hadn't factored in the rain, but it was only a shower, a heavy shower admittedly, but it would pass. Soon... I hoped.

'There are the steps.' I pointed out, with perhaps a bit too much enthusiasm, the large stones spanning the width of the river, their tops just visible above the water. 'Isn't it beautiful?' I said, taking a deep breath. I wiped the rain from my face, the dampness now reaching my extremities, a cold shiver running the length of my body. 'Let's wait until the rain stops and we can walk across to the other side.'

'Hmmm, do you really think that's the best idea? Why don't we head off to the pub instead? We can always come back here some other time, when the weather's a bit better.'

'Oh Max, don't be such a killjoy. It'll be fun.'

My plan was to get out into the middle of the stones and then, holding his hand, ask Max to marry me. With the waterfalls behind us and the river snaking off into the distance it would be the most romantic setting. Of course, if the sun had been shining then it would have been even more special, but you could never guarantee the British weather and, who knew, it was just as likely to brighten up just as soon as we got out there.

'It's lovely,' said Max, flapping his arms around his chest and jogging on the spot in an attempt to warm up, his body language not quite matching his words. I was just beginning to wonder if he wasn't right and we should head for home when the rain miraculously stopped and the sun brightened up the sky as if it realised the significance of the occasion.

'Max, there is a special reason why I've brought you here today.'

'There is? Right. Great. So it wasn't purely to get me completely soaked through then?' He looked all around him, taking in the view. We were totally alone and there was a quiet stillness in the air that lent a spiritual quality to our surroundings.

'No.'

'Okay, so are you going to tell me what it is then?' asked Max bemused. 'Ah wait a moment, it's not bad news, is it?' he asked, making a slicing motion at his neck.

'Well that's for you to decide. Come on.'

I took him by the hand and we trod carefully on the wet ground venturing down towards the gentle shoreline

'Do you want to go first?' I asked, pushing him forward to the edge of the river.

He stepped up onto the first stone, just big enough for him to get both feet on, and looked over his shoulder at me. The water was ebbing back and forth over his shoes, leaving a soggy tidemark around the gorgeous brown leather. I hadn't thought to tell him to wear his wellies or walking boots which would have been a much better choice in the circumstances. Not that it seemed to bother him.

'Are you coming?' he asked, his face full of mischief.

'Yes, I am, just wait for me.'

But it was too late. Arms held out at his side, he negotiated the slippery stones swiftly, his long legs making easy work of the distance between the large pebbles until, in what seemed like only a matter of moments and with all the grace of an Olympic gymnast, he was standing on the opposite bank, having taken a celebratory bow, smiling at me triumphantly.

'Max!'

Oh no, trust him! Why couldn't he do what he was supposed to do for once? I'd wanted him to hold my hand so we could take each of the stones in turn, slowly, carefully, stopping to admire the view around us at each point. I hadn't intended it to be a competition, because there would never be any doubt who would win that particular race.

'Meet me in the middle!' I called across to him, but he was playing silly beggars now. He had his hand cupped round his ear, an expression of confusion on his face, pretending he couldn't hear me. 'Oh for goodness sake!'

I stepped across to the first stone, my shoes feeling desperately unsteady on the wet, smooth surface. My foot slipped away from me and I quickly righted myself, just correcting my balance in time. I looked down at my feet watching as the water seeped through the fabric. Sogginess wasn't something I'd imagined for my big romantic moment, but still what was a bit of dampness between friends. It would be fine. If I just took things slowly. How on earth Max had managed to skip across the river like a gazelle, I had no idea. Carefully and purposefully, holding my breath, I took another large step and landed on the second stone. Easy-peasy. Although, I didn't really have much chance to look around at the scenery because I was concentrating so hard on keeping my balance and staying upright.

I dared to look up and saw Max watching me, although from a distance I couldn't tell if it was with amusement or concern on his features.

'Come here,' I beckoned, realising quickly it was probably best not to wave my hands in the air, not when I was so unsteady on my feet.

'Want a hand?' he asked, when he reached me.

He pulled me forward onto the next stone and I wrapped my arms around him clinging on for dear life. This was more like it. Suddenly I felt so much safer held tightly in Max's embrace. Close enough for us to kiss. Max took the hint as he dropped his head and pressed his lips lightly on to mine. Very romantic.

'Hey?' He pulled away, holding me at arm's length. 'You've not brought me here to get rid of me, have you? I'm not about to suffer some terrible accident at your hands,' he said, dramatically. 'Falling on to one of those rocks and hitting my head in a freak accident. Just so you can get your hands on all my worldly goods. You read about these things in the newspaper.'

At this rate if anyone was going to have an accident it was going to be me. I couldn't remember crossing these stones ever being so difficult before, but then again the last time I was here was probably when I was a teenager and I can only ever recall it being gloriously sunny.

'No, I'm not after your worldly goods. Although now you mention it, if anything should ever happen, I will gladly take custody of your dogs.' I took a deep breath. It was now or never. Time to be serious. We hadn't quite made it out to the middle of the river, but it was close enough. 'No, Max, the real reason I've brought you out here is to ask you if…'

'Ellie! Is that you? Look! It's me, it's me!'

An excitable voice came from behind me. Oh good grief! Who was it? I couldn't believe it. Out in the middle of nowhere and someone spots me. Typical. Whoever it was, there was no chance of me seeing them as they were behind me and I was squashed up against Max only able to see the stubble on his cheek and, if I peeped over his shoulder, the opposite side of the riverbank.

'Hang on!' I took my own advice and did literally that, hanging on grimly to Max, while shuffling around in very small motions so I could face the other way and see who was there. On the bank was a caterpillar of small children dressed in the distinctive green sweatshirts of Little Leyton Primary School underneath clear waterproof ponchos.

'It's me, Alfie!' Gemma's little boy's face beamed out at me from under his rain hat. I couldn't help noticing that all the children were dressed sensibly in rainproof clothing and wellington boots. Unlike some other people.

'Hello, Alfie,' I called brightly, hoping to god that Max wouldn't let go of me. 'Fancy seeing you here.'

'Are you stuck? I've been over those stones. It was really easy. I just jumped and jumped over them.' He gave me a helpful little demonstration of his jumping technique from the riverbank.

'Me too,' said a cute-looking little blonde girl. 'I was brilliant!!' Lovely, we now had an entire audience watching us.

'And me,' said another little boy.

All of the children seemed intent on telling me about their prowess in crossing the river. I didn't doubt them for one moment. I just wished I had a touch of their bravado.

'No, not stuck,' I said breezily, hanging on tighter to Max. 'We were just admiring the view.'

'I want to go over the stones again, but Mrs Walker won't let us. She said it's too dangerous now that it's rained and the stones will be all slippy. We might fall in and hit our head and die!' Alfie said, far too gleefully.

'Ah you see, I was right, it was murder you had on your mind, after all,' said Max, whispering in my ear.

'Right, come along children,' said Mrs Walker, who was eyeing us suspiciously as though we might be up to no good. 'We must leave these people to their walk and get back to the minibus.'

'Byeee!' called Alfie, bouncing up and down on the spot and waving. 'She's really nice, that lady,' he told his friends. 'She's called Ellie and she likes wine and beer. She made a baby with a man in the barn at the pub.'

All of the children giggled and Mrs Walker did a double take at me. In fairness, it was probably a pretty accurate character assessment.

Once the school trip had departed it was just Max and me left on that same stepping stone and I had to wonder what had possessed me to think that this had been a good idea. Any romantic leanings I'd had today had gone home on the minibus with Alfie. Maybe I should just blurt it out now that we were here alone. Get it over and done with.

'I…'

'Come on, Ellie.' Max had extracted me from his embrace, turned his back on me and was off again, striding across the pebbles. 'Just take them nice and steady. You'll be fine.'

Of course I would. I shuffled round tentatively, took a large stride and just managed to reach the next boulder, but my foot slipped off the edge and I toppled sideways unable to stop myself from landing in the freezing cold water. Thankfully it was only calf-deep, but it was still a shock to my system. My hands found the gravelly bottom of the riverbed and water seeped up the arms of my wind cheater. Oh that was bloody great. Now I was going to look like a drowned rat. Hardly the memory I wanted to pass on to Noel about the day Mummy proposed to Daddy.

'Ellie!' Max heard the splash and his head span round to find me flailing about in the water. 'Are you all right?'

'Does it look as though I'm all right?'

'Well I don't know how you managed that,' he said, coming across and offering me a hand up. He bit on his lip and I could tell he was trying to stop himself from laughing.

'Would you stop it?' I scolded him. 'I'm wet through, I've grazed my arm and now I'm cold and grumpy.'

'Well this was your idea,' said Max, obviously still highly amused by the whole scenario. He took off his fleece and wrapped it round my shoulders which went a tiny way to making me feel marginally better. 'Shall we go home?'

Even lunch didn't seem so appealing now. Not when we didn't have anything to celebrate. A bowl of soup and a mug of tea back at home seemed much more tempting. I clung onto his arm as he helped me across the remaining stones to the safety of the shore.

'You know, I'm still not entirely sure why you brought me here, Ellie. I mean it's beautiful and everything, but what was it you wanted to say? Whatever it is, you can tell me you know.'

'It doesn't matter now,' I said, quietly, walking away.

'Come on, spit it out. I'm intrigued. It was obviously something you felt unable to say at home. If there's some sort of problem we need to get it out in the open.' He held his palms up to the sky, which had taken on a dark and brooding quality now.

I fell silent. How was I ever going to explain?

When I didn't respond, he grabbed me from behind, his hands finding my waistline, his fingers tickling me, searching out my hip bone, making me squirm. Despite myself and my grumpiness, I couldn't help laughing and managed to wriggle free of his hold, running off in the direction of the car. He was far too fast for me and caught up with me within a matter of moments.

'Tell me now, unless you want to experience death by tickling.' He wiggled his fingers in front of me to show his intent.

I caught my breath.

Just spit it out. I could hear Sasha chiding me. Deep breath.

'Well, if you must know, I brought you here because I was going to…' I felt a colour tinge my cheeks. 'I was going to ask you to marry me.'

Max's eyes widened, his expression unfathomable, until I noticed the smile twitching at the corner of his lips.

'I thought it would be romantic. Memorable.'

'You are joking?'

'No!' I looked away, feeling cross now. Why would I joke about something so serious?

'Ha, well this will certainly be a day to remember' said Max, gesturing to the growing damp patch I had down one side of my body. 'You know what it's reminded me of? That very first day we met and I found you scrabbling around in the river on the estate trying to rescue your dog.' He chuckled. 'That image will stay forever imprinted on my mind.'

Is that all he had to say? Was he not going to grab my hand and say yes of course he wanted to marry me, that it was all that he'd been waiting to hear?

'Well?' I prompted him.

'Well what?'

'What would your answer be?'

'To what? Oh,' he said, shaking his head as though he hadn't really been concentrating. 'You haven't actually asked me, but…' he narrowed his eyes, pursed his lips and adopted a serious expression, as though contemplating the idea now. Then he shrugged, 'No. I don't think so, do you?'

'What!? Well of course I do or else I would never have dragged you here in the first place to ask you.' The wind had whipped up a pace and was buffeting me unkindly, bringing tears to my eyes.

'We're good as we are, aren't we, Ellie?'

'Are we? You wanted to marry me at the beginning of the year. And now you don't.'

'No, but you were the one who made me realise that we don't have to rush into getting married. I can't see any point now when we're already happy.'

I looked into his eyes, recognising the stubborn defiance there. 'And this has absolutely nothing to do with me turning you down at the New Year?'

'No!' he said fiercely, but I couldn't believe him. My whole body crumpled in on itself, wondering if this was how he must have felt when I'd rejected his earlier proposal.

'Fine,' I said, bristling, a feeling of dread meeting the dampness infiltrating my bones. 'It was a ridiculous idea in the first place.' I stomped off in the direction of the car, my feet squelching in my plimsolls.

'Completely bonkers,' called Max after me.

Twenty-Two

A couple of days later I was back at Arthur's cottage for a meeting with social services who had put in place several strategies to help Arthur cope better in his own home. There was now a high step outside his back door to make it easier for him to get in and out, grab handles in strategic places around the house and a new electric chair that tipped forwards and backwards.

Josie and I had been down last week and had spent a day blitzing the place, throwing out all the rubbish, putting away paperwork into easily identifiable plastic boxes and cleaning the bathroom and kitchen. We put new bed linen on Arthur's bed, plumped up the cushions on the sofa, dusted down the photos and put some fresh flowers in a vase on the windowsill. When Max and I visited a few weeks ago, it had smelled musty and stale. Now it felt fresh and light and airy.

Arthur walked through the front door and lifted his head to look all around him. 'Blimey. You have worked wonders on this place. I would never have recognised it.'

Sarah, the social worker, had a clipboard and a dozen leaflets. She talked about them all individually and then handed them to Arthur in a pile.

'We can also organise meals to be delivered to you, if you'd like us to. You might only want it a couple of times a week or every day, it's up to you.'

'Right, well thank you, love. You've been very helpful.' Arthur turned to me. 'Is it today I'm moving back in?' he asked, looking confused.

Too much information for him to take in, I guessed.

'No, not today. Well, not unless you want to. I'd thought we could gather all your bits together and move back in over the weekend.' I was keeping my tone deliberately bright, but I wasn't sure if that was for my benefit or Arthur's. 'What do you say?'

'Okay, love.' He nodded, but I could see the uncertainty in his face.

Josie flashed me a glance. Arthur was clearly overwhelmed at being back in his old home with the reminders of his past life, photos, ornaments and books, all around him.

'Everyone's been so kind,' he muttered, his hands shaking from the emotion of it all, and I had to turn away to stop myself from buckling too.

Later when we'd returned home, we sat around the kitchen table for tea and biscuits. Josie had joined us, Katy had just come in from college and Max wandered in from his office for what had become part of his daily routine. An afternoon cup of tea and a catch-up, and a cuddle with his little boy. Digby was sitting at Arthur's side hopeful that he might pick up on a sneaky digestive. I didn't like to cast aspersions, but I suspected Arthur had been leading Digby astray and feeding him all sorts of tidbits when I wasn't watching. It was looking as though Digby wouldn't be in luck today though as Arthur seemed distracted and refused all offers of any biscuits, including his favourite chocolate ones.

I'd just been filling Katy and Max in on the changes made down at Arthur's cottage when we all fell silent, lost in our thoughts as we stared into our teas.

'Well, I'll miss you, that's for sure,' I said aloud.

'Oh me too,' said Katy.

Even Digby looked forlorn, looking up at Arthur with those big brown eyes imploringly.

Max meanwhile was slowly demolishing his way through the biscuits, his gaze fixed out the window, clearly distracted by something – work, no doubt. Since our ill-fated trip to Chullingham we'd agreed not to talk about the thorny subject of marriage anymore, and in some ways it had taken some of the pressure away. As Max said, we were happy, so why change things? But things had shifted for me. Since

I'd realised I wanted to marry Max, it was all I could think about.

Now as I watched Max munching his way through the biscuits, I wondered if it was thinking about that conversation that was irritating me so or the fact that he could eat so many chocolate biscuits and still not put on any weight. The biscuit, cake and wine diet only seemed to accentuate Max's lean and muscular physique whereas all it did for me was a squidgy soft tummy and love handles. Mind you, Max did spend an awful lot of time working outdoors, digging the vegetable beds, chopping up logs and walking the dogs around the estate. I shook my head, chasing away an image of Max hot and sweaty, lugging firewood about the grounds. *Stop it, Ellie!* I was becoming distracted and almost missed what Max was saying.

'Well, you do know, Arthur, that you don't have to go,' said Max blithely. He flashed me a quick glance as if checking that I was okay with the idea.

I nodded, my heart swelling at the gesture. His offer may have been casual but I knew it was utterly sincere and once he'd said the words aloud I realised it was exactly what I wanted too.

'No, oh no, goodness me no,' spluttered Arthur, totally flummoxed by Max's comment. 'We all knew this was only ever going to be for a short while. You've been lovely to me and I'm very grateful, but

I've always known I would have to go home some time.' He sighed gently. 'I don't like to outstay my welcome, so I'll get back to the cottage on Saturday. Leave you good people in peace. I'll be fine. Absolutely fine.'

'I wish you could stay,' said Katy. 'I know you're only down the road, but it's not the same as having you here.'

'Well you can always pop down and see me anytime you like. I hope you will,' said Arthur, who was making a good attempt at sounding jaunty.

'Arthur, do you actually want to go home?' I asked him.

He shrugged, looking thoughtful, his chin wobbling from side to side. 'Well, it's better than going in one of those old folks' homes. I'm never going there, that's for sure.'

'No, of course not, and no one's suggesting that you do, but you can stay here if you want to, you do realise that?'

'Pah!' He waved his hand dismissively in front of his face, but I saw a flicker of light appear in his eyes. 'No, not after all the trouble everyone's gone to for me. That house is looking a treat now. Besides, I can't stay here. You've got enough on your plate, young lady, what with the pub and your little baby and the dogs. And I hear there might be another little puppy on the way too.' There were a few startled looks until I reassured everyone that it was an actual Pointer puppy Arthur was talking about and not a human baby. 'You don't want an old fogey living here with you all the time.'

My eyes flickered across to Max, then to Katy and Josie who were all looking at me expectantly.

'Oh, but we do, Arthur. Really we do. If you want to go home, then we're very happy for you to do that. I can understand you wanting your independence and we'll be around to help in any way we can, but, honestly, you're just as welcome to stay here too.'

'Do you really mean that?' Arthur's voice wobbled and tears filled his eyes.

'Of course we do,' said Max. 'If it makes you feel better, we don't have to put a time restraint on it. You're welcome to stay for as long as you like. And then if you want to go home at a later date you can do. But for the time being consider this your home, Arthur.'

Katy squealed. 'Ooh yes, Arthur, please stay! It won't be the same without you.'

Katy launched herself at Arthur and wrapped her arms around him, which was enough for him to break down, and the tears he'd been valiantly hanging on to came out in sobs mingled with warm laughter.

'To be honest, I was dreading going home,' he said through his tears. 'It felt so strange going back to the house today, it just reminded me of the loneliness I'd felt living on my own all that time. Here, well, it's been magical. As though I'm part of a proper family.'

'You are a part of this family,' I told him, trying to hold my tears back now.

'Although why you'd want to be a part of this mad bunch, I'm not sure,' said Max, wryly.

'Well we'll have to sort something out by way of payment. I've got my pension, so I can pay for my board and everything.'

'Don't worry we'll sort something out,' said Max, although I knew full well there was no way he would take any money from Arthur.

'I do love a happy ending,' said Josie, smiling.

It was only later when I'd left Noel at home with Katy and Max, and was walking into the village with Josie that I remembered her happy ending comment.

'How are things going with Ethan?' I asked her.

'Okay,' she shrugged. 'At least we're talking now without taking digs at each other. He's looking after Stella today. He's a brilliant dad, I'm just not sure he's a great husband.'

I wondered fleetingly what made a good husband. Someone caring, thoughtful, honest and respectful? All traits Max had in abundance.

'Maybe the break has made Ethan realise that?'

'It probably has. Well, I've told him in great detail what his failings are, so I don't think he can be in any doubt about that.' She chuckled ruefully. 'He wants to come home again, says he'll try harder this time, but I need to know that he really means it. We'll just have to see how it pans out.'

I didn't want to press Josie any further on the subject because I sensed her sadness and confusion, I just hoped she and Ethan would be able to work it out somehow. Marriage wasn't something to enter into lightly, but it wasn't something to walk away from lightly either.

'Are you looking forward to Polly's hen do on Friday?' I asked, eager to change the subject now.

'I can't wait,' said Josie, her face lighting up. 'It's been ages since I've been on a proper night out. I've even bought a new dress for the occasion. Ethan's taking Stella round to his mum's for the night so I've got a late pass. Cocktails, dancing and sexy hot men!' She scrunched her fingers together excitedly and gave a little squee. 'Well, okay,' she said, laughing. 'Two out of three ain't bad.'

When we reached the pub, Josie gave me a hug and went on her way, while I slipped inside the familiar oak door of The Dog and Duck. Dan was behind the bar and instead of heading for the back, as I would normally do, I took the opportunity to enjoy the relaxed atmosphere out front and pulled out a stool at the bar and sat down. Dan immediately came over to serve me.

'What can I get you, madam?' he asked, a broad smile on his face.

'Oi, less of the madam, thank you. But I'll have a gin and ginger ale please.'

Dan pulled out a Copa de Balon glass, filled it with a shot of botanical gin, added a wheel of orange, a couple of blueberries, ice cubes and topped it up with ginger ale, the whole process proving very therapeutic to watch. Immediately it made me relax, my mouth watering at the delicious amber promise contained in the glass.

'Cheers,' I said, lifting my glass to Dan and taking that first tantalising sip. I felt the tension in my shoulders slip away and the warmth of the pub wrap itself around me.

'Silke is coming along to Polly's hen do on Friday?' I asked him.

'Yep, she's looking forward to it. Eric, me and Andy will be manning the fort in here, but if you need an extra pair of hands out there, just let me know and I can always come and help.'

''Fraid not, entry will be by invitation only. And partners of the hens will definitely not be allowed in. Us girls have some serious partying to do.'

Dan shook his head, and gave a mock shudder. 'Oh crikey, I can imagine it's going to get very messy in there.'

'It will! It's exciting, isn't it? After Friday there's only a week to go until the big day. The thought of the whole village coming together to celebrate the wedding is just lovely.'

I missed my regular chats with Dan. We would talk about anything and everything, the pub, the people, sharing our innermost hopes and desires, our fears and worries. He'd always been a great sounding board. If ever I'd had concerns about the pub or didn't know what to do for the best, then, in Eric's absence, I knew I could rely on Dan to give me honest, sensible advice. He was also good at giving me a male perspective on any relationship concerns I had over Max.

'It's all been very fast, hasn't it?' said Dan, picking up a tea towel and starting to polish some glasses.

'Different strokes for different folks,' I said. 'Will you and Silke get married, do you think?'

He shrugged nonchalantly. 'Actually, we've been talking about it a bit recently. I suppose it's only natural when you see your friends around you getting married and having babies that you stop to consider what it is you want from the future. Silke would like to get married. If it's important to her, then I'm happy to go along with that.'

He was absolutely right, it had just taken me a bit longer to realise it than most.

'And you and Max?' asked Dan.

'We're happy as we are,' I said with a smile, rolling out my standard line, but even as I said it I knew, with a pang, it wasn't quite the truth now. There was part of me, a big part, that wouldn't be truly happy now until I had finally married Max.

Twenty-Three

'What are you doing here?'

It was such a beautiful spring day and the sunshine had tempted me outside. I wandered down the stone pathway to the log cabin nestling in between some trees just behind the main house.

'Is it such a crime to want to come and see my boyfriend,' I said to Max, as I closed the door to his office behind me. Hearing myself use the word boyfriend made me cringe a little. I sounded like a lovestruck teenager. Would partner have sounded any better? No, definitely not. That sounded like a business arrangement. The only thing that might have sounded any better to my ears was husband.

'No, and it's always a huge pleasure to see you, darling.' He reached out a hand to me and I walked over to him, our hands interlocking. 'Where's Noel?'

'Mum and Dad are here. They're entertaining him in the playroom. You should hear the laughter. He's such a lucky little boy to have his grandparents living on his doorstep. And a doting aunty in Katy.'

'I know. It makes you realise just how important family is. The different generations have so much to offer one another.'

'Look, Mum and Dad are staying for a bowl of soup and some fresh out of the oven bread. Can I tempt you?'

'You don't even have to try, Ellie. You tempt me all the time without even realising it.' He pulled me onto his lap and pushed back my hair behind my ears, finding my neck with his mouth, making frankly disturbing noises as my body reacted to his touch.

'No, silly,' I said, giving a half-hearted attempt at escaping his clutches. 'I meant with some soup. Will you come and join us? Say in about half an hour's time.'

'Sure, in that case we've probably got enough time to consider the next addition to our family.' He pulled me back into his side and I soaked up his gorgeous natural scent of the great outdoors mingling with citrus tones. Despite not being able to see eye-to-eye on the subject of marriage, we were getting on pretty well.

'How do you mean?' I said, looking up at him. 'Our new puppy? Is that what you're thinking about? Or are you talking about some livestock, maybe some chickens or goats?' I said, deliberately misunderstanding him.

'I was thinking more along the lines of our next baby. If we're going to have six we need to get a move on.'

'Six? I thought we'd agreed on four.'

'Right you are then,' said Max, triumphantly and I realised I'd fallen straight into his carefully laid trap. He laughed, clearly delighted. When we'd previously discussed the size of our family he'd argued four would be the perfect number and yet I couldn't see beyond two. Now, somehow, I'd just agreed to four, although it occurred to me I didn't really mind at all.

'Shall we just take it one step at a time and see where that takes us.'

'Sounds like a good idea to me,' said Max, kissing me on the lips. His hands caressed my body, as his mouth dropped to my neck and his breathing grew heavy in my ear. My body responded instinctively to his touch and I knew if I stayed there a moment longer then there would be no turning back. I couldn't have that, not when I had my baby, my parents and some hot soup waiting on me.

'Come on,' I laughed, escaping from his embrace. 'Let's go outside, it's a beautiful day out there.'

He took my hand, grumbling about missed opportunities, and we ventured outside, walking along the winding brick pathway that led between the lawns, admiring the flower beds as we passed. The warm air wrapped around us, the sun on my skin invigorating. I loved this time of year when the plants and shrubs suddenly burst into life. The gardens were abundant with promise and soft subtle floral scents wafted in the cool breeze, teasing our senses. This was one of Max's passions, working in the extensive grounds and shaping them into the formal gardens it had become today. We wandered through the archway in the hedge that led through to the raised vegetable gardens, their plots already laid out, with apple and pear fruit trees lining the paths.

'Do you remember when…?' said Max, squeezing his hand around my waist as he indicated to the old wooden shed.

'I knew you were going to say that,' I laughed, the memories rushing back to me.

It had been a scorching hot day last summer, before I'd even found out I was pregnant, and I'd come down to the manor to see Max and found him working in the oppressive heat, his body oiled from the exertion of dragging shrubbery across to where he'd built a fire. Without a shirt on and with his jeans worn low on his hips offering a glimpse of his underwear beneath, he'd been an arresting sight and when he'd beckoned me over, my hands had instinctively reached out for the hardness of his torso. He'd kissed me fervently and I could still remember his salty seductive taste on my tongue. He'd swept me off my feet, literally, carrying me in his arms over to the shed, where, in the hot sultry summer heat, he'd made love to me, the exquisite sensations only heightened by the rays of the sun on my bare skin.

'You know I still have dreams about that day,' he whispered in my ear and my body shivered at the sensation of his breath on my face. 'We could revisit that dream, right here and now, if you wanted to?' He took me in his arms and pulled my body up against his, the firmness of his torso sending shivers of anticipation down my spine.

'Where's your sense of adventure,' said Max breathlessly in my ear.

'Mum and dad are waiting for us. I've got a leek and potato soup bubbling on the Aga. We're going to have to save this for later,' I told him, although my hand couldn't resist gliding over the front of his Levis.

His eyes filled with desire at my touch and a seductive smile spread on his lips. 'How can I possibly compete with a bowl of your home-made soup?' said Max, amused.

We walked back the way we'd come, but it took us several minutes as Max's attention was constantly distracted by something new he spotted in the garden. We had to keep stopping so that he could see to a trailing plant or to deadhead some flowers, his strong large hands surprisingly gentle as he tended his plants.

'How is your dad doing?' he asked, standing up from where he'd been turning some soil over in a raised bed. He wiped his nose with his forearm, black earth falling onto his face and shirt. I wiped it away with my hand.

'Okay. I think. He was at the hospital earlier in the week and they've said they don't need to see him for another few months.'

'Well, that's good, isn't it?'

'Yes it is, and he's really positive and upbeat about things, and so am I, most of the time, but sometimes it hits me, normally in the middle of the night, and I can't help worrying that he'll have a relapse, that something will go wrong.'

Max squeezed my hand, turning to look at me with warm concern in his eyes.

'It's only natural to feel that way, but you can't dwell on those thoughts. Your dad wouldn't want you to. He's here now and he's doing okay, better than okay in fact. We can't sit around worrying what might go wrong. It's a cliché, but we just have to make the most of the time we have.'

'Yeah,' I smiled, reassured by Max's wise words. He always had the ability to yank me out of any dark thoughts and bring me back to reality. 'I love seeing Dad with Noel, I'm not sure who's the biggest kid. I just want him to be around to see Noel hit all those milestones, saying his first words, walking, going to school. They're going to be such good buddies, I know that.' Now my mind was racing off in all directions. 'I've just had a thought, Dad would want to walk me down the aisle, wouldn't he? Every father wants to do that for his daughter. Not that I meant…'

I knew we'd made a decision not to talk about any wedding plans, but the words were out before I'd even had time to think about what I was saying.

'Come here,' he said, pulling me into his embrace. 'Stop worrying. It'll all work out. We've got each other and our families, that's all that matters, isn't it?'

Back inside the manor, putting all thoughts of weddings out of my head, I ladled soup into bowls and we sat around the kitchen table, the smell of the freshly baked bread still wafting in the air. Arthur had joined us, Katy was there too, off from college today, and the dogs were lurking beneath the table. Little Noel was in his baby bouncer, kicking his little legs, watching the proceedings.

With only a couple of weeks to go until the biggest social event on the Little Leyton calendar, it was hardly surprising that the talk would turn to Polly's wedding.

'Has Max seen you in your dress yet?' Mum asked eagerly, as she helped herself to a bread roll. She looked from me to Max expectantly while I hoped that the floor would swallow me up whole. I was excited about the upcoming bash, but Mum's excitement levels were fit to burst.

Max shook his head.

'Oh she does look gorgeous. Wait till you see her in it. She could actually pass for the bride if you didn't know better.'

'I don't doubt it for a moment,' said Max, his gaze lingering on mine, his half-smile giving away the fact that he was as amused as I was embarrassed.

'I can't wait,' said Katy, 'the forecast is meant to be really good for that weekend. I just wish I was a bridesmaid too,' she sighed, exaggeratedly.

Honestly I'm sure the pair of them were scheming together.

'Did Ellie tell you the good news?' Mum said brightly, addressing Max. 'The hospital don't want to see Malc for another three months. Isn't that great? The treatment's been doing its job and they're happy to monitor him for now.'

'So I hear,' said Max. 'That really is marvellous news.'

Dad nodded, embarrassed that the attention was on him. He'd always been the one in control in our family, had taken charge and responsibility for Mum and me, the voice of reason whenever there was a problem, but recently it had been our turn to take care of him. I sensed he wasn't entirely happy with this reversal of roles. 'Now maybe, we'll be able to get back to some kind of normality.'

'Definitely,' said Mum. 'There's so much we have to look forward to. You do know we'll have been married thirty years come November.'

'Wow!' said Max, giving an approving nod of his head. 'That's some achievement, especially in this day and age.'

'I know,' said Dad laughing. 'I must be collecting some kind of medal on this anniversary.'

'What are you like!' said Mum, laughing. It was good to see her so much more relaxed now ever since that last hospital visit.' You might be getting a medal, darling, but I'll be perfectly happy collecting my pearls,' she said, with a mischievous grin.

'Ah right, duly noted,' said Dad sagely. 'I think that may have been a none-too-subtle hint.'

'If you have a loving marriage, then you have everything, I reckon,' added Arthur, and I couldn't help wondering if he hadn't been roped into the campaign too.

I so loved seeing Mum and Dad together, witnessing their teasing and bickering, the way they laughed and quickly got over any grievances, but ultimately what came across was their deep love and affection for one another. Either of them would be hopeless without the other. Thirty years was definitely a cause for celebration and I made a mental note to start thinking how we might mark that occasion once Polly's wedding was over.

My mind flitted towards Max, and I wondered where we might be in thirty years' time. It seemed a lifetime away and yet I could see how those years might slip away from us so quickly.

'Andy wants me to go and meet his partner,' said Katy, staring morosely into her soup.

'Ah, well, that's good isn't it?' said Mum.

'I don't know,' she sighed. 'I'm still getting to know him and now he wants me to become part of his family. I don't know if I'm ready for that.'

'Well I'm sure your dad will be happy to wait until you feel ready,' I said.

'Hmm. I just don't know why he's doing it. Why he wants me to meet his family, I mean? I think he might feel sorry for me and is trying to be nice. That he'll take me round there for tea one time and then that'll be it.'

'Oh Katy, he's doing it because he loves you,' said Max, just managing to keep his exasperation from his voice. 'You're his daughter and he wants you to be a part of his life.'

'Do you think? What if they all hate me though?'

I saw the hurt and bewilderment in Katy's eyes and it tugged at my heart. In many ways she was so grown-up, sassy and confident and in other respects she was still very much a vulnerable young girl.

'Listen here, young lady,' said Arthur. 'Why would anyone not love you? You're a lovely and beautiful young woman with a kind heart. From what I've seen of your dad he seems a pretty decent fella. He'll be as proud as punch to have you as his daughter. He'll want to show you off to his family, that's all.'

'Oh, Arthur.' She looked genuinely touched by his words. 'Do you really think so?'

'Yes!' We all tried to reassure her.

'It's so scary. I'm just worried that I might be a novelty to him, and when he gets to know me and finds out what I'm really like, he won't want to hang around.'

'I wouldn't mind betting that now your dad's found you, he'll never want to let you go,' said Dad. 'He'll love all of you, not just the good bits. I mean, I love the bones of Ellie, including all her peculiar ways.'

'Oi!' I said, mock-outraged. 'What peculiar ways?'

Katy laughed, looking relieved to be able to talk about it. 'It won't change anything here, will it? I don't want you thinking I'm abandoning you all.'

'Nah, you can't get rid of us that easily. You're one of us and there's no escaping the fold.' Max laughed maniacally and I shook my head at his antics.

'It won't,' I told her. 'We'll always be here for you, but you're lucky to have found your dad. Why don't you give it a try and see how you get on? You know you're always welcome to invite Andy and his family here if you want to.'

'Thanks Ellie,' she said, jumping up to see to Noel, which I knew was her way of avoiding the tears building in her eyes. She pulled him out of his bouncer and lifted him up in her arms, holding his little body above her face, the two of them chuckling at each other.

Honestly, I know we had our moments, but sometimes we could actually pull off the fully functioning family thing.

Twenty-Four

'This is amazing! Are you sure this is even the barn? It looks like I've been transported to a New York cocktail bar. Thank you, Ellie. You're the best friend a girl could have.'

Polly was dressed for the occasion in a little black dress, strappy high heels and fuchsia pink lipstick, and looked like a woman intent on enjoying herself. She went around the room sharing hugs and kisses with all her friends, who had turned up bearing bottles of wine, chocolates, flowers and gifts, to help her celebrate this special evening.

I looked all around, feeling a real sense of satisfaction at what we'd achieved. I'd roped in Sasha to help and her experience as an interior designer had paid off hugely. It was amazing what some black and gold drapes, twinkly lighting and well-chosen accessories could do to a place. We'd brought in some high stools, put a shiny reflective top along the bar, placed a mirrored covering on the walls and hung a row of small but absolutely essential glitter balls from the centre beam.

'What are you going to have to drink?' I asked Polly. 'A Porn Star Martini?'

'Bring them on,' said Polly gleefully.

'Young man!' I said, in my best posh voice, lifting a finger in the direction of one of our specially arranged waiters for the evening, which amused Polly no end. A couple of Ryan's friends had jumped at the opportunity to earn some extra cash and looked very dapper in their black trousers, white dress shirts and black bow ties. One such man, young, ripped and eager to please, arrived at Polly's side with a tray of cocktails held high in the air.

'Psst, Ellie,' she whispered. 'Please tell me he's not going to whip his clothes off, is he? If he is, then I need to prepare myself mentally for that possibility. I'm already beginning to feel a bit queasy.'

'I promise you,' I said, squeezing her hand. 'There will be no naked bodies in this room tonight.'

'Good, I'm so pleased, although if I was going to have to see some naked flesh, then I suppose his might not be too bad to look at,' she said wistfully, her gaze following him across to the other side of the room. 'Although, of course, I'm so over all that crass and unbecoming behaviour these days.' She gave a knowing wink. 'Since I've met George I've become so much more worldly-wise and sophisticated, you know. I've been on a book tour and everything,' she said, laughing, and helped herself to another cocktail from a passing waiter.

I left Polly chatting to Gemma and Janet, the woman who helped Polly out at the florists, and went back into the pub to collect the food. I checked my watch. It was still early so I had enough time to do a sweep of the place first, just to check who was in and to make sure there weren't any problems. It was a habit of old that I always found hard to resist, and besides, I liked to have a little chat with any customers who were in.

The pub was heaving tonight, the party atmosphere from the barn infiltrating into the bar, probably due to the fact that most of the hens' partners were in too, taking the opportunity to have a pint with their friends.

Eric was keeping an eye on the proceedings and was now deep in conversation with Dad and Paul. It was great to see Dad back among his friends, laughing and joking, looking as though he didn't have a care in the world. Andy had called in to see Katy this afternoon and had been persuaded by Arthur and Max to join them for a quick drink, and was chatting away animatedly as though he had always been a villager. It was still early days, but Katy's relationship with her dad was taking positive tentative steps forward. She was calling the shots and Andy seemed happy to take things at the pace Katy dictated.

Ryan was in too, with some of his other friends, having absolutely refused to dress up and be part of our waiting staff tonight. Johnny and George had made an unlikely friendship and were engaged in some good-hearted banter.

Max was looking as devastatingly handsome as he always did. I couldn't help but notice that a woman, probably about thirty-ish, with glossy black hair falling in soft waves on her shoulders and wearing a black fitted cat suit with a plunging neckline was giving her undivided attention to him, her hand resting proprietarily on his arm. The only pop of colour was the red of her lipstick matching her nails and the soles of her black patent high-heeled shoes, that she had a tendency to flick coquettishly in the air. I'd never seen her before in my life and I wasn't particularly happy to see her now.

I sauntered over. 'Hi Max, everything okay here?'

'Yep fine,' said Max, a bemused look on his face. Up close I noticed that the woman had very much infiltrated Max's personal space so that her impressive décolletage was right in his line of sight, even if he was doing a pretty good job of ignoring it. Could she be a work colleague, a client or an old friend, I wondered, and if so, why had Max never mentioned her before?

I hovered awkwardly a moment or two, exchanging pleasantries with some of my customers, and then when there was no introduction forthcoming I did the honours.

'Hi there, my name's Ellie. Welcome to The Dog and Duck. I don't think we've seen you in here before, have we?'

'Oh right, you're a barmaid then, are you?' she said, haughtily.

'Landlady, actually,' I said, adopting my megawatt smile, reserved for my really special customers.

'Brilliant. Could you take these from me,' she said, picking up a clutch of glasses from the table and thrusting them in my face. She didn't look me in the eye, dismissing me with the turn of her body and immediately returned to focus on Max, who was doing absolutely nothing to dissuade her attentions. From behind her back, I glared at him, but he only gave a resigned shrug, a half-smile playing on his lips. Well if he was happy chatting and getting up close and personal with Miss Cat Woman then I wasn't going to stand in his way.

I wandered off and it was only when I was putting the dirty glasses in the dishwasher behind the bar, looking slyly across the room, that it suddenly dawned on me who the woman might be. Of course! She must have come for the party. I sauntered back over again, channelling my best friendly landlady impression.

'Sorry, I didn't catch your name?' I said, laying a hand on her arm.

'Darcy,' she said, with a tight smile, her gaze dropping to my touch, before her heavily kohled eyes flashed back at me by way of a warning. Still I wasn't about to take the hint. If she could be touchy-feely with Max, then I was more than happy to extend the same level of friendliness towards her.

'Are you here for the hen night, Darcy?'

Clearly she was, her sophisticated and sleek outfit wasn't the kind of garb you'd choose for a casual visit to the pub. She sighed heavily, probably at the realisation that I wasn't about to go away and the fact she would have to engage in conversation with me whether she liked it or not.

'Yeah, although to be frank with you, it's not my idea of fun, spending the night with a bunch of cackling women. I've only come along to show my face. I'll go through in a while, but I might just have another drink first,' she said, raising her glass at Max by way of invitation.

There was a pause while we all looked at each other awkwardly.

'Right... okay,' she said when there wasn't an offer forthcoming from Max. 'I'll go and get it myself... Oh,' she said, suddenly remembering my presence, 'could you get me a bottle of Prosecco please?'

'Sorry.' I smiled sweetly. 'We don't offer waitress service. You'll need to put your order in at the bar.'

She tutted and shook her head disdainfully before wandering off.

Max shrugged his shoulders at me. 'What?' he laughed, seeing my pursed lips and wide-eyed expression.

'She's coming on to you,' I whispered. 'You know she is and you're doing nothing to stop it.'

'I'm just having a quiet drink,' he chuckled. 'It's not my fault if she's drawn to my devilish good looks and innate charm. What am I supposed to do?' His hand reached out for my waist and he pulled me into his side. 'That's not a hint of jealousy I'm detecting, is it?'

'No, of course not,' I said, bristling.

'Good, because you do know that I've only got eyes for one woman and that's the extremely hot and sexy landlady of this pub?'

'Hmmm, I should think so too,' I said, marginally appeased. I just spotted Darcy out of the corner of my eye making her way back to us again, so I turned and draped my arm over Max's shoulder, giving him a big kiss on his cheek, before nuzzling my head into his chest.

'Oh…' Darcy was back and surveying the scene critically. 'Are you two a thing then?' she asked, without batting an eyelid.

I nodded while Max said, 'Yes. Ellie's my…' He paused as his gaze swept over my face, that familiar half-smile twitching at the corner of his mouth. 'Well, Ellie's my… girlfriend.'

'How cute,' Darcy said, laughing, picking up on Max's light-hearted and casual remark.

'Right, well I should get on,' I said tightly, feeling my skin bristle. 'You should come through when you're ready. I'll tell Polly you're here. I'm sure she'd love you to join the party.' *Instead of hitting on my man!* I felt like saying.

Girlfriend though? It didn't quite cover it. Mother of his child, soulmate, life partner, housemate even. He could have said any one of those things. Still, I'd leave Max to fight off Darcy's attentions and for her to find out the truth in her own time.

Back in the barn, the party atmosphere had gone up several notches and there was an impromptu game of pass the balloon going on with Polly at the centre of the fun as she tried valiantly to pass the balloon between her legs to the good-looking waiter who seemed to be wholly distracted from what he was supposed to be doing. Never mind, just by looking around, I could tell that everyone had a full glass, a smile on their faces and was having a good time.

I laid out the food platters on the table, peeling off the cling film. Chorizo sausage rolls, smoked salmon blinis, arancini bites, mini vegetable kebabs, olives, asparagus wrapped in prosciutto, all of Polly's favourites were there, and when she managed to escape the compromising position she'd got herself into with a balloon and a young man, she came rushing over.

'Oh my goodness, Ellie! Is there anything you can't do? What a wonderful spread. It all looks delicious and I suppose I really ought to have something to eat now to soak up all those Martinis I've been knocking back. I blame that young man. He's a very bad influence. No sooner have I taken a sip from my drink than he's refilled my glass.'

'He's only doing his job,' I laughed. 'So, tell me, what's the gossip on your friend Darcy?'

'Is she here? I haven't seen her. To be honest, I wasn't convinced she'd come. We used to work with each other years ago in an office in town, long before I started the flower shop. I'll tell you a secret, her real name is Dawn, but she started calling herself Darcy because she thought it sounded more sophisticated. Do you think we should do that? I could call myself Pandora and you could call yourself...' she waved her fingers in the air, clearly thinking, '...Evangelina... how does that sound?'

'Mad,' I laughed.

'Anyway, Darcy – she left the company we were working for under a bit of a cloud. Had an affair with her married boss and it all got very messy. At the time I felt really sorry for her, he kind of used her and hung her out to dry. We've always kept in touch ever since. Where is she then?'

'Out in the bar, working her charms on Max,' I said, rolling my eyes.

'Don't worry, she's harmless enough,' said Polly. 'Just one of those women who needs constant affirmation from men. Besides, you've got no worries about Max on that front. He's totally devoted to you.'

Polly was right, I knew that, and I didn't like to think of myself as the jealous type, but that's exactly how I'd felt seeing this unfamiliar woman being so up close and personal with Max. Maybe it was the fact we had Noel now. It wasn't just about the two of us anymore, it was about protecting our little family. Huh, who was I kidding? This wasn't about Noel at all. It was about Max. My man. My soon-to-be-husband, even if he wasn't quite up to speed on that particular development.

'Talk of the devil,' said Polly, looking across to the door where Darcy had just swept in looking like the sexy villain from a Bond film. 'I should go and say hello.'

Watching Polly dash across the room, I piled a plate high with lots of the delicious goodies I'd prepared earlier, helped myself to a glass of champagne from a passing tray and went and found a seat at the table, where Sasha joined me.

'You know, I think we've done a pretty good job here. Polly seems well pleased and well on her way too,' she said, giggling. 'All our hard work has been worth it.'

'I know, it's great, isn't it? Although probably one boozy night in a cocktail bar is enough for me. It just reminds me that I did absolutely the right thing coming back to Little Leyton. I'm definitely a country girl at heart.'

'Me too. Perhaps we're getting old, eh?' Sasha laughed. 'So, I didn't like to ask the other day as you seemed a bit distracted, but dare I ask how the big proposal went?'

'Oh god, Sasha,' I said, my turn to laugh now, 'it was a complete disaster. I don't know how I got it so wrong. For one, it completely pissed it down and we both got drenched though, then I found getting over those stones much harder than I remembered. I'm clearly not as agile as I once was. Just when I thought I might be getting the hang of it, I jumped onto a stone and promptly fell off straight into the river. When I asked Max if he would marry me, he just laughed. He thought it was hilarious.'

'Oh…' Sasha was trying her darnedest not to laugh too. 'Perhaps he didn't realise you were serious.'

'I don't know. He said it was a mad idea. It wasn't such a mad idea when he asked me though.'

'Who knows what goes on in Max's mind,' said Sasha. 'We were together five years and I really never got to grips with how his mind ticks. You and him have a much better and deeper connection though than we ever did.'

'Yes, but I've still no idea what's going on in his brain!' I laughed.

'So, does it really matter about getting married when you're so happy together?'

I pondered on that question for a moment. 'I'll tell you a secret,' I whispered in her ear. 'Actually, it's become really important to me.' The rhythmic sounds of the soul music were rousing me. 'With everything that's happened this year, I really would love to make it official now. To stand up in front of our families and friends and take our vows. Don't tell anyone though,' I said, holding a finger to my mouth. 'Especially not Max!'

'Come on you two, this is a party and we should be dancing. I won't take no for an answer.' Polly rushed over and grabbed us by the hands, putting an end to my wistful reflections. She dragged us up on to the dance floor, the music seducing us with the beat. We danced as though no one was watching, fuelled by the champagne and cocktails we'd been drinking, our arms and legs flailing in the air. We paused for breath every now and again, to hug each other, to tell everyone in our close-knit group of friends just how important we were to each other, before picking up the beat again.

I felt an arm around my shoulder and looked round to see Darcy strutting her stuff beside me.

'Your boyfriend is pretty damn hot,' she shouted in my ear above the noise of the music. 'If you ever get fed up with him, then send him my way, won't you?'

'It's not going to happen, Darcy, I'm afraid,' I shouted back at her, the alcohol I'd consumed making me feel more relaxed in her company. She was attractive, sassy and full of sex appeal, but there was a sadness and vulnerability in her eyes that was noticeable even in the dark shadows of the barn.

'Story of my life,' she said with a hint of wistfulness, before twirling her way off into another corner of the room.

I took the opportunity to slip out of the barn to take in some fresh air. The sharp coolness to the night made me realise just how light-headed I felt. It was the first time I'd had a proper drink since the arrival of Noel and those delicious potent bubbles had gone straight to my head. I gave myself a mental shake before walking back into the pub, the hubbub washing over me in a warm welcome. It was even busier now and I literally had to move people out of the way to get through the crowds.

'Hello you,' I said, when I reached Max.

'Well hello you,' said Max, his voice full of warm humour. He slipped an arm around my waist and kissed me on the cheek. 'How's it all going in there?'

'Great, judging by how merry they all are. Everyone seems to be having a fantastic time, especially Polly, who is high on excitement and several Martini cocktails.'

'Another successful evening organised by the delightful Miss Browne then?' he said, running a finger down my face.

'Well, I do try. I had a bit of a moment in there with your not-so-secret admirer. She told me that if I ever get fed up with you then she would be more than willing to take my place. Wasn't that nice of her?'

'Really? Well I do hope you told her that that was never going to happen.'

'Of course. Come here,' I said, pulling him away by the hand to a quiet corner of the pub. 'You know I love you, don't you?' I rested my hands on his waist, my fingers finding their way beneath his shirt to feel the definition of his hip bone beneath.

'Yes.' Max's dark eyes lit up with warmth, a smile on his lips. 'I love you too, Ellie.'

'And you know how happy you've made me since I moved into the manor and we've had our precious baby boy together.'

'I do. I told you it would all work out for the best, didn't I?'

'All right, smart-arse. Just sometimes it takes me a while to come round to these things. I must admit though, you were right and I was wrong.'

Max pulled me into his body and I rested my head on his broad chest.

When I first discovered I was unexpectedly pregnant I'd been full of doubts, and moving into Braithwaite Manor had been a huge stumbling block for me. I'd been living at The Dog and Duck, running the pub and I loved it there. Then I was being asked to give up everything I knew, my home and my security, to move into what looked like a cold and unforgiving stately home from the outside, with a man, who I hadn't known that long, but had fallen madly in love with. It had seemed fraught with danger and I'd been tormented by the what ifs. What if what I was feeling was based purely on lust, what if we found out we didn't really like each other, what if it failed, what if the success of the pub crumbled if I wasn't there to see to it on a daily basis? There were so many variables and yet…

'Isn't that always the case…?'

'What?' I said, my mind was off wandering, thinking about everything that had happened in such a short space of time.

'That I'm always right,' he said, teasing me with that familiar half-smile on his lips. He'd been right so far. Moving into the manor hadn't been the upheaval I thought it might be. Now it was a proper family home, filled with baby clutter, dogs and regular visitors, with all the mess and untidiness that came with that. A happy family home.

'No, it's not,' I said, chiding him with a shake of the head. 'You're not always right, but... well, you were right about me moving in and having your baby, and we are very happy, aren't we?'

His brow furrowed and his eyes narrowed in contemplation. 'Are you drunk?'

'No,' I said, digging him in the chest. 'No, I'm not drunk. Maybe a tiny bit tipsy, but that makes no difference to the way I feel. I would be saying exactly the same thing if I was absolutely stone-cold sober.'

'Good.' He looked totally bemused by my unexpected show of emotion. 'Is this all because of that woman... Darcy?'

'No, not at all. I think it's just important that you know exactly how I feel.'

'Ellie!' My name rang out across the crowded bar and everyone turned to look. Katy was stood on a chair beckoning me over. 'You need to get back in the barn now, I think we could have a problem,' she giggled.

'Max?' I held out a hand to him.

'Go,' he laughed.

'But…?'

'Just go,' he told me. 'I've got it,' he said laughing. 'You're madly in love with me.'

There'd been so much more that I wanted to say, but perhaps it was just as well I'd been called away or else I may have ended up regretting my actions again.

'What's going on?' I asked, when I reached Katy.

'It's all got a bit wild in there. I think you should come and see.'

We pushed open the door to the barn to be met by the throaty and sexy tones of Tom Jones blasting over the speakers singing 'Sex Bomb'. All of the guests had made a big circle around the edge of the room, jiggling in time to the music, while Waiter No. 1 was currently doing a very good job of interpreting the music, swirling his shirt around his head in a provocative manner, displaying abs that were defined, bronzed and frankly should have come with a health warning.

'He's only about twenty,' I gasped.

'Old enough then,' laughed Katy.

'Ellie, where have you been?' Polly was at my side, hands on her hips, looking at me accusingly. 'I thought you said there wouldn't be any naked bodies.'

Blimey. My eyes widened as the waiter wiggled his bottom in our direction.

'Polly, I'm so sorry.' I took hold of her hands and squeezed them tight, looking at her imploringly. 'I really don't know how this has happened. But don't worry, I'll get it sorted straightaway. Right young man…'

'Are you kidding?' She grabbed me firmly by the arm, stopping me in my tracks. 'Don't you dare! It's not every day a girl has a hen night, and this fella is only just warming up.' She leapt up in the air to catch a bow tie flying through the air in her direction, snatching it in triumph. 'Well, if I can't indulge in some light-hearted innocent fun on my hen night, then when can I?'

Twenty-Five

'Ugh, my head.' It was the next morning and Polly was sprawled over my kitchen table cradling her head in her hands, making pitiful animal noises. 'I think I'm dying.'

'I think it's called a hangover. Here drink this,' I said, handing her a black coffee, trying not to sound too smug. I was feeling remarkably bright-eyed this morning, but then again I'd stopped drinking long before Polly and her friends, knowing I'd be up early with Noel.

'What's your aunty Polly like?' I asked him now, kissing him on the cheek.

'Please don't tell George about this. He'd probably disown me if he knew how many of those lethal cocktails I drank. He's such a lovely man, cultured, kind and respectful. I mean, I try to be all of those things to him too, but it's bloody hard and sometimes, like last night, the real me decides to put in an appearance. Honestly, Ellie, I don't know how a nice man like George has ended up with someone like me. Oh god, and if he saw me dancing with those waiters, it doesn't bear thinking about!' She buried her face in her hands again. 'Mind you, I suppose it could have been worse.'

'It could have been a lot worse if I hadn't stepped in when I did. Those guys did a great job at serving the drinks, but they didn't take much encouragement from you lot to get their kit off.'

Polly grimaced and blushed. 'I blame Darcy. She always was a bad influence. The last time I saw her she was huddled up in a corner with that waiter, snogging the face off him. I do hope she got home okay. She was pretty wasted when I last saw her.'

'Did someone mention my name?'

Darcy padded into the kitchen barefooted, bare-faced and with her catsuit looking completely at odds with the bright sunshine filling the kitchen this morning. The look of shock on Polly's face was priceless.

'What...? How...?' But Polly just couldn't find the right words.

'Darcy needed a bed for the night. We were having trouble finding a taxi so I said she could stay here. You clearly don't remember us all walking home together then.'

'No, it's all a bit of a blur, although some things are still very vivid in my mind.' She shuddered and shook her head regretfully.

'Thanks for putting me up last night, Ellie,' said Darcy. 'I'm not sure I would have been quite so generous in your shoes. And I can only apologise for my bad behaviour earlier in the evening, if I was rude to you at all.' She took a moment, clearly revisiting the events of the night. 'Oh, and I must apologise for my bad behaviour later in the evening too. In fact, blanket apology for all the bad behaviour.' She cringed. 'That poor young man. I do hope I haven't scarred him for life.'

'Don't worry,' said Polly laughing. 'The last time I saw him he was looking very pleased with himself. And what happens in the barn at The Dog & Duck stays at The Dog & Duck. All your secrets are safe with us.'

Darcy took a sip from the mug of coffee I'd handed her, reflective for a moment. She appeared much less confident and more vulnerable in the cold light of day.

'I envy you two,' she said, her gaze distracted by the gardens through the windows of the kitchen. 'I'm older than both of you and yet you both seem to have it all sorted. Solid relationships, good jobs, and then there's me, still working in a series of temporary jobs and spending my weekends pretending I'm a teenager and getting off with a string of unsuitable men.'

Polly grimaced. 'Well it can't be all bad.'

'Oh, but it is. It seems fun at the time, but waking up the next morning and realising you have to go home to an empty flat in your clothes from the previous night can be pretty soul-crushing. I want all this.' She chuckled, looking around her. 'It doesn't have to be on this scale, obviously, I'm not greedy, I'd just like to find someone special to spend the rest of my life with. It's not a lot to ask for, is it?'

'If it can happen to me it can happen to you, Darcy. This time last year I hadn't even met George and now look us.' Polly wiggled her engagement ring as if she couldn't quite believe it herself. 'And Max and Ellie have only known each other a couple of years too. Keep the faith.'

'I'll try,' said Darcy, laughing.

'It's funny how things work out,' I said. 'You can make all sorts of plans, thinking you'll go in one direction and then suddenly fate has a way of barging in and taking you off in a different direction. I never thought I'd be running the pub, and yet if I hadn't come back to Little Leyton, then I would never have met Max, and this little man wouldn't even be here,' I said, blowing raspberries on Noel's cheek. 'I wouldn't want it any other way though.'

Max took that moment to wander in the kitchen. 'I should hope not,' he said with a smile, coming over to kiss me and Noel in a warm show of affection.

With a clear head and away from the hubbub of the pub, I wondered why I'd ever felt ruffled by Darcy's behaviour last night. In the heat of the moment, I'd over-reacted when I'd had no need to. Not when I trusted Max completely.

When we'd got home last night and after putting our drunken party revellers to bed, we tiptoed into Noel's room to check on him, before Max and I had poured ourselves a glass of Pinot Noir and curled up on the sofa together. I smiled, thinking how close I'd come to asking Max to marry me again last night, once in the pub and later, back at home, wrapped in his arms. Now, I just felt relieved that I hadn't gone through with it, possibly spoiling what was an otherwise wonderful evening. It wasn't that I'd changed my mind about marrying Max, quite the opposite, but if I wanted to make sure that he definitely said yes the next time, then everything had to be absolutely perfect for my next proposal. There was no rush. First of all there was Polly's wedding to get through, and then, after that, well, I might just think about how I'd go about persuading Max that I really did want to marry him after all.

Later that morning after several more coffees, Darcy left in a taxi, dropping off Polly on the way, and I made my own way into the village, with Digby walking obediently at my side, while I pushed Noel in his buggy.

At the pub I checked out the barn just to make sure it was still standing and there weren't any drunken revellers hiding inside. Most of the clearing up had been done the night before by the staff, but I grabbed a black rubbish bag and filled it with the remaining bits of debris that were scattered over the floor, mainly scrunched-up napkins, party poppers, deflated balloons and, inexplicably, a pair of underpants. My New York cocktail bar looked decidedly seedy this morning, but once the glitter balls were down and the mirrors were gone, it would be back to being a blank canvas ready for its next transformation into an English country barn for Polly's wedding reception.

Back in the pub, I was chatting with Eric as he poured me an apple juice, when I spotted Ethan and Johnny sitting in the bay window and they beckoned me over.

'Hello you two, I haven't caught up with you in ages. How are you both keeping?' I pulled out a chair and sat down with them, handing Noel over to Johnny, who was only too eager to hold Noel in his arms and chatted away to him as though he could understand every word he was saying. Johnny was a natural with children and I'd always thought what a lovely father he would make one day.

'Okay,' said Ethan, looking pretty downcast, and not really very okay at all. 'How is Josie?' he asked me.

'She's okay,' I said, my turn to be evasive. 'Haven't you seen her?'

'Oh yeah, I see her a couple of times a week, but I have no idea how she really is. She won't open up to me. I go round there, collect Stella and drop her off again a few hours later. I just wish I knew what to do to make things better. I can't believe that she would give up on our marriage without giving it another try.'

'You're not at that stage yet?'

'Aren't we? I don't know where we are. You probably know more than I do.'

I shook my head. 'Josie hasn't said very much about it to be honest.'

And if she had, I wouldn't tell Ethan, but my stomach twisted with guilt at the thought that I hadn't provided more support for Josie during this difficult time. She'd split up from her husband and every time I asked after her, she would always deflect my concern, saying that everything was fine, and that she was sure they'd sort it out eventually. I wondered if I was guilty of just accepting what she told me because it was easier to do that rather than putting in more effort to help.

'Don't give up on her yet, Ethan,' I told him. 'I really don't know what's going on in Josie's mind at the moment, but I know that she loved you very much. I can't believe things have changed that dramatically.'

Ethan shrugged despondently. 'Neither can I.'

'Maybe you need to spend some time together, just the two of you without little Stella, so that you can rediscover what it is you first loved about each other. I'm happy to have Stella overnight if you want me to. A break away, just the two of you, might be just what you need, to get things back on track.'

'Thanks, Ellie, that means a lot. I'd love to do that, if only Josie would agree.'

'Hearing this sort of stuff makes me very nervous of relationships,' said Johnny, pulling a face. 'We were talking about it before you turned up, Ellie. We both reckon neither of us are very good at this sort of stuff.'

'I thought you were getting on well with Sasha.'

'I am. She's a great girl. I really like her. I find her easy to talk to and we have a good laugh together, but you know what I'm like, Ellie, I'm liable to cock it up at any moment now.'

'No, you won't. What makes you say that?'

'Well I managed to mess things up with you, and then Polly. Whenever I meet someone I really like it's as though I have to go and sabotage it.'

'Oh Johnny! It doesn't always have to be that way. You and me, you and Polly, that was never going to work out, and hey, we still have our brilliant friendships intact, and that's what counts. But Sasha, she's lovely and I think you'd be really good for each other.'

'Do you?'

'Yes, I do. Sometimes you have to take a risk for something that's so important.' I smiled ruefully, hearing the words on my lips that Max had told me so many times in the past. However, Johnny and Ethan remained downbeat. They were both sitting there morosely staring into their colas. The pair of them reminded me of how Polly and I were a couple of years ago when we'd sit and discuss our relationship woes, gradually making ourselves more and more depressed by the moment. I'd always thought that was just a girly thing, but now I realised that men shared all the same doubts and concerns, and sought the same solace from each other. 'I should get going, but let me buy you both a pint before I leave.'

Up at the bar, Eric smiled knowingly as he poured two beers. 'You know if you ever get fed up being landlady of this pub you could always take up a new career as a life coach.'

I laughed. Thinking about it, wasn't it time Eric found someone special to share his life? I made a mental note. That could be next on my list. *Sort Eric's love life.*

Twenty-Six

On the morning of Polly's wedding, we gathered at Mum and Dad's house to get ready for the big day ahead. Caroline had come round from next door with the dresses and Polly and I were sat in our robes, sipping champagne while Janice, the hairdresser, put gentle soft waves into our hair and carefully fitted the flower crowns made from white baby's breath and yellow daisies. Angie, the make-up artist, applied foundation, bronzer and eyeshadow to our faces in light natural strokes, finishing off with a lick of mascara and a kiss of peach lipstick.

'Have you seen what the weather is doing out there?' asked Mum. 'It's absolutely gorgeous and the forecast is sunshine all day.' She'd been fluttering about all morning, her excitement palpable.

'At least it's something less to worry about,' said Polly. 'I didn't expect to feel this nervous. Mum and Dad are here, I saw them only briefly last night when they arrived, so I can't wait to have a proper catch-up with them later. Dad's going to be waiting for me at the lychgate and I know as soon as I see him, I'm going to burst into tears.'

'No tears until after the ceremony please,' said Angie firmly.

'I'll try, it's just that with all our friends, family, and neighbours turning up to see us, it feels like such a responsibility.'

'A few butterflies in the tummy are to be expected, but try not to worry too much. Once you see George waiting for you at the altar everything will fall into place. It's your special day and you're not to worry about a thing, we'll all do what we can to make sure that everything goes off without a hitch.'

'Ellie, you're such a star. I really don't know what I'd do without you.'

Carefully we stepped into our dresses as Angie and Janice fussed around us, putting the finishing touches to our hair and make-up.

'Oh my goodness, I'm going to cry,' said Mum when she saw us ready to go. 'You two look absolutely beautiful.'

'No, don't cry, not yet,' I said to Mum, giving her a very careful squeeze. 'You'll ruin your make-up too.'

A car beeped its horn outside the front of the cottages and we ran to the window to look. Parked on the kerb was the most adorable white VW Beetle which had a bright pink ribbon tied in a bow on the front and white and pink heart-shaped balloons floating from the back.

'Look at that!' Polly flapped her hands excitedly. 'This is George! He's organised all of this for me. He must have remembered. I told him about my first car, a beaten-up old red Beetle that I absolutely adored. It was a real wreck but I always hoped that Dad and I might be able to renovate it and bring it back to its original condition. We spent many Sundays working on it, sanding down the rust, putting in new parts, it was a real labour of love until I had to sadly get rid of it in the end. It was costing too much money and time that I didn't have to spend on it. To think that George has gone to all this trouble.'

'That's reminded me, George asked me to give you this.' I handed her a little white box held together with a pink bow. She looked at it perplexed.

'What is it?'

'I don't know, maybe a necklace,' I said, disingenuously. 'Open it.'

She pulled open the bow and lifted off the lid, her expression when she saw what was inside the box was even more puzzled. She took out the key that had been nestling in some pink silk and looked at it, disbelieving, and then looked from me to the key again.

'What is it?' she asked, giving a half-laugh.

'The key to your new car. That sweet little car outside is your wedding present from George.'

'No!'

'Yes! Obviously you're not expected to drive it today. There's a chauffeur waiting to take us to the church, but after today it's all yours.'

She opened her mouth to scream, but no sound came out, she just shook her head, before finally emitting a small squeeing noise.

'Oh my god, my gorgeous lovely husband-to-be! Did he really do this for me? I think I'm going to cry.'

'No!' We all screamed at her. 'Don't cry. Think of the make-up!'

She waved her hands in front of her face in an attempt to stem the tears, but in fairness we were all struggling with our emotions this morning. We only needed to share a look, a kind word or a hug and the tears would present themselves again, threatening to fall on to our cheeks.

'Look at the time! We're going to have to go,' said Mum. 'Good luck, Polly, that George is a lucky man to be marrying you. We'll see you at the church.'

'Thanks, Veronica, but really it's me who's the lucky one.'

Mum, Caroline, Janice and Angie each hugged Polly in turn and then hugged me too, before leaving the cottage to walk the short distance to the church.

'Well Polly, it's just you and me now,' I said, when we were left alone. 'This is really happening and in less than an hour you will be a married woman.'

'I won't believe it until I have that ring on my finger.'

I lifted up her left hand to see where the ring would go, trying to imagine how it might look on her lovely manicured hand.

'You do know that this doesn't change anything between us,' she said, urgently.

'Of course, it doesn't,' I laughed, not entirely certain what she meant.

'We're always going to be here for each other, aren't we, through marriage, children and anything else that's thrown our way?' She squeezed my hand tightly. 'Your friendship means the world to me, Ellie – we've been through so much together, happy times, desperate times and very drunk times too. I'm just excited for these next grown-up steps in our lives and all the good times we'll have ahead. I've still got that date in my diary, you know?'

I looked at her quizzically.

'You can't have forgotten about the Leyton Girls' Grand World Tour of 2050?'

'Oh yes, of course, how could I?' I said, giggling.

One evening a couple of years ago, Josie, Polly and I had, over several bottles of Prosecco and a magnificent cheese board, been putting the world to rights. We'd been bemoaning our sorry love lives at the time and decided that whatever the future held for us individually, we would, after we'd brought up our children, go off on a belated gap-year adventure. It had started as a joke after a throwaway comment, but the seed had been planted and we all still talked about it occasionally, keeping the dream alive.

There was a knock at the door from the chauffeur, telling us it was time to go. Outside, we stood together for photos, the sun casting a golden glow onto the warm stone of the cottage, the yellow rambling roses climbing over the porch providing the perfect backdrop for the first of many photos today.

I followed Polly down the pathway to the waiting car and we both let out the biggest sigh as we stepped into the lovely little gleaming white Beetle which had been restored to its original condition with gorgeous red leather seats.

'This is so amazing,' gasped Polly.

I managed just about to hold onto my emotions until I stepped inside the hallowed walls of St Cuthbert's church. When the organist began to play, I bit on my lip and took a steadying breath before following Polly and her father down the aisle to the warm appreciation of a full congregation. Seeing all my friends and family gathered in the pews, the sun filtering through the stained glass windows, brought it home to me, the sanctity of this wonderful occasion. My eyes searched out the one special person I wanted to see and my pulse took up apace spotting Max standing towards the front of the church, with little Noel in his arms. My heart swelled at the sight of them, and a huge ball of emotion lodged at the back of my throat. Everyone else faded from sight as Max looked over his shoulder to meet my gaze. It was almost as if…

Polly joined George at the altar. They made such a stunning couple, their faces alight with happiness, and the hushed anticipation in the church sent a shiver running down my spine.

Under Rev. Trish Evans' thoughtful direction, Polly and George took their vows and I felt as though I might burst with pride. When the service was over and the newly married pair walked back down the aisle to the magnificent sound of the church bells pealing above us, there couldn't have been anybody present who wasn't filled with an overwhelming joy and happiness at seeing these two lovely people married now.

Outside, the solemnity of what had taken place inside the church was replaced by laughter, congratulations, tears – happy ones – and much bubbling chatter and enjoyment, as Polly showed off her wedding ring to anyone who wanted to see.

Max wandered over to my side and whispered in my ear. 'You, Ellie Browne, look absolutely stunning.'

'Thank you, Max. You look pretty damn good yourself.'

In fairness, everyone looked amazing in all their finery, but Max especially so in a soft grey Italian wool suit, white double-cuffed shirt, purple tie and silver initialled cufflinks. I was so used to seeing him in his casual work clothes, with holes in his jeans and those old much-loved checked shirts that had seen better days, that the sight of him suited and booted literally took my breath away. His tall and lean figure enabled him to carry off expensive Italian tailoring with style and panache. Standing next to him in the seductive warm heat, I felt a longing and desire for him that wasn't entirely appropriate for my surroundings. Instead I gave myself a mental shake and focussed my attentions on little Noel who looked just as endearing in his smocked navy and white romper suit.

I had to stop my mind from entertaining all sorts of fanciful thoughts that it could so easily have been Max and me walking down the aisle today. The dress I was wearing could double as a wedding dress and Max was perfectly attired to play the part of the dashing groom. I could have taken up Polly's invitation to make this a double wedding or accepted Max's first proposal of marriage – *why didn't I?* – and we could have been making our own wedding plans or even be married by now. But it wasn't to be. There had been an opportunity and I'd missed it.

'You all right?' Max took hold of my hand and shook it, bringing me back to the moment.

'Yes, I was just thinking what a lovely service it was and how lucky we've been with the weather.'

'Perfect! Isn't this exactly how you imagine an English country wedding to be?'

'Yeah,' I sighed. If only Max knew just how much imagining I'd been indulging in. 'Look, I should get along to the pub to make sure everything's ready for the wedding party.'

'Well, I'll come with you,' he said.

'Ooh, look at you lot!' Mum came rushing over just as we were about to leave. 'What a gorgeous family you make.' She covered us in a shower of kisses. 'Wasn't it such a beautiful service. They make a fabulous couple, don't they? Takes me back to when your father and I got married. It was such a happy day. Those memories stay with you forever. Mind you, if you didn't know, anyone would think you were the bride and groom.'

'Ha, ha, ha!' Max and I looked at each other and smiled. Mum was the first one to tell us that today, but she wouldn't be the last. I just hoped she wouldn't come out with any other embarrassing comments or unsubtle hints.

Down at the pub, the doors to the barn were open, white and pink bunting hung from the rafters, balloons bobbed gaily from the backs of the chairs and confetti was sprinkled across the tables. The garden was an abundance of blooms, hand-reared and tended by Polly, and the sweet scent of roses and honeysuckle wafted in the air.

The waiters were ready with trays of champagne to greet the soon to be arriving wedding guests. After a lot of deliberation, I'd decided to rehire the lads who had been at the hen night, with strict instructions that they were there to serve the drinks and not to actually partake of them, and all clothing was to stay firmly in place. I only hoped Darcy wouldn't feel too embarrassed at coming face to face with Waiter No. 1 again.

After we'd eaten from a banquet of creamy cider chicken casserole, roasted salmon topped with a herbed crust, or a vegetable terrine with oregano tomatoes, Polly's dad raised a toast to the bride and groom and George gave a heartfelt and touching speech which had us all dabbing at our eyes with our hankies. Not to be outdone, Polly stood up and addressed all her family and friends.

'I just wanted to say a big thank you to you all for turning up today to share the happiest of days with me and my new husband. My husband,' Polly repeated the words as though she couldn't quite believe them to be true. 'Honestly,' she said, taking a moment to compose herself as her chin wobbled precariously and tears gathered in her eyes. 'Today, I really do feel like the happiest and luckiest girl alive. I have to thank George – my husband – for making all my dreams come true.' A spontaneous roar of approval came from the increasingly merry and good-natured guests. 'Also, I have some other thank-yous to make. This place, The Dog and Duck is very special to me, not only because it's right next door to my shop, serves the best coffee and Prosecco for miles, and has the most amazing landlady who I can also count as my best friend, but because this is where George and I met for the first time.'

'Yep, she tried to seduce me with some pork scratchings,' George piped up.

'It's true,' Polly laughed. 'The early days of our romance were conducted in that lovely building just there and if it hadn't have been for my lovely friend, Ellie, here, then I wonder if George and I would have ever got together in the first place.'

'Ah, right, it's you I have to blame for all this then,' said George good-naturedly.

'Thank you, Ellie, for being the best friend a girl could have. You've always been there for me through the bad times and through the good times too. Relationships like ours aren't always easy to find and I feel truly blessed to count you as my friend.'

I dropped my gaze to my lap, hoping she would shut up soon or else I'd be in desperate danger of breaking down into an unbecoming blubbery mess of tears on the floor.

'More than that, you have taken all the stress and strain away from me in the organisation of today and you have made a reality of all those pie-in-the-sky dreams I had. I wanted the perfect English country wedding and that's what you've delivered and from the bottom of my heart I can't thank you enough. To Ellie!' Polly raised her glass of champagne in a toast and everyone stood and joined in, a roar of approval rippling around the barn like a Mexican wave.

I laughed away my embarrassment. I hadn't done anything out of the ordinary. It was my pleasure organising my best friend's wedding, it hadn't been difficult in the slightest. I'd known exactly what Polly had wanted because it was what I wish I could have chosen for myself.

Twenty-Seven

It was a few weeks after the wedding of the year in Little Leyton and Polly and George had returned from their honeymoon in the Maldives looking bronzed, relaxed and incredibly happy. Immediately George returned to his computer to start work on his next book and Polly went back to work at her florists next door. I'd got into a habit of popping into the pub most mornings to check on stock and staffing levels, so we quickly fell back into our daily ritual of Polly calling in for a morning coffee and a catch-up. It was just like old times.

Katy was doing really well at college and had passed all her assessments with flying colours. She and Ryan were seeing a lot of each other, hanging out in the barns in the village where Ryan and his band, The Leyton Boys, practised, or meeting up with friends at the pub or sometimes just heading off on Ryan's motorbike for a ride around the lanes, which was still a bone of contention between Max and Katy. I was of the opinion that if she was happy, then that counted for a lot and I liked to think Ryan was a sensible and careful rider when he had special cargo on the back.

Katy was in regular contact with Andy too, who texted her every day and popped round frequently, always ringing to check first that it was okay with Katy. She was enjoying building a relationship with her biological father and although they had a lot of years to catch up on, she was gradually opening up to him, seeming so much more relaxed in his company. He'd become a regular visitor at The Dog and Duck fitting in with the locals as though he'd always been a part of the village. Katy also spoke to her mum on the phone at least once a week and with Rose already making plans for her next visit to Little Leyton, I was hopeful that their relationship was moving forward in the right direction.

Arthur continued to thrive at Braithwaite Manor and loved being part of a busy family. He spent his days generally pottering around the house, although he loved to sit at the kitchen table and enjoy a pot of tea with whoever happened to be passing through at the time. Max had given him a small plot of the vegetable garden that he could oversee and it was lovely to see him so interested and engaged in how the rhubarb and courgettes were coming along. There'd been no more mention of him returning home, and we were all very pleased about that fact.

Josie and Ethan were still not back together, but had been talking more openly, sharing their grievances and discussing ways they might be able to make a go of things. They'd come together at the wedding and I'd actually seen them laughing, which was something of a miracle. A few days later Josie came to me and asked if I wouldn't mind having Stella overnight so that she and Ethan could go away for a night or two. That was happening this weekend and I was looking forward to looking after Stella, and hopeful too that Josie and Ethan, with some time alone together, would be able to get their relationship back on track.

Sasha and Johnny's fledgling relationship was going from strength to strength. They too had been out on more dates and Johnny had been spending time with Sasha and Ruby at the weekends, going for country walks and sharing meals. When I caught Sasha alone, she told me that she was excited to be with Johnny but was trying to play it cool and when I caught Johnny alone he told the exact same thing. I suspected that they wouldn't be able to maintain the mutual coolness act for too much longer and my fingers were firmly crossed that they would soon be able to come out as a couple.

Mum and Dad seemed happier than ever now that the shadow of Dad's illness had lifted and they were making up for lost time by cramming as much as they possibly could into their days. They were always out gallivanting, with trips to the seaside, visits to stately homes and had even started playing golf together, which had given rise to lots of friendly rivalry between the pair of them. I loved having them close on hand so that I could pop in to see them whenever I wanted and, of course, Mum was always quick to volunteer for any babysitting duties.

Max was as busy as ever, working on several property development projects, while also building more formal gardens in the grounds where he intended to grow some ornamental plants. He was a law unto himself really. The man was such a powerhouse and his relentless stamina and enthusiasm filled me with both inspiration and admiration. Working from home, or more accurately the Swiss-style chalet office in the grounds, meant that I got to see Max occasionally during the day, even it was only for a cup of tea and a quick cuddle with Noel. I could barely keep up with all of Max's comings and goings. He was forever dashing in and out, off to a site meeting here and a development meeting somewhere else, so it was always a bonus when he did put in an appearance. Like today. Even if it was only a very fleeting appearance.

'Sorry,' he said, putting a whole fairy cake in his mouth at once and munching away at it greedily. 'I have a very important meeting to go to. I'll be back later. In about two hours. You will be around, won't you? There's something I need to discuss with you.'

'Er, yes, of course,' I said, wondering firstly what sort of meeting he'd be going to dressed in his ripped jeans, old shirt and wax jacket, and then secondly what it was he needed to discuss with me. It sounded ominous. 'See you later then.'

He popped his head back round the door again. 'You do know what today is, don't you?'

I looked at him blankly. 'Tuesday?' I said, suspecting as I said it that it probably wasn't the answer he was looking for.

'Ah, you see, I thought you wouldn't remember. Today is 742 days since I first met you.'

My mind went all fuzzy as I tried to compute that fact. 'Really? How do you even know that?'

He grinned. 'That would be telling.' He tapped his finger against his nose. 'Laters!'

What? There were so many questions I had for him now, but he was gone. Max was always likely to surprise you with a random and intriguing fact when you least expected it, but could that be really true? That we'd known each other for that many days and if so, was that somehow significant? Everything inside me tensed with excitement and goosebumps spread along my limbs. Could this really be what I'd been hoping and waiting for? Oh my goodness!

'Oh Noel,' I said, picking him up to kiss his gorgeous unsuspecting face. 'What's your daddy up to?'

I couldn't help speculating, but didn't want to get carried away just in case I got hold of the wrong end of the stick entirely. It wouldn't be the first time. Was he really off to some business meeting though? If so, he was acting very peculiarly. I tried to put it out of my mind as I bounced Noel up and down on my knee, watching the dogs through the kitchen windows as they scampered about the grounds.

'Say, 'hurry up daddy'' I told Noel now, jigging my foot up and down on the ground.

I hated surprises and I didn't much like it when Max was being mysterious. I knew him well enough by now to know that he was up to something. I walked over to the calendar, and looked up at the date hoping it might give me a blinding flash of comprehension that would make all of Max's behaviour fall into place. Only it didn't.

I paced around the kitchen, cradling Noel on my hip. I couldn't settle to anything because my mind was so caught up in what Max had said to me, hoping that if I went over each sentence it would eventually make sense to me. Only I failed on that front too.

This was ridiculous. At that moment I could have throttled Max for playing with my emotions, leaving me all agog. I couldn't help myself from hoping that this was indeed a special anniversary, one that I'd overlooked and Max would come running through that door with a special surprise for me. Ugh! I gave myself a mental telling-off. I was getting carried away now.

When, much later, I heard Max's car scrunch onto the gravel of the drive, I literally jumped, as anticipation ran down my backbone.

'Come on, Noel, let's put you in your rocker and see what your daddy's been up to?'

My heart was pounding in my chest, my skin was tingling with excitement and if Max didn't hurry up and get in here right now, I might just faint onto the lovely tiled kitchen floor.

He wandered in, completely oblivious to the high-octane adrenaline experience my poor body had been going through in his absence. He looked seriously sexy in his scruffy work clothes and I wanted to rush over to him and pound my fists on his chest, to tell him to stop teasing me and just let me know what was going on. There had clearly been no business meeting. I could tell that just from looking at him.

'Hiya,' he said, so casually I might have screamed at him.

'How was the "business" meeting?' I asked.

'The business meeting?' He looked at me puzzled. 'Oh yes, that! All good. All sorted now.'

'Right.'

A silence simmered between us. Was that it? Was that all he was going to say?

'What was it you wanted to talk about?

He raised a questioning eyebrow. Had he completely forgotten everything he'd told me before he left the house?

'When you left you mentioned this being a special day.'

'Oh right, yes 798 days since we first met. That's something to celebrate, don't you think?'

'Noooo!' I said, rather too vehemently. 'You said it was 742 days.' I knew because that number had been etched on my brain ever since Max had uttered it. How could it possibly be significant when he couldn't even get the number of days right. There'd been no hidden meaning to his words, after all. It had been an off-the-cuff comment and I'd read far too much into it.

'Did I?' he asked, a smile twitching at the corner of his mouth. 'Well what's a few days here and there between friends. Still worth celebrating, don't you think?'

I shrugged my shoulders, not knowing what to think. I turned away, trying to hide my disappointment as I focussed on filling the kettle.

'Do you want a cuppa?' I asked.

'No. We should have something proper to celebrate this special day. Maybe a glass of champagne? First of all though, I have something for you. A present.'

'A present?'

Champagne and a present? I wish he'd stop with the riddles and just get on with it. He didn't have any bags with him so I could only assume that it was a present of the small variety, something that would easily fit into a pocket. Like a little box. Honestly, I had to cross my arms in front of me to stop my body from shaking.

'Yes. I hope you like it. Although now I'm wondering if you will.' He sighed. 'Maybe this isn't such a good idea, after all.'

'No, it's a brilliant idea. Honestly I'll love it, whatever it is, I know I will. Just give it to me.' I paused, realising I might be coming across a bit strong, but could he really blame me? 'Please?' I added.

'Well, look, don't feel obliged to say you like it, if you don't. It can always go back if it's not what you want. I don't want to force you into something you don't want to do and now I'm thinking I may have misjudged this whole situation.'

It was only natural for him to be reticent. After all, he'd already asked me on previous occasions to marry him and I'd said no. He was probably thinking I would turn him down yet again.

'No, you haven't! Can I please just have it, Max.'

'Okay close your eyes and open your hands.'

I knew it, something small enough to fit into my hands. My fingers tingled expectantly as I imagined the sensation of that small velvet box in my cupped hands.

'Keep your eyes closed and don't move. I'll be one second.' I heard him disappear out of the door again and I heard the door to the car open and shut. What was he doing? I couldn't believe he'd left an engagement ring in the car when he could easily have hidden it in his pocket. There was a bit of scuffling and other noises I couldn't quite work out. Then some heavy breathing. Clearly, Max was as excited about all of this as I was. Then a wet damp feeling in the palm of my open hand. *What the...?*

'Right, you can open your eyes now.'

I opened one eye tentatively, and then the other, to be met by a pair of the biggest brown eyes looking back at me, eyelashes to die for and a flurry of wet kisses that I simply hadn't been expecting.

'Oh my goodness, what is that?' I said, jumping backwards to get a better look. A stupid question I knew when there was a long tongue licking my hand eagerly, the two brown eyes looking up at me longingly and two paws scrabbling on my thighs.

'A dog, Ellie. It's a dog. An English Pointer. You've been saying for ages that you wanted one.'

The black and white flecked dog was leaping around my kitchen as though it had a sugar rush, it's tail wagging as though it was battery operated.

'That's never a Pointer!' It was the first thing that came into my mind.

'It is,' argued Max. 'She's come from Spain after she was found abandoned and hungry in a disused building. She was brought over by a rescue society and is currently being fostered by a friend of one of my contractors. She's about nine months old they think. She's had all her jabs now and has been spayed. She's looking for her forever home.'

'Really?' I couldn't quite take it in. I'd been dreaming of a big diamond ring, and even that cute little expression and exuberant personality couldn't quite quash all my disappointment.

'Look, Ellie, she's not here to stay. I said I'd bring her home to see what you think and to see if she'd get on with Digby and the other dogs. But I can tell you're not keen. She can go back tomorrow… well, if you'd want to do that to a poor and defenceless puppy.'

The poor and defenceless puppy was currently scooting around the kitchen, jumping in Digby's bed, had said hello to Noel in his rocker and was now trying to remove my socks by nibbling on my toes. I didn't know what to think. Only that my heart was swelling at the sight of her. Adorable didn't even come close.

'Come here,' I called, and she came padding over, all long legs, big eyes and endless enthusiasm. She was utterly beautiful and had on a swish red leather collar that complemented her black and white markings.

She licked my face as if saying 'pick me, pick me', and I wasn't sure whether to laugh or cry, but I knew that Max's plan was working, I was falling in love with her with each passing second.

'What's her name?' I asked.

'Not sure,' he said, dismissively. 'It'll say on her name tag. Take a look.'

I bent down and was rewarded with some more wet kisses, legs that were clambering all over me and a tail that kept thumping against me. I reached out for the silver metal tag on her collar, all the time wrangling with the dog's exuberance, and turned it over to see. It wasn't easy when I was being licked to death at the same time. Her name was… I strained to see, before looking up at Max tears swelling in my eyes, looking for confirmation that I understood what I was looking at. He nodded.

'Don't all the best surprises come in small black and white packages?' he asked.

'Oh goodness, Max, do you really mean it?' I read the words aloud on the tag. '*Will you marry me?*

'Yes. Obviously that's not her real name. Her name is Flora, but she thought all of this would be a good idea.'

'Oh Max, I honestly thought you'd changed your mind and you wouldn't ever want to get married.' I ran into his arms, squeezing him tight, while Flora tugged at my socks, unaware of the importance of the occasion.

'Are you crazy?' He pulled away, holding my face in his hands. 'I've never stopped wanting to marry you.' He kissed me on the lips. 'But I'm an old-fashioned guy, Ellie, I wanted to be the one doing the asking. Is that such a bad thing?'

I shook my head. 'No, not at all. I just wished you'd said!'

'I was waiting for the right moment and well, now, there seems no better moment.'

He reached inside his jeans pocket and pulled out a small black and white box, opening it with his thumb to reveal the most gorgeous diamond ring I'd ever seen.

I gasped. 'Oh Max, of course I'll marry you!'

'Hey, you didn't even give me a chance to ask you properly,' Max said laughing.

'You don't have to; the answer is yes.'

His face lit up and I saw the love and happiness in his warm expression, matching my own soaring feelings. He pulled me tight into his arms, as the tears gathered in my eyes. 'I should have said,' he said, taking a step back to look into my face. 'There is one condition attached. You do realise Flora will have to stay.'

'Don't worry,' I laughed, 'she's already one of the family. Oh dear, look!' Flora was happily depositing a little puddle by my feet.

'I reckon that's a lucky omen,' smiled Max.

I thought so too. I went across and lifted Noel into my arms and Max pulled us into his embrace. I was overjoyed to be extending our little family. Flora would fit in absolutely perfectly, I knew, but wasn't one piece of good news enough for one day? I closed my eyes, dropping my head onto Max's chest, resting my arm around the gentle swell of my tummy. The other piece of good news? That could wait until tomorrow.

We hope you enjoyed this book!

The next book in the Dog & Duck series will be
released in spring 2018

More addictive fiction from Aria:

Find out more
http://headofzeus.com/books/isbn/9781786698070

Find out more
http://headofzeus.com/books/isbn/9781786697967

Find out more
http://headofzeus.com/books/isbn/9781786699008

Acknowledgements

To my brilliant publishers, Aria Fiction, and in particular Sarah Ritherdon and Jade Craddock, for their detailed and insightful editorial comments, I owe a very big thank you.

To my long-suffering family for 'bearing with' as deadline day approaches (although I'm sure you don't really mind the endless takeaways) and asking, at what seems like five minute intervals, 'have you finished that book yet?', your encouragement, love and, ahem, helpful comments, are very much appreciated.

To all my fellow author and blogging friends (you know who you are!) - thank you for all the amazing tweets, and shout-outs and hand-holding, it means a lot.

And finally I must mention my lovely readers. I'm always so thrilled to hear from you and to know that you've enjoyed catching up with the characters from The Dog and Duck. It makes it all worthwhile, and I am really so grateful for your continued support. THANK YOU xxx

About Jill Steeples

JILL STEEPLES lives in a small market town in Bedfordshire with her husband and two children.

When she's not writing, she enjoys reading, walking, baking cakes, eating them and drinking wine.

Find me on Twitter
https://twitter.com/jillesteeples

Visit my website
http://www.jillsteeples.co.uk

A Letter from the Author

Dear Reader,

It's so lovely to see you here at the end of my story. I really hope you enjoyed the read!

One of life's great pleasures, I believe, is to lose yourself in another world for a couple of hours, within the pages of a book. I like to write feel-good, heart-warming stories which provide an escape, with characters you would want to sit down with over a cup of tea and a natter.

If you have enjoyed this novel, then I hope you might consider leaving a short review online - they really do help to spread the word - and I'd love to hear your thoughts!

To find out what I'm up to next, and for news on upcoming releases, you can follow me on Twitter. Just follow the links below.

Much love, and see you next time!

Jill

xx

Find me on Twitter
https://twitter.com/jillesteeples

Visit my website
http://www.jillsteeples.co.uk

About the Dog & Duck Series

Find out more
http://headofzeus.com/books/isbn/9781786691781

Find out more
http://headofzeus.com/books/isbn/9781786691798

Find out more
http://headofzeus.com/books/isbn/9781786691804

Visit Aria now
http://www.ariafiction.com

Become an Aria Addict

Aria is the new digital-first fiction imprint from
Head of Zeus.

It's Aria's ambition to discover and publish
tomorrow's superstars, targeting fiction addicts and
readers keen to discover new and exciting authors.

Aria will publish a variety of genres under the
commercial fiction umbrella such as women's
fiction, crime, thrillers, historical fiction, saga and
erotica.

So, whether you're a budding writer looking for a
publisher or an avid reader looking for something to
escape with – Aria will have something for you.

Get in touch: aria@headofzeus.com

Become an Aria Addict
http://ariafiction.com/newsletter/subscribe

Find us on Twitter
https://twitter.com/Aria_Fiction

Find us on Facebook
http://www.facebook.com/ariafiction

Find us on BookGrail
http://www.bookgrail.com/store/aria/

Addictive Fiction

First published in the UK in 2018 by Aria, an imprint
of Head of Zeus Ltd

9 7 5 3 1 2 4 6 8

A CIP catalogue record for this book is available
from the British Library.

ISBN (E) 9781786691804

Aria
c/o Head of Zeus
First Floor East
5–8 Hardwick Street
London EC1R 4RG

www.ariafiction.com

30551562R00217

Printed in Great Britain
by Amazon